One Pound

By

randall 'Jay' andrews

JaCol Publishing Inc.
Copyright 2023 © by JaCol Publishing Inc.
Illustrations Copyright © 2023 by JaCol Publishing Inc.
FIRST PRINTING
May 2023
All rights reserved
JaCol Publishing Inc.
195 Murica Aisle
Irvine, CA 92614
818-510-2898
Editor-in-Chief: Randall Andrews
Managing Editor: Roman A. Clay
www.jacolpublishing.com

ISBN: 978-1-946675-75-0

Cover Work: Erin Flanagan and Randall Andrews

Acknowledgment

To all of Writers World who have helped me keep up my writing habits. Somewhere out there a backdoor exists that I can find all those inside laughing and having a good time. Thank you, Erin M. for listening and editing. Thank you to Erin F for all the cover work in getting this ready to print. All my friends who have worked to keep me here, thank you. Thank you, Nettie, for listening to everything I have in my head. Thank you to my family who has no idea what I do when I am up there typing away but are generous enough to let me do it.

Table of Contents

Chapter 1

Everything in life has consequences, and consequences don't always happen from action, sometimes they happen from someone testing our reality.

People with quirks irritated Mindy. She snapped the clip off her Coke; the sizzle echoed from her office like Old Faithful. "God damn," she liked her Coke.

"Knock, knock?" Number Two poked his head in. "Got a moment?"

Mindy pushed away from her desk and put a sore foot on top of a heap of papers. "Care to massage my toes?" She waved in Brent Smith, the company pulse.

He stepped in. "I wanted to discuss Mr. Templeton."

Mindy pulled her foot down, stood, and hurried to the door. "Is he still here?"

"Relax, no, you had him escorted out."

"Fucking freak. Good riddance."

"Why?"

"I didn't like him." She canvassed the outer room through the window slats of her office.

Brent took a seat. "He was funny. I sort of liked him. So did everyone else."

"No they didn't."

"Actually, they did."

"No they didn't. He irritated everyone. He couldn't get anything right, and he always asked questions."

"And that's a bad thing?"

Mindy turned and leveled her view. "It is when time is production."

"Well, you hired an attorney, not a computer expert. He was supposed to make sure the material we disseminate is properly worded, and that he did well."

"Be that as it may, we functioned pretty well before he got here, and we will do just fine now that I have rid us of that payroll." She found her seat, and her Coke. "Besides, he'd only been here through probation anyway. It's not like I'd fired some tenured employee." She wagged a finger at Brent, "And he turned out to be way older than he looked. Did you ever hear him talk about shit in the past? You'd have thought he was a hundred."

"The guy knew a lot."

"He was weird, and I wanted him gone."

"What did Mr. Stripling say?"

"Told me to do what I thought was best."

"What reason did you give?"

She smiled. "I might have helped the process along a little."

"How?"

"I noticed he'd come in a half hour early and make coffee, never go to his desk until eight. So, I wrote him up, and said I wanted him to keep all appointments on time. I'd see him leave in the evening, and I'd send an email to his office account and tell him to see me first thing in the morning. God, what a tool. I must have done that ten times, and when he'd come to my office, I'd chew his ass out for having been in the office for thirty minutes, yet just now getting in to see me."

"You know that's sort of a bitchy thing to do. It's also not much of a fireable offense."

"I had more. I didn't like his production. I didn't like him asking so many questions, I didn't like him."

"Fair enough. You're the manager."

She gestured. "Yes, I am."

"What did he say when you let him go?"

"I wasn't there. I sent Carl. He's HR after all, it's his job."

"Doesn't he have the right to speak to you?"

"I don't give a shit. I just wanted him gone, and I didn't want some old man begging me for his job." Her eyes widened. "And I'm guessing he must have begged, because Carl came in here out of breath and unable to speak."

"What?"

"He couldn't speak, just stammered out some nonsense, stuttering the entire time."

"What did he say?"

"Best I could make out, he pointed at me and said, 'one pound.'"

"One pound?"

"Yeah. It felt like charades. He'd point to himself and say, 'sssssssstutter,' then at me and say, 'one ppppppound.'"

Brent stood. "Just for the record, I'd like you to know, and no disrespect intended, but I'm disappointed that you fired him. He sat back there in his cubicle and never complained. When he did surface, he'd ask me to show him something, and every time I did, he imparted some sage advice that made my day."

"Oh my God, you had a bromance."

Brent chuckled. "Shut up. It wasn't that. It was like having my dad in the office. He just seemed to understand when people were down."

"How come I never saw that?"

"Because you're never here."

"Every time I was here, he always seemed to get under my skin."

"How?"

"He'd say things like, 'You shouldn't drink so many of those.' As if I need him telling me how many Cokes I should drink."

Brent turned to a wall with two cases of Coke. "Yeah, well, he's sort of right."

She tossed back the can and drained it. When she finished she held it out and gave it an ironman squeeze. "I don't care."

"He was very kind when he left. He smiled and said, 'My work here is done. May you find the riches you so richly deserve.' He bowed his head, smiled at Tina and Margaret, and walked away, Carl following him to the elevator."

"You don't think he'll come back here with a gun do you?" She cracked another Coke. "Do you?"

Brent shook his head and walked toward the door.

"Okay, okay, okay. So he wasn't as bad as I made him out to be, but come on. This department is ten members who are like family. He was never going to be that."

Brent slid out the door, and turned, "If you say so," and closed her off to herself.

"Damn straight," her voice echoed off the walls, "Damn straight."

Chapter 2

"Mr. Templeton. I was wondering if we could meet in Ms. Docket's office?"

"About?"

Carl smiled. "Nothing, just some procedural work."

Mr. Templeton stood. He drew closer to Carl and winked. "I'm glad; you had me worried with the expression on your face."

Crazy coot has a sharper awareness than I gave him credit for.

"Just procedural."

"Good." Mr. Templeton kept a spotless desk, his cubicle tucked back in the far corner, his view of everyone. He pulled a pad and pen from his desk. "Red or black?" He held up two pens.

Carl stared, what a peculiar question. "Doesn't matter."

"I see." Mr. Templeton sat back down and closed a screen, followed by another.

Carl noticed. "What are you doing?"

"Sensitive material. If I'm going to step away, I need to secure it."

"I wouldn't worry about it."

Mr. Templeton swiveled in his chair and tilted his head. "Please, tell me again, what is our meeting about?"

Carl hesitated. The old man wanted the truth as if he knew the truth. "Just some procedural work." His conscience warmed his ears and lifted hairs up off the back of his neck.

"Then I shall continue." Mr. Templeton returned to his screen. Blip, blip, blip.

"Please hurry, Mr. Templeton."

"All done." He removed a wayward dust bunny that sullied his desk. "Do you prefer Carl, or Mr. Wickmire?

This is what I hate about my job. What a nice old man. "What do you feel comfortable with, sir?"

"I feel comfortable with the truth."

"The truth?"

Mr. Templeton smiled. "The truth of what you prefer?"

"Oh, well, I guess Carl is fine."

"Carl it is. So, Carl, do you like your job?"

They walked the corridor, Carl wondering if the old man knew it was the green mile. "Yeah."

"It must be tough being in HR."

"How so?"

"I mean, you always have to be above board. Oh, what am I saying? We should be above board in whatever we do in life, huh?"

The hallway heated up. Carl inhaled and exhaled. A thin perspiration beaded against his temple and ran down his cheek. "Yes, that's important."

"You're perspiring, Carl." Mr. Templeton removed a handkerchief from his pocket and offered.

Carl used his palm to wipe his face. "No, thanks."

They made it to Ms. Docket's door. Carl reached for the knob and Mr. Templeton caught his wrist. "Just procedural?"

Carl continued through and opened the door. "Yes."

"So be it."

When the door closed behind them and they were secured inside, the only participants, Carl moved to a round table in the center of the office. Atop lay a bevy of papers. "Mr. Templeton, I'm sorry to tell you, but Losan and Gellis of Longmont incorporated will no longer be retaining you."

"I thought this was just procedural?"

Carl rested his hands against his eyes. "I'm sorry about that. I needed to remove you from your desk without incident."

"What incident were you afraid of?"

"It's just how we do things."

"I see." Mr. Templeton sat across from Carl, hands locked, resting his arms on the table. "May I ask why I'm being terminated?"

"Yes, here is a report from Ms. Docket."

Mr. Templeton took his time. Read the litany of remarks cast down from his boss. "I'm confused. None of these appear worthy of being let go." He pointed to one remark in particular. "Asks too many questions. Is that a fireable offense?"

"I don't take sides, Mr. Templeton."

"Why not? Aren't you the advocate for employees?"

"I'm sent in when someone wants to execute a termination."

"Then you do choose sides."

"No, I stay neutral."

Mr. Templeton leaned into the conversation and studied Carl's face. The old man's chiseled eyes stayed fixed and his lids didn't blink. "You've chosen the wrong side."

Carl sighed. "I don't choose sides."

"But you have."

"Be that as it may, I have some exit paperwork I need you to sign. You have accrued a fair amount of PTO, and with your last check, you'll have plenty of money to hold you over for at least thirty days."

"I liked this job, Carl. Liking a job should be something an employer celebrates in their employees. Don't you think so?"

"Look, I'll let you know that I'm not going to prevent you from unemployment. When they call, I'll tell them you were not fired for cause."

"So if you are going to do that, then why am I fired?"

"It's all in the paperwork."

"Okay." Mr. Templeton relegated his posture to resignation. "I suppose there isn't anything else you can do."

"I'll have to see you out of the building, and you won't be allowed back to your cubicle."

"That's okay. I have everything I need."

Carl stood, but Mr. Templeton remained seated. "Do you need a moment?" He sat back down. "Is there something you'd like to say?"

"Can you relay a message to Ms. Docket?"

"As long as it isn't threatening."

Mr. Templeton's eyes gleamed, and a smile ripened. "Oh, never."

"What would you like to have me say?"

"One pound."

"One pound? Meaning?"

"Just one pound. In time, its meaning will become clear."

"Anything else?"

Mr. Templeton reached across the table and tapped his finger on Carl's hand. "For you...stutter."

Carl held his breath and his tongue. He bowed and stood, waved Mr. Templeton to the door. They were through.

Carl delivered Mr. Templeton to the elevator in silence. Mr. Templeton entered and Carl followed. Carl pressed 'ground' and the elevator closed off the location Mr. Templeton had called work for the last six months. Mr. Templeton exited at the lobby but Carl stayed behind. Before the door closed, Mr. Templeton turned and smiled. "Call me in a month and I'll come back." As the door closed, he continued, "But you'll have to give me a raise."

Chapter 3

Brent's wife had a glow. "Okay, what did you do?" He set down his briefcase and loosened his tie. Becky nursed a tea and patted the cushion. "Come sit for a minute."

That meant she wanted something. "How much is it going to cost?"

"A lot. A lot of money and eighteen years of your life!" Her stare penetrated.

"Get out." Brent smiled. "Really? Really and truly?"

"Really, truly, really."

She stood and Brent stopped her. "No, stay there, I don't want you exerting yourself."

"Honey, I'm pregnant, not injured."

"Well, I want to make sure you stay that way."

She laughed. "I shouldn't have told you until the laundry was done." She moved to the kitchen and Brent followed.

"So how do you know you're pregnant?"

His wife turned, her back against the counter, and pulled his tie until they snuggled. "Well, I'd missed my period and decided to take a test."

Brent rubbed his nose against hers. "Did you pass?"

She kissed him. "I suppose I did."

"I guess the old man was right."

She arched her back and caught his expression. "What old man, and right about what?"

He danced around her and made his way to the refrigerator. "Mr. Templeton, the guy we hired this year to write up our proposals." He found the milk and leaned over the door. "Fucking Mindy fired him today."

"And what did he say that he was right about?"

"This morning on the way up the elevator, he said, 'I think you need something wonderful, and you shall get what you deserve.'" Brent cracked the milk and drank from the carton. "He never said anything unpleasant—to anyone."

"So why did he get fired?"

He shrugged. "He didn't fit in. I get it. Mindy has developed a family in there, and she's the mom. I don't think she cared much for a father figure." He wiped his lips. "And he wasn't very tech savvy. Everyone liked him, but everyone covered for his lack of understanding of the computer." Brent pointed at Becky, "Let's go out and eat."

"I'm thawing hamburger."

"Forget hamburger, and forget cooking. You are carrying now. You need to be gentle."

"Oh, Lord. Is this how it'll be for nine months?" She took his hand and pulled him into the hallway. "Go change and we can go to Denny's."

"Denny's? Forget that. We're going out for real. I'll find a real restaurant." He typed in 'Five Star Restaurants' on his phone. "The first name up is Italian restaurant, 'Destino.'"

"Get ready then, and I'm ordering double, because I'm eating for two."

"I'm pretty much ready, Hon; you are the one who needs to get ready. This restaurant isn't a Denny's."

Life as a married couple was about to change. Gone would be dress-up nights. Brent took it in on one quick breath. He went to her side of the closet and slid the hangers to the formal wear. He pulled out the dress he loved on Becky and laid it on the bed. "Here, will you wear this?"

"Um, I don't know. You always seem to screw the hell out of me when I wear that dress. I think it has aphrodisiac effects on you."

"Not anymore, I don't want to hurt junior."

She took his shoulders and stopped him. "Please relax. I'm not fragile all of a sudden, and I hope the ixnay of the exsay is a joke."

"I just don't want to have anything bad happen."

She pinched his cheek. "Didn't Mr. Templeton say that you were going to get what you deserved?"

"Yep."

"So, if he said it, it must be true, right?" She laughed. "Now, if I wear this dress, are you wearing the turtleneck?"

He winked. "Is that what you want?"

"Yeah, I do."

"Why do I get this feeling I'm going to have to take a cold shower tonight?"

"You better not."

They dressed and left the house. When they got to the restaurant, Brent realized he'd stepped into a part of the world he couldn't afford. "I'm not sure we can get in."

"Why?"

"I didn't call in a reservation, and by the looks of this crowd, I suspect reservations are hard to come by." They stepped inside the door, and the ambiance reeked of million dollar lifestyles. "I don't think you can walk up and say table for two, Honey."

Becky squeezed his hand. "Denny's?"

He nodded and found humor in his embarrassment. "Yeah, looks like it."

He turned and opened the door.

"Excuse me?" An Italian voice called them back. "Table for the Smiths?"

Becky turned. "We're the Smiths."

"First name?"

She hurried to the maître d. "What name does it say?"

"It doesn't work that way, Miss."

"Well, you can't fault a girl for trying."

"Unless your husband's name is Brent, then the table belongs to someone else."

Brent stepped forward. "Brent is my name."

The maître d sighed. "License."

Brent was a step ahead. "Here."

"It looks like you, yes; I'd say that's you. Very well." He snapped his fingers and a woman stepped forward. "Table Paradiso."

She led them past tables with wealth times two, past faces he'd seen on T.V., up to an exclusive perch overlooking the entirety of Destino.

"Honey, has it dawned on you that another Brent Smith is about to come to this table and ask why we have his spot?"

"Becky, I'm just running with this until that happens."

She put the cloth over her lap. "This could get mighty embarrassing pretty fast."

A sommelier rolled a cart to their table. "I believe it is champagne to celebrate for you, sir. No? And I suspect the young lady will have a sparkling water?"

"How do you know we are celebrating, and how do you know she can't have any?"

His Italian poured through his words. "Look at her glow."

She did glow. Brent wanted her to never leave his sight, to always have that touch of love. "Yes, but she's always glowed to me." A passionate play between him and his wife.

"And thus the champagne."

"Oh, I can't afford a bottle of that."

"Afford? But I don't understand. You aren't paying for this."

Oh shit, not only have I taken someone's table, but I'm about to eat food they have already paid for.

"I think there's been a mistake. We will be paying for our meal tonight."

The sommelier put the champagne back on the tray and shook his head. "Very well, sir." He turned and carted his tray to a lone elevator, servicing the only table in the loft.

Becky viewed the patrons below. "I think the man who has this table is really important."

"Not important enough for the sommelier to know who he is."

"How much do you think this is going to set us back?"

"I don't know, but I suspect I'm spending at least four bills."

"Hundreds?"

"Yeah."

She whistled. "Should have let me make Hamburger Helper."

He waved her off. "It's fine. If this," he motioned to her belly, "isn't worth a few hundred bucks, I don't know what is."

The elevator opened, the sommelier and another man approached Brent and Becky. From his attire, he had to be somebody's boss.

"Mr. Smith." He held his hand out, "I am Amedeo Abatangelo, proprietor of Destino."

Brent was in too deep. "I can explain." He took Mr. Abatangelo's hand and stood.

"I'm sure you can. What would you like to explain?"

"My name really is Brent Smith."

"I know it is; this is your table, reserved for you, tonight." He pulled a paper from his pocket. "Reserved last week. To celebrate your wife's pregnancy. No?"

Brent stiffened. He tried to catch his thoughts. "Wha...what?"

"Is this beautiful young woman not pregnant?"

"Yes, yes she is. But we just found out tonight. Also, I suspect another Brent Smith is going to walk in that door, and through some act of incredible coincidence, has a wife who is pregnant."

The owner belly laughed. "How do you know this reservation wasn't for you?"

"Because I didn't make one."

"This reservation wasn't made by you, Mr. Smith."

"Then perhaps we can contact the person who made the reservation and find out who the other Mr. Smith is?"

"We don't have to contact the gentleman, because he's right here."

"Where?"

They stepped to the railing and looked down. Mr. Abatangelo pointed to an empty table. "Where did Mr. Templeton go?"

Chapter 4

"My fucking puppies are killing me." Mindy Docket cursed the room.

Her husband lowered the paper and made contact. "Feet hurt?"

"Yes." She waddled in and plopped down on a recliner. "Tough day today."

He lifted the paper back to his face. "I'm sure you shined."

"Why do you read papers? Don't you know you can get your news faster and more in depth, on your phone?"

He spoke, shielded by newsprint, "I'm old fashioned."

Mindy hopped out of the chair and pulled the paper down. They were eye to eye. "You want to know what is really old-fashioned?"

"What?"

"I fired that creepy old man we had at the office."

"Which one?"

She sneered. "We only have one."

"You mean that attorney guy? The little man with gray hair?"

"Yes. Old as dirt and twice as slow."

"So you fired him, huh?"

"Yeah, and I loved every minute of it."

Mindy's husband took an interest, leaned into the chair and rested an elbow. "What did you tell him?"

"Well, I actually didn't tell him anything. I had HR do that."

"That's kind of chicken shit, Honey."

She pointed. "You never know. He might have gone ape-shit on me and hurt me."

Her husband drew a blank stare. "Really? You think that old man would have punched you?"

Mindy looked around the room. "I don't know. He might have pulled a gun out and shot me."

"Oh, I'm sure a few ex-employees have thought about it, but something tells me he isn't one of them."

"You never know." She stood and scooted into the kitchen. "There better still be some Cokes in the reefer. I've been drinking warm ones all day."

From the other room, Mindy's husband pointed out, "If there aren't, you have no one to blame but yourself."

"One! One God damned cold one." She huffed. "It will take an hour to get some more cold ones." She worked her way to the pantry and removed a case of Coke. Only four cases left. "We need to make a run."

Her husband found his way into the kitchen. "I'll make a run tomorrow. I'm sure we're safe until then."

"So guess what he said."

"Who?"

"The old man."

"Doesn't he have a name?"

"Templeton, but you can call him fired ex-employee."

"So, what did fee say?"

Mindy tilted her head. "Fee?"

"You said, 'fired ex-employee. F-E-E."

"Oh, good one, Ron." She cracked the top and tilted the can to her lips.

"I thought you said you didn't talk to him."

"I didn't, but Carl said he uttered two words for me." She wiped her forehead with the can. "Shit, I hate hot days."

"What were the two words?"

"One pound."

"One pound?"

"Yeah, I know, right?" She put the can down. "I told you he was a freak."

"So did Carl know what he meant?"

"Carl couldn't talk. He comes in, out of breath, stammering like a retard. Uh, uh, uh, uh, one ppppppound. I wanted to slap him, but he is HR and you know how those cretins are."

"Honey, what are you trying to accomplish at your work? Do you want everyone to think alike, act alike, be alike?"

Mindy hesitated, considered his question. "As long as they think like me, then yeah, that's the idea."

"Don't you think that takes the spice out of life?"

She hesitated a second time. "Nope."

He shook his head. "I ordered pizza."

"Great, I'm starved."

He put his hand on her shoulder and pulled her close. "You look good. How are the workouts?"

She flexed a bicep. "Feel that, they're like cannons."

He squeezed her bicep until she yelped. "More like pea shooters, but keep trying."

"One-ten, five-five, solid muscle."

"Keep drinking these," he grabbed her can off the counter, "and you might find yourself at two-ten and no teeth."

Mindy retrieved the can and cradled it like precious cargo. "You leave my Cokes out of this."

The doorbell rang. "Pizza must be here."

Mindy ducked under her husband's arm and hurried to the door.

"He's not going anywhere."

She dug into her purse. "I don't care, I'm hungry."

She paid for the pizza and shooed the boy away. "Here, it's all I have; don't spend it all in one place."

The delivery boy counted out forty-five cents. "Gee, I'll try not to."

She closed the door and carried the box to the kitchen. "What a shitty job. They must have to deal with assholes every day."

"You mean like change tippers?"

"Hey, it's all I had."

"You could have asked me."

"No, I couldn't have. He didn't deserve a tip."

Her husband pulled two plates down and joined her at the table. "And why is that?"

"Because he didn't smile." She bit into a slice. "Monday is going to be so much more relaxing."

"Why?"

"Because I won't have to see that toothy grin anymore."

"Do you ever listen to yourself?"

Mindy gave her husband full attention. "About?"

"You just said the kid didn't deserve a tip because he didn't smile, but you will be happy that you won't be seeing a smiling face when you get to work."

She sighed. "Completely different. The kid is selling something, he better smile. He is a puppet on a string, playing for his next meal. Mr. Templeton needed to look and act a little more professional. Smiling is what you do when you are selling or hiding something, and the old man isn't selling anything."

"So what was he hiding?"

"I don't know, and I no longer care, because he is a fee!"

Her husband shook his head and kissed Mindy. "I don't know what I'm going to do with you. You are a hellion."

"And you are the luckiest man alive." She kissed him back.

Chapter 5

"Ms. Wickmire, We'd like to keep your husband overnight for observation."

Carl sat, tight lipped, and clinging to his wife's hand. The solemnity of white walls, certifications and degrees, and a gentle giant physician assured his wife that his issue wasn't at the hand of suggestive powers.

"This may be a slight stroke. We won't know until we do some tests."

Carl grabbed a paper, scribbled a note and slid it across: 'My faculties are fine. I'm not disoriented.'

Dr. Morehead smiled. "Not all strokes take your mental capacity away. In fact, most don't." He leaned back and reached for a booklet. He thumbed through the pages and set the book to rest in front of Carl. "This is the brain. When a mild stroke affects the left side, you can develop Apraxia. I suspect that the story your wife has relayed about this employee telling you to stutter is one of those incredible coincidences."

Carl relaxed. His world, as he knew it, began to return. *Yeah, how stupid of me to think someone could will me to stutter.* He scribbled another note: 'How long a recovery process will this be?'

The doctor pursed his lips and shrugged. "I wish I could say. We have to go in and find out how much damage was done. However, diagnosing the problem is the first step."

Carl's wife put her arm around her husband. "Honey, I'll stay until they get you situated, okay?"

Carl shook his head. He'd been reduced to gestures. *A stroke, shit, I should have known.* Carl smiled. His day had gone from one extreme to the other.

The hospital checked him in and while his wife waited in his room, they wheeled him down to have a CAT scan. He processed his life: wonderful wife, two high school-aged daughters, parents close by, house, cars, dog. He didn't pay enough attention to the small things. Missed most his daughters' soccer games, work did that. Work was okay. It wasn't what he expected in life, but it paid the bills. Maybe Mr. Templeton's words helped create the stress that led to a stroke. The whole 'feeling comfortable with the truth.' It unsettled him then, and still weighed heavily. Too many people escorted out the door, some undeserving. People just trying to make ends meet, but not meeting the cliques of social dynamics. He'd become the henchman for the wrong side.

A tech rolled him into place, a chamber they'd slide him into and take pictures from all angles. They moved him from gurney to table. "We're going to place this shield over your waist, okay?"

Carl nodded. The tubular chamber slid into place and his head rested inside a contraption that hummed, whirled, and clicked.

The tech's voice interrupted technology, the sound piped, "Please remain as still as possible, Carl."

He hasn't even introduced himself and he's calling me Carl.

More hums, more whirls, more clicks. "Do you think they will find anything?"

Did he just ask me that? Carl shrugged.

"Please stay still, Mr. Wickmire."

He asks a question and then tells me to stay still?

"You really don't need these tests. You know what to do, you know what is right."

Carl crawled out and sat up. The tech came around a corner, "Mr. Wickmire, if we are going to do these tests, you can't move."

Carl motioned for something to write with. The tech removed a pen from his breast pocket and handed him a chart.

Carl scribbled: 'How much longer?'

"We haven't started."

Carl had heard the machine. He continued: 'You haven't taken any pictures yet?'

"You'll know when we do. You will hear clicks, and the rotation of the cameras."

Carl ground the pen into the paper: 'I did!!!'

"Just relax, Mr. Wickmire. This won't take long." He put pressure on Carl's shoulder and guided him back to rest. "Just relax."

Carl slid into place and the quiet solitude left him helpless. No hums, no whirls, no clicks.

"Okay, we are going to take some pictures, so you will hear some soft noises, okay?"

Carl raised a thumb.

Click...camera whirled...click...a positioning arm hummed...click...camera whirled...another hum...click. On and on. "You're doing great, Mr. Wickmire."

Fifteen minutes. A long fifteen minutes to contemplate life as the core where those thoughts came from had a camera charting its territory.

"All done." The technician came back and slid the chamber forward and off of Carl. "Kind of a pleasant experience, huh?" He smiled. "No shots, no pressure, tiny bit of radiation, but nothing that will hurt you." He helped Carl up. "I'll get these images to processing, and the doctors will find the issues and fix you up in no time." He patted

29

Carl's shoulder. "Let's put you back on the gurney and roll you to your room. Give Doctor Morehead about thirty minutes, and he'll have your results.

Carl's thoughts crashed. He didn't need the results, he knew what the answer would be; the voice had told him.

Chapter 6

Brent rolled out of bed. Saturday, pregnant wife, beautiful day. "Honey?" He peered around the door and bacon floated upon a velvet stream rippled with coffee and fresh linens. "What are you doing?" He came into view. "Will you take it easy. I don't want you straining yourself." He hurried in and tried to interfere with her morning rituals.

Becky turned. "I can see we need to enroll in a Lamaze class." She flipped a hoecake. "I won't be able to survive if you make the first seven months all bed rest."

Brent put his arms around his wife and kissed her cheek. "I realize you can do things, but try not to overdo it."

She pushed away and returned to her efforts. "Making breakfast isn't overdoing it. Trust me."

Brent accepted defeat and retreated to the table. "Pretty weird about last night, huh?"

Becky waved the spatula like a baton. "Um, weird doesn't actually fit." She stopped and came around the counter. With her arms akimbo, she stood over Brent. "What do you know about Mr. Templeton?"

Brent followed the intricate lines in the wood, age rings coursing through the tabletop. He navigated them as they twisted with rhythm, each telling a year in the life of a tree no longer living. "Not enough, apparently."

"I think you should talk to HR about this."

Brent recoiled. "Why? Just because he guessed? He knew we were trying."

His wife slapped his shoulder. "You told him we were trying for a child?"

"I told you he had a disarming way about him. He'd soothe you and get your life story out of you. You felt he wanted to know you, and you spilled it out as though somehow his experience could guide you through tumultuous times. It's just how he was. I liked him."

"Still, last night is unnerving, and all the variables don't add up—not even a little."

"Becky, I'm extremely aware of that. Even if he'd guessed, which I suspect he did, unless the owner was in on it, and just bullshitting about the reservation being a week old, our home would have to be—" Brent turned to his wife.

"What?"

"Bugged." He put his finger to his lips and motioned for her to follow. They stepped out to the backyard. "For him to have set that up, he had to know where we were going, and we didn't know where we were going until an hour before we got there."

"Brent, why would he bug our house? What possible reason? You have nothing anyone wants. You don't hold secrets for anything of importance. You think he would bug someone he works with just to do random acts of kindness?"

"Any way you look at it, Becky, that's the only way he could have known. Unless you're suggesting he picked that restaurant a week ago, and told them it was for a pregnancy celebration. Who's the crazy one here?"

"But why?"

"I don't know why, but I'm not down with wizards and magicians. Everything in life has a logical answer, and unless you can give me a better one, I'm working on the assumption that he's hearing what we are saying in that house."

Becky turned. "Oh, shit."

Brent held her arm. "What?"

"The hoecake." They turned and the smoke detector ripped into high gear.

Brent laughed. "I thought maybe you knew where the bug was." He stormed around her and into the house, the velvet layer gone and replaced with a dense darkening cloud. "Black, just like I like it." He turned the stove off and put the pan in the sink. "How many did you make?"

"Two. It's okay. I made a smorgasbord of other stuff."

Brent canvassed the counter. Eggs, bacon, hash browns, waffles, squeezed orange juice. "I see that. Damn, are you getting the munchies already?"

"I wanted to celebrate. I want to celebrate for the next nine months." She changed course. "So what do you want to do about—"

Brent cut her off. "Generic, Honey. Everything generic." He winked. "I'll look into the back patio."

"The back patio?"

"You know," he winked again, "the back patio."

"What…oh, oh, yeah. Okay. Today?"

"Yeah." He sat her down. "Let me serve us. You've done enough already this morning." He replaced her spot in the kitchen and dished up her breakfast. "You want to go shopping today?"

"For what?"

"Well, let's see. You are about to need a new wardrobe, and we're going to have to accessorize one of the bedrooms."

She leaned on her elbows. "Maybe we should name our child after the mysterious Mr. Templeton?" She scanned the room.

Brent shook his head.

Becky smiled. "Generic enough"

"I suppose."

"What was his first name?"

"Gabe."

"Sounds Jewish."

"I have no idea. He never mentioned religion. He didn't involve himself in politics, in movies, in music. He didn't lean toward anything concrete. He was more about you, and what you were doing. He didn't preach, other than to remind Mindy that she drank too many Cokes."

Becky wrinkled her nose. "She does."

"I know, but she's my boss, so she can do whatever the hell she wants."

"Including firing nice old men."

"Yep, including that."

Becky changed the subject. "I have my final tonight."

"Final?"

"Yes, that's what it is called."

"How's it graded?"

"If you get laughs you pass, if you don't, don't quit your day job."

Brent shrugged. "You'll get laughs."

She pecked him on the cheek. "Thank you."

Chapter 7

"Come on, girls!" Mindy urged the Zumba class to keep going.

"Mindy, I think you piss Lyndsey off every time you do that." Mindy's Zumba mate, Kelly, squatted, raised, kicked right, kicked left.

"I can't help it; it's the leader in me." Mindy, swung an arm out, circled it over her head and did a half turn. "Would you guys give me your best effort!"

A voice from across the room grumbled, "Thank you, Mindy, I'll control the pace."

Mindy winked to Kelly. "She's such a twat."

"She runs the class."

"Not very well, if you ask me."

"What are you going to do this weekend?"

"Shopping, movie, putting an ad in for a new legal writer."

"Another employee quit on you?"

"No one ever quits on me, Kelly. They get trumped."

Kelly came to rest at the leader's call to stop. "What did he do? Steal?"

"Hardly. He was too stupid to steal. He couldn't have stolen a heart let alone money." Mindy took a breather against a mirrored wall, sat, and patted a spot next to her for Kelly. "Stripling hires some bad employees. I bet his track record is twenty percent keepers."

Kelly exhaled and fanned herself. "You have anything left in that water bottle?"

"Here." Mindy snapped the top and offered her canister.

Kelly took a drink and stopped. "What is this?"

"Coke."

"What the hell? Why don't you have water?"

"Coke makes me exercise harder."

"You drink these things too much."

"Hey, careful. That helped get the last guy fired."

"You fired your attorney for telling you the obvious?"

"Among other things, but that was on the list."

"Tell me you aren't taking steroids while you're working out?"

"What's that supposed to mean?"

"You seem to be getting kind of mean, Mindy."

Mindy smiled. "It's all for show."

Kelly lifted herself off the floor. "Let's go."

"You want to sauna first?"

Mindy leaned in. "Are you worried about your weight?"

"I don't know. I just feel like I need to push some water out of me." Mindy stood, rolled her tank-top over her abs.

Her friend smiled. "You look great."

"Thanks. Ever since I started this routine, I feel great." She picked up her bag. "I'm thinking about a running routine on the weekends, you want to join me?"

Kelly faced Mindy. "You're lucky I Zumba with you. I'm not going to run, nor all the weightlifting you've started, or the stair climber. This," she waved her hand around the mirrors, "is enough."

"Suit yourself, but when I start looking like Jillian Michaels, you might reconsider."

"You know she's a lesbian? Is there something you want to tell me?"

"Ha! You want to shower and find out?"

"Now I know why you want me in the sauna."

Mindy squeezed Kelly's arm. "Don't worry, you aren't my type. You're too chubby."

Her friend pulled back. "Hey, that's not funny."

Mindy waved her off. "Lighten up. I'm just kidding."

"That's my point. It's not funny."

"Sorry."

Mindy found the vending machine on the way to the showers. She put a dollar in and hit E-3. The tumbler didn't move. She pushed E-3 again. Nothing. She tapped it, punched it, and started pounding on E-3. "God damn it." She pushed on the machine, the bottles inside rocking. "Get the fuck out."

Kelly pulled her arm. "Stop."

"This machine has my Coke."

"No, it has your money."

"I don't give a shit about the money, I want my Coke."

A fitness center employee stopped. "Excuse me, can I help you."

"This machine isn't working." She pointed at the employee. "I need you to get your key, open this up and give me my drink. Is that too much to ask?"

"I can't do that ma'am. We don't own these machines."

"Did you just call me ma'am?"

"Yes, ma'am."

"Do I look like a ma'am to you?"

He stood apprehensive. "Uh, yeah?"

"You would be the luckiest guy in this place if you had a woman like me on your arm."

"Maybe, but you're ten years older than me. I'm pretty sure my parents wouldn't be happy if I took you to my senior prom."

Mindy stopped. "You're in high school?"

"Yes, ma'am."

Shit, she had fifteen years on the squirt. "Very well, but don't call me ma'am. It's rude."

He remained stiff. "Okay."

"And get me a Coke, please."

"I'll make a call right now."

Mindy and Kelly followed him to a station. The kid picked up a booklet and thumbed through the pages. He picked up a phone and dialed. "Hello, is this Templeton Distributors?"

Mindy stopped the kid. "Did you say, Templeton?"

He cupped the phone. "Yes. They are the vending machine owners."

Mindy turned to Kelly. "Oh, the irony of life."

"What's that?"

"No wonder the pop machine hates me. It has the same name as the guy I fired."

Mindy left the kid talking on the phone. That machine wouldn't be fixed until Monday, so she had to hurry and get home. "No sauna tonight."

"Why?"

"I need to get home."

Chapter 8

Doctor Morehead entered Carl's room and the ambiance deflated. The doctor's face spoke volumes for his thoughts.

Carl's wife stood. "So, how bad is it?"

Doctor Morehead shrugged. "We need to redo these." He pulled a scan out and slipped it onto a screen. "This is your husband's brain."

"And?"

"And according to these takes, it's normal."

Carl scribbled on a piece of paper and urged the doctor to read it.

Doctor Morehead scoffed. "You did not meet the devil. I deal in science. Science, real science, the kind of science that can figure this out. These tests may be faulty, or, or there are other possibilities. I'm going to do a toxicology run. Your 'devil' may have poisoned you."

Carl continued. He handed the doctor another sheet.

The doctor answered. "They make poisons that can do all sorts of odd things." He stepped closer, and pulled out a penlight. He tested Carl's pupils. "How are you feeling?"

Carl wrote: 'Other than the fact that I can't talk, fine.'

"No nausea?"

Carl shook his head.

"Hunger normal?"

Carl gave a thumb up.

"Everything in life is explainable." He turned to Mrs. Wickmire. "Depending on what we find. It might be wise for you to contact the authorities."

"Yes, Doctor."

Carl slowed down. He wrote with purpose. He gave the doctor a more complete understanding: 'It's not like that. Mr. Templeton didn't offer me a drink. He didn't offer me a bite of food, or a piece of candy. He didn't shake my hand. I made no contact with him.'

The doctor dismissed it. "You were in the same room with him." He challenged Carl. "You don't know that he didn't release some sort of aerosol poison."

Carl sighed and wrote some more: 'Doctor, he isn't that kind of man. He's just a little old man who did our legals. He was polite, kind, and didn't wish ill will on anyone.'

The doctor shared glances with both Wickmires. "I guess that begs the question, why was he fired then? Someone must not have thought he was too great."

Carl's eyes glassed over.

For the love of God, what have I done?

He wrote: 'His boss isn't the most endearing person in the world. She's tough, she's smart, she's great at her job, but puppy dogs and bambis are to be stomped on.'

"What kind of shape is she in tonight?"

Carl handed the doctor another verse: 'Fine, nothing can hurt that woman.'

"Are you sure? Have you spoken to her? Maybe she's in the same condition as you?"

Carl added: 'He didn't wish stuttering on her.'

"Did he wish anything on her?"

Carl wrote: 'He didn't see her. He relayed a message through me. He told her "One pound".'

"What's that mean?"

Carl shrugged. The pencil broke and the doctor motioned it was fine.

"I want to hear you read this." He handed Carl a note.

Carl formed his lips into motion. "Mmmmy nnnname is dddddoctttter Mmmmmorehhhhead." Carl's lip quivered and he shook his head.

"Okay, that's fine." The doctor crossed his arms. "I've read of people who can succumb to suggestions. Psychosomatic conditions prevail into ever increasing stress. It builds on itself and renders a person incapable of coping. Are you easily convinced of things, Mr. Wickmire?"

Mrs. Wickmire interrupted. "My husband is a strong personality. He's not given to suggestions, doctor."

"Depends upon one's state of mind. Anyone can have enough stress in their lives to be ripe for this sort of conditioning. Have you had a death in the family? Anything that could have weighed on you?"

Carl shook his head.

"Did Mr. Templeton suggest a reason why maybe you should be sad?"

Carl hesitated.

"What?"

He motioned for something to write with. He scribbled a note: 'He made me question my sense of right and wrong.'

"And did you question it?"

Sorrow overwhelmed him. He wrote: 'I still am.'

The doctor exhaled. "I'm going to call a colleague to come in tomorrow to see you. He's a psychiatrist. As much as I want to believe this is biological, I might have to hand the ball off on this one." He turned to Mrs. Wickmire. "All the more reason to call the authorities. And find out if the woman is okay.

"Yes, Doctor."

Chapter 9

Brent's wife waited for her slot. Brent waited backstage with her. "Who was that last one?"

"Leslie. She's really good."

A nervous hand squeezed Brent's arm. "Stop shaking. You're fine."

"I don't feel fine. Getting up in front of a class is one thing, but those are paying customers."

"Those are also drinking customers. Just be your sarcastic self and you will be fine." Brent faced his wife. "Have you been rehearsing?"

"You hear me every morning in front of the mirror."

"Then just do what I hear, and you will be fine. I sit in the bedroom as you are talking to an imaginary crowd and howl. You're funny. No matter what happens out there, you liven up every room with your wit and your sincerity. Do your gig. I have faith in you."

The red light came on; his wife would be next. She squeezed Brent's hand one more time. "Wish me luck."

"Break a leg." He lifted her hand and kissed it.

Over the speaker, a voice boomed. "Now introducing a first-time performer, Becky Smith," followed by a bio she'd written up. Brent went out front and stayed in the dark recesses, not wanting to make his wife more nervous.

It didn't help.

She wilted and a lull hovered over the audience. His wife was about to panic, he knew that fight or flight; he'd seen it in her before.

Brent screamed. "Be funny, Honey!"

The crowd snickered and she turned to where he hollered from. "Come out and say that, mister."

Brent stepped out from the darkness.

"Just as I thought; my husband."

The crowd perked with another chuckle. His wife didn't stop, she lit into everything Brent, and the audience slid into that place where they were digging Becky. Brent laughed along with them. When she finished, she got the grade, she got the laughs, and they wanted more. Brent's wife couldn't ask for much more than that.

Brent met her backstage. "You were awesome."

She hugged him. "Thank you for coming to my rescue."

"I didn't do anything. I just started the engine. That was all you."

"I'll need to book you for my next one."

"Next one?"

She grinned. "I'm taking that class again."

"Take mystery theater. I'll take that one with you."

"How about you take a comedy class."

"Nope. Not my thing."

"We'll talk." She took his hand and they made their way out to the edges to watch her other classmates sink or swim.

When her instructor came to the mic, he offered a round of applause for the comics, and for the audience who'd come. "I want to thank all of you for being here, and for the gracious funding from Templeton Entertainment."

Brent whispered. "His name pops up again."

Becky raised her eyebrows. "I hadn't thought of that, but they have been sponsoring it for years."

"Good things seem to happen with that name, but why?"

Becky tilted her head. "If you are a Smith. I'd say Wickmires and Dockets would disagree."

"True, but this seems staged." Brent stood with the crowd. "Shall we have a late snack?"

"I thought you'd never ask. I'm guessing that urchin in me is begging for food, because I'm starved."

Budgeting for a child, Brent found the nearest pancake house.

Becky stepped out of the car and stopped. "Look; it's closed."

Across the street a high-end hotel restaurant had the only open sign on the block. "Guess we are splurging again."

Becky confided. "We'll make it. Let's enjoy."

He took her hand and they chose to walk. "Car will be fine here." He felt pressure. Spending money frivolously had never been his forte.

"Stop looking like that. Just like the car, we'll be fine."

Brent pulled Becky closer. "You're right." They crossed the street, entered the hotel and found the restaurant doors. Brent stepped up to the dais. "Is there a reservation list?"

A woman nodded. "There is, but it's ten at night. You're fine."

Becky whispered. "Hear that, everyone has said we're fine."

They seated Brent and his wife and brought them water, bread, and menus.

"They're quick. They must want to wrap this up. I see they are putting up the rope to the dining area."

"When the waiter arrived, Becky asked, "Would you prefer we eat at the bar?"

"No, ma'am, you are fine here." He motioned to the menu. "Have you made a decision?"

Before they could answer, two more employees came close enough to hear the conversation. Brent felt oddly watched.

"Um, yeah. We'd like the Grilled Chicken with Banana Pepper Dip and Fattoush, and the Harissa-Spiced Salmon with Israeli Couscous."

Our waiter appeared to have been expecting that with doom, while the other two high-fived each other.

Brent's wife turned to the jubilance, "What's going on?"

The waiter shook his head. "A man came in here earlier tonight and said someone at this table would order this at ten, and that we should have it ready to go at ten-o-seven." Through the kitchen door, as the clock ran to ten-o-seven, another waiter pushed a cart through with two dishes. He rolled it up to the table and motioned. "Is this what they ordered?"

Their waiter eyed it. "Exactly."

Brent stopped the waiter. "Who said we'd order this?"

"Some man from a company called Templeton Entertainment. Said this woman had performed at Funny Bonez, and that she'd be celebrating her performance."

Brent cut in. "What'd he look like?"

Their waiter turned and motioned to the Maître d.

When she approached, he asked, "What did the guy look like who paid for this?"

Brent stopped her. "Paid for?"

"Well, we wouldn't have had it ready if he hadn't."

"What did he look like?"

"Older gentleman. Pleasant."

"Did he say anything about us?"

She stepped closer. "No, but he did tell me to relay a message to the party that ordered this food. He said, 'Tell them that good things come in threes.' With that, he paid the bill, turned, and left." She hesitated, "Although he was adamant about what time to have it rolled out." She smiled. "I thank you for not being late."

Chapter 10

"I need to work out this morning."

Mindy's husband rolled over. "Do you know what time it is?"

"Six."

"In the morning, on a Saturday. If you are going to work out on the weekend, a note beside my made-breakfast would be sufficient."

"Very funny, Ron. Now, you should get up with me and do the stair climber."

Her husband edged his eyes open. "Nope. Body says more sleep, and I'm listening to body."

She shook him. "I want you to go with me."

"Call your friend Kelly."

"She already said no."

Her husband rolled away and pulled the blanket to his neck. "You're out of luck then."

"You ever want sex again?"

"With you?"

She flicked his ear. "Very funny."

"Blackmail me and find out how funny."

Mindy put a leg over her husband's hip. "Come on, Ron. Please? I don't want to go alone."

He patted her leg. "Make it eight and I'll go."

"Promise?"

"If you let me sleep, I promise."

She kissed his lobe and rolled out of bed. She made her way to the bathroom and jumped in the shower. She toweled off and stepped on the scale. "Shit!" She stepped off, exhaled and stepped on again. "Damn it." She wrapped herself in a robe and drew anger with each step back to the bedroom. "Ron."

"I said, don't wake me."

"I need to go now."

He sighed. "Why the change of heart."

"I need to check my weight."

"And our scale isn't good enough?"

She sat on the edge of the bed and danced a crossed-leg up and down in irritation. "It says 112."

"And?"

I weighed 110 two days ago. When I went to work out last night, after Zumba, I weighed 111. I came home, didn't eat—"

"But drank a shitload of pop."

She snapped his butt. "Perhaps, but still, a night's sleep after a workout, and I wake up to 112." She stood and pinched her ribs. "And I swear to fuck I can feel that pound."

"Have a good workout."

"You aren't going?"

"Nope."

She let her robe slide off. "Even if I promise you this?"

"You know the drill. Eight and I'll go. Anything earlier and the answers–nope."

Patience wasn't her virtue. She waved her hand. "I'm seriously disappointed."

He closed his eyes and hugged his pillow. "I'm sure you are." In the throes of drifting off, he offered, "Have a good workout."

"I'm leaving without you."

"I think we established that already."

She used noise as a rallying cry. He might not go, but he'd hear every moment of her putting clothes on. Drawers opened with abruptness, and closed with a slam. Hangers slid across the bar with the grating of chalkboard fingernails. Elastic panties snapped. "Get up!"

"Nope."

"Fine." She circled around the bed and headed for the door. As she passed the end of the bed, she took a fist full of blanket and yanked. Like a magician's dining table, the cloth shed away from the bed. "Have a good morning."

Her husband didn't move, fetal and uncovered. "You too."

She tapped a number on her phone. "Kelly?" She woke her friend.

"What do you want?"

"Heading to the club. Get your sweats on."

"I told you last night, I'm not doing more than Zumba."

"I know what you said, but I'm going to start training you. Besides, you need it."

The phone went dead.

She dialed back but it went to voice mail. "Don't be mad. I really need someone to talk to this morning. Call me back, please."

She's weak, she'll call me back.

Her phone chirped. "Thank you for calling back."

"What do you need to talk about?"

"Meet me at the club, and I'll tell you."

"If you are yanking my chain, I swear we will never be friends again."

"No, really. I need someone to talk to."

Mindy waited twenty minutes. When Kelly drove up, Mindy wanted to bitch.

"Keep that look out of your mouth, Mindy. I'm here for you, so be grateful."

Mindy held it in. "You're right." She opened the door for her friend.

"So what did you want to talk about?"

"Hold on." She passed the kid's station. "Hey, did you get my pop?"

"Man came last night and fixed it. Restocked it too." The kid laughed. "Old and strong."

"Who?"

"The guy who restocked it. Little old distributor, but carried stacks of cases in his arms and didn't want help."

The kid had worked the nightshift but was there bright and early. "Hey, why are you here? Didn't you get off about seven hours ago?"

"Six actually."

"So my question stands, why are you here? Go home and enjoy your weekend."

"Funniest thing, the distributor gave me a piece of advice that I thought I should take."

"What's that?"

"He said, 'a good employee addresses the problems presented to him.'"

"Meaning?"

"He said I should be the one to give you back your dollar, and give you a complimentary Coke."

"But that doesn't explain why you're here. You had no idea I'd be here this morning."

"He said you'd be here bright and early."

"Why?"

"He said, you'd come in to work off that one pound."

Mindy's friend turned. "Mindy, you look like you've seen a ghost." She pulled Mindy aside. "What is it that you needed to talk about?"

"About that one pound."

Chapter 11

"Mr. Wickmire, my name is Dr. Coldsnow." He entered Carl's room with two assistants. "This is Mr. Pearl and Ms. Ping." The two junior associates took seats and opened computers. Ms. Ping tapped out a steady rhythm of stenography, while Mr. Pearl called out personal questions that Dr. Coldsnow relayed.

"Age?"

Carl held up four fingers on one hand and two on the other.

Height. Weight. Eye color. Hair color. Diet. Physical conditioning. Members in the household. Boys or girls. Ethnicity. Prior illnesses. History of mental issues. On and on, and Carl fingered what he could and scribble the rest.

"Religion?"

Carl hesitated.

"Religion?"

Carl wrote: 'Why is my religion important?'

"Carl, often religion plays a role in what we are willing to accept as real."

Carl tilted his head.

"In the early seventies, a movie came out about a little girl possessed by the devil. After that, the rate of exorcisms coming out of the Catholic Church spiked. People believed that bodies could actually be possessed."

Carl emphasized: 'They can.'

Dr. Coldsnow smiled. "I guess that's what we are going to find out." "Mr. Pearl, bring up test samples 223 and 224."

Mr. Pearl asked, "Suggestive reasoning, yes?"

"Exactly."

Carl pointed to his question: 'What does that mean?'

"You believe in heaven and hell?"

Carl nodded.

"You believe that if you do the right things, you'll get into one or the other?"

Carl nodded.

"Do you believe it with your heart and soul?"

Carl nodded.

"Well, that means you believe it with the most dynamic organ in your body—your brain. If your brain believes it, it's been conditioned to accept the unknown rather unquestionably."

Carl said, "Sssssssssso."

"So, you may have experienced a very crafty employee."

Carl wrote: 'He's a meek old man.'

"Exactly the kind of man who could suggest something innocuous and not raise any suspicion." He patted Carl's hand and smiled. "We are going to step out and discuss how to get your speech back." He winked. "Your mysterious employee isn't a match for me. I've seen this before, and I'll get you auctioneering in no time."

Carl exhaled.

"Just relax."

Left alone, outside the day glistened under a cloudless sky. A gentle breeze circulated chilly air through the room. He pulled his blanket up. He couldn't stem the guilt. His phone rang.

800 number. Hmm.

"Hello."

Carl tried to speak but nothing came out.

"It's okay. I understand you are in need of speech therapy. We can get you auctioneering in no time." The person on the other end paused. "Your mysterious psychiatrist is no match for me. I've seen this before. You know what to do."

Carl hit end. He viewed the number and hit redial. "Sorry, but you've reached a number that is not in service. If you feel you've reached this number in error, please try again, and you know what to do. You know what to do, Carl."

The doctor stepped back in.

Carl held the phone up and waved his doctor over.

"What is it?"

He scribbled: 'He called.'

"Who?"

Carl scribbled: 'Mr. Templeton.'

"What did he say?"

Carl redialed the number and put it on speaker phone. "You have reached the office of Dr. Coldsnow. If you have been directed by a medical facility, please call our number—" Carl hit end.

"How did you get our number?"

Carl wrote: 'This number just called me.'

Dr. Coldsnow motioned to Ms. Ping. "Call the office and see if anyone has made a call from the 800 number."

I'm going crazy.

Ms. Ping shook her head.

"Mr. Wickmire. Let's get you out of this hospital. We have a place for you. I think you'll find it more comfortable."

Carl wrote: 'I'm fine here.'

"Still, I'm going to have you brought to our facility."

Carl shook his head.

"It's not your decision, Mr. Wickmire." He turned to Mr. Pearl, nodded, and his assistant left the room.

Ms. Ping, Carl, and Dr. Coldsnow occupied space but no one spoke. Ms. Pearl tapped on her computer, and Dr. Coldsnow studied a series of charts.

Two orderlies, big men, came in with Mr. Pearl.

"Mr. Wickmire, Dr. Coldsnow has signed off on you, and we have to release you to him. I realize this is very sudden, but your wife signed off on this last night."

Carl wrote: 'Can I speak with Dr. Morehead?'

"Dr. Morehead is off today."

Carl continued: 'I'd like to wait until he gets her before I make this decision.'

One of the orderlies stepped forward. "You don't have any decision to make."

He panicked: 'WHAT ABOUT MY WIFE?'

Dr. Coldsnow smiled. "She'll meet you there, we'll call her now and have her picked up if you like, or she can drive there."

Carl went on: 'Have her drive. She can drive me home.'

The doctor's smile broke. "Let's cross that bridge when we get there."

Carl's guilt deepened.

Chapter 12

Brent's boss marched down patterned carpet of green checks and brown circles. To her right, she caught Brent leaning back in his chair, a grin as big as Texas. "Why are you happy?"

He stepped out of his cubicle. "You want to hear the good news?"

"There is no good news." She kept walking.

He followed her. Inside her office, he cornered her. "What's the matter?"

She pulled the cases of pop from her shelf. "I need to have these looked at. Do you think they could be tampered with?"

"Why?"

"That fucker said 'One pound,' and it's been three."

"You mean Mr. Templeton?"

"Yeah." She relayed her bizarre conversation at the club.

"You aren't going to believe this."

"You have some shitty event happen to you too?"

"No, far from it."

The restaurant story and Brent's wife being pregnant didn't make Mindy feel better. "Why the fuck did he pick up your meal, but he's trying to ruin my life? I never did anything to him."

"Uh, you fired him."

She dismissed Brent. "He deserved it, and he knew it was coming." She waved him off. "Why am I having this conversation? We are starting to sound like he's mystical. Somehow he's a little more sneaky than we thought." She leaned over and caught Mr. Stripling's office. "You think the boss is setting us up for a grand prank?"

"If he is, you are the only one being pranked, and seriously, you gaining three pounds isn't too mystical, mysterious, or a very funny prank. Besides, he didn't do anything to us, just predicted our pregnancy."

"And paid for your meal." She reminded Brent. "You know that kid is going to ruin your life? Not to mention rip that poor wife of yours wide open."

"Thanks for the congratulations. You make it seem so wonderful."

"Just keeping it real, and if I didn't, who would?"

The jingle of keys turned their attention across the hall. "Frank?"

Mr. Stripling turned, his expression weighted. He walked across and popped in. "You two have a minute?" He sat on the edge of Mindy's desk and laid out the news. "Carl is in a mental hospital."

Brent interrupted, "Why?"

"He can't speak."

"Why a mental hospital?"

"I don't know all the details, but he's hallucinating." He turned to Mindy. "How was he on Friday?"

"He seemed pretty out of breath right after I fired Mr. Templeton."

"You fired Mr. Templeton?"

"Frank, I told you I was going to fire him." She shook her head. "Don't you remember?"

"You said you were going to write him up for slow productivity."

"I did. I then gave him one week to improve and he didn't. So I let him go."

"One week? This strikes me as more personal than professional."

Mindy had no response.

"Anyway, so Carl had issues on Friday?"

"Yeah."

"Did he say anything? Like maybe his head hurt?"

Brent stepped in. "Mindy, I think it would be best if you told Frank."

Mr. Stripling crossed his arms. "About?"

"He threatened Carl and me."

Brent's face dropped. "That's not exactly true, Mindy."

"What would you call it then, Brent?"

Brent turned to her boss. "He said two things, neither of which were threats; however, they seemed to be prophetic."

"And they were?"

Brent turned it over to Mindy. "You care to tell him."

"Stutter and one pound." She shrugged. "More specifically, he said, 'stutter' to Carl, and told him to tell me, 'one pound.'"

"What does one pound mean?"

Mindy offered, "I didn't think anything until Saturday." She relived her story a second time. "So you can see, he seems to have made something happen to Carl and me."

Mr. Stripling sighed. "Okay, I'll call the authorities, and it looks like I may have to get a hazmat team in here to see if he's done something to you and Carl."

Brent stopped him. "But no one else has been affected."

Mindy volleyed to Brent. "Don't you have something to tell Frank as well?"

Brent studied his boss. *How much do I want to tell him?*

"Did he do something to you, too?"

"No."

Mindy spoke up. "Now who isn't telling the whole truth?"

"Very well." Brent pressed forward, and gave the account of his weekend.

Mr. Stripling slapped Brent's shoulder. "Although congratulations are in order, I'd be concerned that he knows a little too much about you and your family."

Brent resigned. "I suppose. However, I have nothing but nice things to say about Mr. Templeton. Just know that. If the police ask me, that's what I'll tell them."

Mindy sneered. "Just tell the story as it unfolded. They will know what a freak he is." Mindy gloated. "I told you, Brent. He was a freak. I always peg them quickly."

"Doesn't change the fact that I liked him."

"Well you can go visit him in prison."

Brent put his hand up. "Hold off on prosecuting him until he's spoken to."

Mr. Stripling reminded the two. "I don't have to tell you two that this is not to be discussed, right?"

Brent nodded. "Yes, sir."

Mindy bristled. "Yes."

Chapter 13

Carl struggled against restraints. He lay on his back, a cuff securing him to a gurney. Alone inside a room with a mirror, bare pea green walls, his echo bounced around in space.

A voice reassured him, "Relax, Carl."

"Pppppppplease."

"Okay." The door opened and Dr. Coldsnow entered. "Carl, I'm going to remove you from this room. I'll take the bindings off as well." He stepped closer and peered over the top of Carl. "However, I'm going to need your help."

Carl nodded.

"Good." Dr. Coldsnow nodded into the mirror and Mr. Pearl and Ms. Ping entered the room. "My associates will make you comfortable. If you agree to remain until Monday, I'll process you out the door."

Carl nodded.

Mr. Pearl swung Carl's gurney feet first to the door and rolled him out. Past shrieks of pain and displeasure, beyond doors of hysteria, Carl, Ping, and Pearl rolled to an elevator. "Taking you topside, Carl."

Ping had her laptop hung from her neck and positioned like a cigarette girl. She never spoke and Carl wondered if she might be mute. Her fingers danced over the keyboard. Everything said, every inference made, she typed.

When the door reopened, the ambiance went from hell to sublime. A chandelier passed over Carl, followed by another.

"You like?"

Carl exhaled.

"Welcome to Coldsnow Manor." Pearl winked. "It's not really called that, but we've dubbed it that." Carl flowed along, wheels on carpet, quiet. "This is the family unit of Eastern State."

They stopped and Pearl knocked on a door. When it opened, he said, "Here you go, Mr. Wickmire."

He craned his neck and Mrs. Wickmire stepped closer.

"Let me unhook him." Pearl uncuffed his arms, and Carl sat up. "He's all yours. Remember, Dinner is at five, and Dr. Coldsnow would like to dine with you."

"Thank you, Mr. Pearl." Mrs. Wickmire helped Carl off the gurney.

Mr. Pearl turned to Carl. "You are obligated until Dr. Coldsnow clears you. Trust me; that will be sometime Monday."

Carl put his hand on Mr. Pearl's sleeve. "Thhhhhhhhank y—"

"Relax, I know. You're welcome."

Carl retreated to his room.

"Honey, are you okay?"

Carl shook his head and wept into his wife's arms.

"I contacted the police."

Carl retrieved a pad and pencil: 'What did they say?'

His wife's eyes carried a burden. "They said they would look into it, but I didn't hear a lot of concern in their voices."

The room phone rang. Mrs. Wickmire answered. "Yes, one moment." She cupped the phone. "Dr. Coldsnow wants to talk to you."

Carl took the receiver.

"Carl, I wanted to personally call you and let you know that we will unlock what was done to you. The more comfortable you get with daily routines like answering the phone, and not panicking when you have to speak, the quicker you will lose the block you have with enunciating without a stutter."

Carl pointed to his wife and motioned to thank him.

She took the phone. "Carl says, 'Thank you.'"

Carl listened. "Okay, see you at five."

She hung up. "Well, he seems like a nice man."

Carl scribbled on his pad: 'I don't like him.'

"You don't? Why?"

He wrote: 'He doesn't talk to me, he talks at me.'

"He wants to help you."

Carl shook his head and composed: 'No he doesn't. He wants something else. I can feel it.'

His wife rubbed his shoulder. "You've been through a lot, why don't you take a nap."

I've been pinned to a bed for four hours, and she asks me to take a nap?

Carl shook his head. He took his wife's hand and pulled her toward the door.

"Where are we going?"

He motioned out. He grabbed his pad and they exited.

Sconce lighting, movie theater carpet, wide halls. The place was grand. They made their way to an interior courtyard. On a bench, Carl penned his thoughts: 'It is my guilt that silences me. Over the last four years, I have not always been the husband and father that I should have been. I didn't say all the things I should have said, and now that I can't say them, it is extremely evident that I missed some wonderful opportunities to tell you how much you and the girls mean to me.' He slid the note to his wife.

She held it and sighed. "I don't know what that evil man did, but he won't get away with it."

Carl stopped her. He scribbled: 'He has shown me something I didn't see before.'

She frowned. "Don't thank him for this."

He shook his head and wrote: 'I'm not.'

Chapter 14

The clock couldn't move fast enough.

"Brent, you look preoccupied today." His webmaster peeked over a cubicle wall.

"Want to get home to Becky." He leaned back in his chair. "I can't concentrate. It's as if this job has moved to nothing more than a paycheck."

"Seriously?"

"Yeah. Suddenly, so many other things are more important." Brent twisted kinks out of his back.

"Just remember all those important things take money."

Brent tossed a crumpled piece of paper at his webmaster. "Hunter, you're one to talk. You've threatened to quit fifty times."

"That's only because I have leverage. I know they aren't going to fire me."

Brent cocked his head. "What would you do if they did?"

"Move on. Somebody will take me."

"Yeah, but would you feel slighted if you didn't think you deserved it?"

Hunter winced. "No." He smiled. "But I'd get even."

Brent nodded. "So you would feel slighted."

"No. I'm just antisocial and prefer to go out on my own terms. People can do whatever they want, but that doesn't mean I'm not going to get the last word." He rested his chin on the lip of the wall. "I prefer to be my own God." He changed the subject. "You know what happened to Carl, right."

"Maybe."

"Ooh, you aren't talking?"

"I've heard the rumors, same as you."

Hunter came around the corner and walked into Brent's cubicle. "You've heard more than that."

"Excuse me?"

"That rumor, the one you say you've heard, you haven't come over to my desk and said, 'Hey, guess what I heard?' So, I suspect, you've been told a whole bunch, and that Stripling has said mum's the word."

Hunter's stare needled Brent.

"What I may or may not know is no more or less than what you probably know, besides, secrets tend to not stay secrets around here."

"It's me you're talking to."

Brent pushed off the desk and his chair rolled to his cubicle opening. He slid his partition closed. "What are your thoughts of Mr. Templeton?"

"How did he creep into our conversation?"

"Just answer the question."

"I didn't interact with him. We were sort of at the opposite ends of office duties."

"You never spoke to him at all. Not once in the six months he was here?"

"Of course I spoke to him, but just chit chat shit."

"Such as?"

"Family stuff. How my kids were doing, how my wife was doing, chit chat shit."

"Did he ever wish anything for you?"

"Like what?"

"Like anything."

"Not that I recall."

"Think. Anything? A raise, a good test score for the kids; that a store would have something you were looking for?"

"Nothing." He hesitated. "Unless you consider talking me down when we were held over late for that annual review."

"What did he do?"

"I'm running to catch a train, one that I can't catch. He said, 'Don't let it stress you. You can only do what you can do.' He then said, if you have to get home, it'll wait for you. When I got to the station, there was my train. I think it was late, but the conductor joked when he saw me, 'Finally, we've been waiting for you, mighty hunter.' Mighty hunter was sort of a weird coincidence, but I do have that kind of name. However, it wasn't that he meant it as a joke, but rather that he seemed to mean it. Is that what you mean by wishing me something?"

"Exactly what I meant."

"I can see why you need to get home. You are thinking way too deep."

"Am I? What did you hear in the rumor mill?"

"Nothing about Templeton. I heard something about Wickmire."

"They are inextricably tied together, Hunter."

"Templeton made Carl go insane?"

"Carl isn't insane. He can't speak."

"Not what I heard."

"Well, then you did hear a rumor, and a false one."

Hunter winked. "An HR who can't speak. Wow, what a novel concept."

"There's so much more than you know." He stood and faced Hunter. "Can you do a little sleuthing for me?"

"Depends on what it is."

"Can you hack into HR's files?"

"Why?"

"I need Mr. Templeton's address."

"I can get that."

"Also, where he last worked, why he left, and—" Brent pointed. "His age."

"What are you looking for?"

"I have no idea, but take a seat." He motioned to his chair. "I have a story to tell you about what happened when Becky got pregnant."

Brent laid out everything, including the information Stripling said to keep quiet about. Hunter offered, "I have a cousin who can locate a bug in your house. He's got some equipment that detects energy sources. I'll bring him over and find it for you."

"Fine."

"You look puzzled."

"I am."

"Let me guess, you think we won't find anything."

Brent shrugged. "You better."

"Then what?"

"I love a good mystery, but if you don't find anything, then he has a huge network to make this happen."

"Well, then from what you're describing, the only logical answer is he has your house bugged. Otherwise, how would he know to get you the reservation?"

"The owner said the reservation was made a week in advance."

"Brent, that's the easiest way to scam someone. It's called collusion. Clearly, the owner is in on it."

Brent nodded. "I think you're right about that."

"What's the owner's name?"

"Amedeo Abatangelo."

Hunter smiled. "That's funny."

"You know him?"

"No, but it's ripe with meaning."

"Like?"

"Amedeo means 'lover of God,' and Abatangelo means 'angel priest.'"

Chapter 15

"Hunter, get in here."

Bullshit Stripling. You are never fucking here and if you think I'm not solving this issue myself, you are out of your mind.

"Yes, Boss."

"Sit down, we have to talk."

Hunter didn't move. "About?"

"Hopefully, a raise."

"Well then," he scooted in and took a chair, "I'm all for that."

"I need you to do me a favor."

"Such as?"

"I want information on a former employee, and I figure you have the wherewithal to get it."

"And who might that be?"

She stared down Hunter like staring down the end of a barrel. "Really, you have to ask?"

"Uh, yeah."

"And in that thirty minute piss break you took in Brent's cubicle, you never discussed shit you shouldn't be discussing?"

"I have no idea what you are talking about."

"I bet." She slapped herself down into her chair. "Listen, I need you to hack into HR and get me every detail about Mr. Templeton that you can. I want to know what he ate for breakfast this morning. Can you do that?"

"If you mean you want his personal information, I'm pretty sure I can get that for you."

"Good; and I'm sure I don't have to tell you that this is not to be mentioned to Mr. Stripling, or anyone else, right?"

"Your secret is safe with me."

"Our secret, Hunter. Our secret." She shooed him away.

He stood and bowed. "How soon?"

Mindy tilted her head, exacerbated. "Yesterday."

"I'll get right on it."

She opened her drawer and pulled out a Lasix.

Fucking pound. We'll take care of that right now.

She cracked a Coke and downed the water pill.

The phone rang.

"Losan and Gellis, Mindy speaking."

"You have a package down here in the lobby, Ms. Docket."

"Open it."

"Excuse me?"

"I said, open it."

"Ma'am, I'm sorry, we can't do that. You'll have to come down here and do that yourself."

Just what I need is that freak sending me a bomb or something.

"Who sent it?"

"Mr. Docket."

"Why didn't you say that before? I'll be right down."

Before she made it to the elevator, the water pill kicked in and she wormed her way to the ladies room. "Happy days!" Her words echoed across porcelain fixtures.

Someone in a stall next to her coughed. "You sound happy."

"Sorry, just sort of bloated and this feels great." Her piss drilled the water like a squirt gun.

So much for those three pounds, Templeton.

Mindy finished, washed up, and made her way to the lobby. "Okay, where's the package?"

The security guard swiveled in his chair. "Are you talking to me?"

"Yeah, you called and said you had a package from my husband."

"No I didn't."

"Hardy har har. Jokes on me. Is there a package or not?" Mindy stood in front of the station.

"Not that I know of." The guard never wavered.

"You're serious?"

"Like a heart attack."

She slapped the countertop. "Very well. Thanks." She turned bumped into the UPS man.

He continued through and put a package down for the station guard. "Sign for this, please."

Mindy shook her head.

Fucking prank. Just what I need right now.

Her fists balled and her teeth grinded.

"Ms. Docket?"

She turned and the guard held a package out. "This just came for you."

"Who's it from?"

"Doesn't say, just has your name."

"UPS doesn't do that." She turned to the deliveryman. "Do they?"

"No, we show the sender."

Mindy asked again. "So who's it from?"

The UPS man took the package. "Hmm, it's too faded to read." He pulled his Telzon out and checked the screen. "That's odd; it's not on here either."

"Take it back."

"Are you sure?"

"Take it back." Mindy backed away, "I don't want it in the building, take it away."

The UPS man shrugged. "Okay." He twirled it to each side, one last time, "No name. Very well," and hurried out the door.

Mindy swiped her badge and headed back up the elevator.

When she made it to her floor, she rushed to the bathroom for another long drain of her lily.

Shit, I might be under a hundred by tonight.

She stopped by Brent's cubicle. "You didn't by chance play a prank on me did you?"

"What?"

"That's what I thought." She worked her way to her office, stopping at everyone's station to see how they were doing.

I don't talk to them enough. I really need to put time in with everyone.

She closed her door and opened her screen to employee projects. Inside, she took note of everyone's progress. Good people, all of them.

Her phone rang.

"Losan and Gellis, Mindy speaking."

Her husband asked, "Did you get the package?"

"That was you?"

"I hope it was a surprise. I paid to keep them from putting my name on it."

"You dick. I'm so frazzled about my weight, and that freak we fired, and you send me something without your name on it?"

"Sorry, just wanted to surprise you."

"Well you did a great job, because I sent it back."

"No, too bad, you would have liked what I sent."

"What was it?"

"A fruit bouquet."

"I can't eat that anyway. I'm now officially dieting."

Her husband sighed. "You're welcome, dear, thank you for the kind gesture."

"Yes, honey, thank you, but seriously, I am now dieting, so don't send food."

"Does that mean no dinner tonight?"

"Depends on what I weigh. I'll stop by the club and let you know."

Chapter 16

"Honey, I'm home." Brent held a dozen roses behind his back. "You here?"

Becky called from the kitchen. "In here."

"Can you come here a minute?"

She peeked around the corner. "Yes?"

"I have something for you."

"Is that why your hand is behind your back?"

"Could be." He stepped farther into the room and swung red roses out and held them in front of her.

"Oh, Brent, they are so beautiful."

He circled his arms around her and kissed her. "Not nearly as beautiful as you."

She twirled in his grasp and pulled the roses to her bosom, resting her back against his chest. "You are such a wonderful man, what did I do to deserve you?"

"That's pretty self-deprecating. Trust me, I'm the lucky one. You? You have merely made me a better man."

"Either way, you are a great husband."

He put his hand on her stomach. "Are you ready for a family?"

She pulled away and locked her fingers into his. She pulled him into the kitchen. "Of course I am. Now, time for dinner, Mr. Smith."

He guided her to the table. "Can I tell you about my dream I had last night?"

"If you let me tell you the one I had first."

Brent nodded. "Go ahead." He winked, "But mine is pretty fantastic."

"Let's see if it tops mine." She exhaled. "Okay, I'm in the delivery room—"

"No fair! Mine was in the delivery room too."

"Yes, but I delivered triplets in my dream."

Brent paused, he took in his wife's face, and his heart skipped. "What?"

"I had triplets in my dream."

Brent studied his thoughts. "Three girls, the trinity, they grow up to be seekers of truth, helpers of the poor, humanity's wealth of life."

Becky stared at Brent. "That was your dream?"

"Yes, and you?"

"The same."

Brent rubbed his thumb in gyrations over the back of her hand. "Interesting."

Becky shook her head. "Do you think—"

Brent shook his head. "No, I don't. I think we both want kids so bad that we coincidentally dreamt of triplets."

She stared at him. "Really, you believe that?"

Brent's voice cracked, "Yes, yes I do."

"Why?"

"Why not, we watch the same movies, we have the same conversations, we do the same thing. Of course we could think the same thing. It's all suggestive—"

She cut him off. "Suggestive reasoning? Do you think the idea was planted in our heads?"

Brent leaned in, careful to keep his conversation between them. "Are you aware that Carl can't speak since Mr. Templeton said 'Stutter' to him, and that Mindy has gained a pound a day since Mr. Templeton told her 'One pound'?"

"Every woman can gain a pound a day, believe me"

"Fair enough, and she is working out like a cross trainer. Maybe it's just muscle weight."

Becky waved him off. "Exactly."

He continued, "And Carl?"

"Maybe his is suggestive reasoning."

Brent winked. "I'll give you Carl, but a pound a day is difficult to accept, and for all I know, none of this, outside of what's happening to us, is real. I'm leaning that our friendly old man has lots of skills and lots of cohorts."

"What did he say to you that he could have access information?"

Brent shrugged. "He just said nice things. Told me nice things."

"I guess that's a good thing, right?"

"Let's hope. Let's hope that he doesn't show up and demand a pound of flesh for being good to me." Brent cringed. "I hope he didn't hear that?"

"Are we still under the assumption the house is bugged?"

He lowered his voice, "I think we'll find something. Hunter is bringing someone over to check out the place."

"Oh Lord, I better clean up."

"No. No, no, no. The place looks great, and besides, it's a dude, not the Better Homes Society." He held her from standing.

"This is all so confusing."

"What is?"

"If this man really is torturing those two, nothing about him is good. Why would he be nice to us?"

"I don't know, maybe he's vindictive."

"A man like that could turn on a dime."

"Stop. Wait, wait, wait. Think for a minute. These aren't natural things we are suggesting. If we really think about what we are saying, then we are suggesting he has access to a lot of equipment, so let's not shake the tiger's tail."

"Honey, we dreamed the same things."

"If he could make Carl stutter, he could make us believe we dreamed the same dream. Hell, we may not have dreamed at all, it may have been put there."

"I haven't spoken to him, only you have."

"You don't know that, he might have spoken to you one day at the store, and you didn't know who he was."

She screwed her face. "That's a stretch."

"Okay," Brent smiled, "Your options are earthly or celestial. One is a man, the other is a God. Choose one."

"What if I choose God?"

"If we are going to go on the assumption he's a God, what's his purpose?"

"To give us a child!" She winked.

"I'm serious. Think about the other two people involved. Is God a vindictive creature? I doubt it."

"Says who?"

"I think pretty much everyone who is into God says that. You know, absolute love, the whole nine yards."

"And what if that's not true? What if, religion as we know it, and agnostics as we know it, are both wrong. What if it's something entirely different?"

Brent crossed his arms. "Like what?"

Becky nodded. "Like some flute playing Pan who is as altered by his surroundings as we are?"

"Honey, listen to you." He broke a smile. "You are getting caught up in your own imagination."

Becky smiled. "You're right."

Brent offered, "As soon as Mr. Templeton is investigated, this is going to make for a great story to tell our child."

Becky winked. "Our three daughters."

Chapter 17

"Carl?"

Carl turned, and coming up the walkway, Dr. Coldsnow motioned for him and his wife to follow. "Let's get dinner." Mr. Pearl and Ms. Ping trailed behind.

If the complex was beautiful, the dining area was magnificent. Chandeliers draped from a carved wooden ceiling. Forty foot windows cast views to the setting sun and ambience of wealth.

"I hope you have an appetite, Mrs. Wickmire. I've made this facility the finest recuperative facility in the state. Mental illness often can be tied to failed dreams, the stress of lost hope."

Carl's wife took exception. "My husband's not mentally ill."

"Oh, of course not. Sorry that I came across so rudely. However, the majority of my patients are recovering from mental disorders."

Mr. Pearl had his laptop open and exchanged views with Dr. Coldsnow. Ms. Ping typed as voices spoke.

Carl scribbled a note: 'How do you suppose a man can will someone to stutter?'

"Let's eat before we get into therapy." Dr. Coldsnow picked up a menu, nodded to Mr. Pearl and suggested to Carl, "Stop stuttering."

The fivesome shared a moment, stares planted on Carl. He tilted his head.

"Stop stuttering."

Carl relaxed, closed his eyes, and exhaled. "Wwwwwwhat dddddid you sssssay?"

Dr. Coldsnow turned to Mr. Pearl and nodded. Ms. Ping joined in their silent session. Dr. Coldsnow smiled. "Carl, Mrs Wickmire, can you excuse us a moment?" He stood and bowed to Carl and his wife. "We'll be right back."

Carl wrote: 'Guess he's not as convincing as Mr. Templeton.'

He slid the paper to his wife.

She winked. "Must have been a blow to his ego."

A waiter came to their table. "Will Dr. Coldsnow be returning?"

Carl's wife smiled. "Yes, they took a moment for some business."

He put a bottle of wine on the table and slid a coaster over to Carl. "Compliments of the chef."

Mrs. Wickmire thanked him.

When the server left the table, she offered. "That waiter sure was tall."

Carl wrote: 'I'd guess that kid was seven feet.' He noticed his coaster had something written on it: *'Friends are enemies, enemies are friends. Servants are your masters, masters are your servants.'*

He grabbed his pad and wrote: 'Guess our waiter is a philosopher as well.'

He slid the paper and coaster to his wife.

"How peculiar at a time like this."

Dr. Coldsnow and his assistants came back into the room. Carl's wife nodded as she tucked the coaster into her purse.

"Thank you, Mr. and Mrs. Wickmire." He lifted the wine bottle. "Nice selection."

"It—"

Carl nudged his wife under the table.

"It is Carl's favorite."

Another waiter made his way to the table. "Dr., would you like the usual?"

"I would. Please get Mr. and Mrs. Wickmire whatever they wish. And," he twisted the bottle's label to the server, "Another of these."

The waiter leaned in and lowered his glasses. "We don't have that selection here."

"You didn't bring this bottle to the table?"

"No. First time I've seen it."

Dr. Coldsnow turned to Carl. "Who brought this?"

Mrs. Wickmire interrupted. "Another waiter."

Dr. Coldsnow put his elbows on the table. "What did this waiter look like?"

"Tall."

"Tall as in my height tall?"

"Much taller."

"Much? I'm six-two."

"Much taller."

"Did he open the bottle at the table?"

"No, sir."

Dr. Coldsnow leaned back, turned to Mr. Pearl, and viewed his screen. "Find out who our visitor is."

Mr. Pearl closed his laptop, dropped it into his briefcase, and took his leave. Ms. Ping continued typing.

Dr. Coldsnow stroked his cheeks. "As you have gathered, we don't have a tall waiter here. Don and Carol are the only two waiters we have tonight." He continued, "A waiter who doesn't work here brought an opened bottle of wine to the table. Probably not a great idea to drink it." He sighed as he viewed the label one more time. "Even if it's one as nice as this."

"Perhaps you should call the police?"

"Of course. I'll have the bottle retained and give it to the authorities to test." He smiled. "In the meantime, let's not let this spoil our dinner. We still have a lot of things to go over."

Mrs. Wickmire frowned. "This appears it is getting dangerous. You don't suspect a disgruntled employee is tracking my husband, do you?"

"Don't worry Mrs. Wickmire. This is a lockdown facility. It's safer than a prison."

Carl bowed his head.

That's what I'm afraid of.

Mr. Pearl returned. He and Dr. Coldsnow engaged in a conversation of motions and nods. Mr. Pearl gave a confirmative and Dr. Coldsnow's face paled.

Dr. Coldsnow squared off with the Wickmires. He pressed his temples and covered his face. The silence slid into uncomfortable as Carl waited for a sign the doctor intended to continue a conversation.

"Sorry, I'm distracted by the pressures of running an institution like this." He waved his hand in the direction outside the walls. "I have to deal with protesters, and sometimes they figure out ways to infiltrate here." He promised. "But you don't have to worry. They are never violent or dangerous. However, they might need to be here more than the patients."

Carl nodded.

"Did the guy say anything?"

Carl pressed into his wife and shook his head.

Ms. Wickmire agreed. "No, he didn't say anything at all."

"Really? He didn't say, 'Here's your wine?'"

"Well, he did say that."

"So he did say something." Dr. Coldsnow leaned closer. "So if you forgot that, is there anything else you forgot?"

"I thought you meant other than that. He actually asked if we wanted a menu, and we said we were waiting for you." Carl's wife leaned in so she matched Dr. Coldsnow's intensity. "Other than that, he didn't say a damn thing." She tilted her head to Ms. Ping. "Did you get the swear word in your typing there?"

Ms. Ping stopped, looked up and smiled. "I did."

Dr. Coldsnow eased the throttle. "Sorry, Mrs. Wickmire. I'm just stressed about the man who brought the bottle. I suspect it was meant for me, and depending on what's in that bottle, it could mean the stakes have changed." He removed his table napkin and spread it out across his lap. "Let's enjoy dinner."

Chapter 18

"Meet me at the club." Mindy pushed her way into a lane.

"Are you driving right now?"

"Yeah, why?"

"Do you have the car Bluetooth on?"

"I can't figure out how to sync it."

"Then you should get off the phone."

"Please. Worry about yourself." The lane next to her opened up and she slid in.

An irritated driver gave her the finger, and pointed out she was on the phone.

"Hold on, Kelly." She lowered her window. "Up your ass, fucker!" She returned to her phone. "You there?"

"Yeah, I'm here, and I heard that. You are so lucky you aren't a guy."

"Will you quit worrying about me? Just meet me at the club."

"What are we going to do?"

"Don't worry, Zumba." She slammed on her brakes; her phone jarred loose and fell to the floor.

Holy shit, that was close.

"Can you still hear me?" She shouted at the receiver. She tapped her foot, searching for her phone. She slid it to the front of the baseboard and leaned around the steering wheel. She fumbled for the phone and swerved into another lane. Horns honked and voices flared. "Yeah, yeah, yeah. I hear you, moron." She picked up the phone. "You still there?"

"What are you doing?"

"Trying to kill myself."

"I'm hanging up. That may be the only way you make it."

Mindy laughed. "Okay, see you there."

She disconnected and avoided the pair of eyes she knew drilled into her from the next lane. Mindy rolled into the club, not a parking spot in sight. "Shit." In the distance, a car's taillights lit up and she hurried around a row and noticed another driver putting her turn signal on to take the vacating spot. From her position, if the leaving driver pulled out to the left, he'd block the other woman from getting in. Mindy inched forward and joined the other driver with competing turn signals. Facing off in a duel. Mindy could see the woman mouthing that she was there first. "Fuck you."

The guy did leave left, and Mindy took the slot as he pulled away. She blew a kiss to the woman.

Too bad, honey.

She had to pee. The last of the water pill ran through her system and her bladder filled like a waterbed.

Kelly waited at the entrance. "What's your hurry?"

"I gotta' piss." She scooted past Kelly without waiting. When she finished, she entered the changing room and stripped down to her panties.

Kelly sat on a bench and pulled on her sweats. "What are you doing?"

"I'm weighing myself." Mindy stood next to the scale and exhaled. "Okay, here we go." She stepped on. "One-ten, fuck ya!" She turned and pointed at Kelly, "Take that, Templeton."

Kelly tilted her head. "It says you lost weight?"

Mindy studied her curves. "Yeah, why?"

"I don't know. It just seems like you are still a little thick."

"Excuse me? Coming from you?"

"Never mind." Kelly stood and walked past Mindy. "I'll see you in the Zumba room."

"Hey, step on the scale."

Kelly shook her head. "You are such a bitch."

"Oh, come on. Hey, wait for me."

"No, just get ready and meet me in there. I better start early so I can look like you."

"You might want to—"

"Don't say it, Mindy."

"Okay. I'll be there in a few."

Mindy pulled her gear out and put her tights on, her top, and tied her shoes.

"Knock knock, is anyone in here?" A male voice sounded off from the door.

"Yeah, but if you need to get in here, I'm decent."

A manager entered. "Sorry, just have to grab this scale."

"Why?"

"It's broken."

"It worked for me." Mindy met him at the scale.

"Yeah, if you weigh one-ten."

"What you mean?"

"It weighs everyone one-ten. It's stuck on one-ten."

"I just used it yesterday and it read different."

"Maybe, it was reported today, and sure enough," He stood on the scale, much more than one-ten, and looked down, "One-ten."

"Are you bringing in another?"

"Yeah, it's out in the lobby."

"Can you bring it in?"

"Sure."

"Where are you taking this one?"

"Sending it back to the company." He pointed to a label on the side. "Templeton Scales."

"What did you say?" Mindy crowded him to get a view of the label.

"Templeton."

"Rhetorical, dude, rhetorical." She huffed. "Bring that other scale in here. If you don't hurry you're going to see me naked."

"Just a minute."

When he returned with the scale, Mindy told him to scram, and she stripped to her panties.

The truth is, I've peed so much, I think I'm probably one-oh-five.

She stepped onto the scale and closed her eyes. With a wince she opened them. "One fucking fourteen! How is that possible?" She stepped off and stepped back one. The same.

She put her clothes back on, left Kelly in the Zumba room and drove home.

Chapter 19

Alternating walls of baby blue and pink, 'Highlights' scattered on end tables, children fidgeting, and couples in various stages of pregnancy.

"Mr. and Mrs. Smith, Dr. Love will see you."

Brent nodded and took Becky's hand. He winked. "You ready?"

"As I'll ever be."

The receptionist guided them through a door and into an inner area. "Mr. Smith, you can wait in Room C. I'm going to take your wife to the nurse for a general exam."

Brent kissed his wife and settled into a room with an examining table, a couple of cabinets, and not a magazine in sight. A poster of a uterus drew his attention.

What a small first apartment. No wonder you move out after nine months.

His phone chirped. He had a message. He viewed the number. He didn't know it, probably a salesman. He didn't open it. Three Otoscopes stood like sentries on a rack. He lifted one out and ticked on the light. He put it to his hand and studied his lifeline.

Looks like you'll have a long life, Mr. Smith.

His phone chirped again. He had two messages. He viewed the number. Same number.

Hmm.

Brent opened his messenger: Faith, Hope, and Charity. Both times.

Great, are the Jehovah Witnesses doing phone visits now?

He slid the phone back in his pocket and continued playing with the earpiece. He eyed the pleather on the examining table, looked at the fibers in the sanitary cloth on top, and tried to view the sun out the window. "God damn, that's stupid."

His phone chirped again. He dug it out, another message, same number. He popped up the message: 'How was the celebration dinner?'

A vacuum sucked the air from the room, his heart jumped, and he lost his breath. He tapped the number, and hit dial.

All right, Mr. Templeton. What game are you playing?

The phone rang once, twice, answered, "Coldsnow Manor, can I help you?"

"Coldsnow Manor?"

A woman's voice kicked back, "Yes?"

"I'm sorry. What is Coldsnow Manor?"

"We're a wing of Eastern State Mental Facility?"

Brent paused. Was Mr. Templeton in a mental facility? "Do you have a patient named Abe Templeton there?"

"I'm sorry, we aren't at liberty to give out patient names, and only patients can initiate calls."

"But you guys messaged me?"

"Messaged you?"

"Yes, from this number."

"That's not possible. This is a landline, traditional phone."

Brent viewed the number and repeated it to facility operator. "Is that the number?"

"Yes."

"Well, that is who sent the message."

The woman paused. "What name did you ask for?"

His phone chirped. He pulled it away from his ear and viewed another message. It was from the number he was on the phone with.

What the fuck?

He read the message: The path is your own, but the light is lit where you should go.

"Excuse me, sir, what name?"

Brent weighed the words.

The path?

"Sir?"

"I'm sorry, Templeton."

"Please hold."

Elevator music piped through the receiver. His phone chirped. Same number, another message: 'It's best to go down that path unknown.'

A male voice opened the line. "Hello, may I ask who this is?"

Brent studied the message, considered the man's request, and disconnected the line.

The door swung open and his wife entered, followed by a short elderly woman in a lab coat.

Becky swung between Brent and the woman. "Honey, this is Dr. Love."

"Are you playing with my toys, young man?" She reached out and snatched the Otoscope. "Now I have to sanitize it."

"Sorry." He stood and her diminutive stature leapt out. "Pleased to meet you."

She put her arms akimbo. "I might look meek and tiny, but I can promise you, when we deliver this baby, you'll find I'm a tough old broad. You play with my things again, and you will learn how loud I am."

Brent smiled. "Copy that."

She turned and closed the examination room. "Besides, if there are any issues with the pregnancy, I can climb in there and help the kid get out."

Brent laughed.

"Don't laugh; five years ago I was five feet. Today, I'm four-eleven. If I practice until I die, I might be able to."

Brent liked Dr. Love. "So, how is my wife? Are we on our way to a healthy baby?"

"Weighs one-ten now, she shouldn't experience much weight gain the first trimester. Maybe five pounds."

Becky raised her hand.

"Honey, I'm a doctor, not a teacher. Don't raise your hand."

"Sorry. I was wondering about keeping stretch marks from forming?"

Dr. Love pulled her glasses off and leaned into Brent's wife. "I was sort of hoping your first question was about vitamins for the baby. You are going to treat the baby as the most important cargo, and not a nuisance, aren't you?"

Becky stiffened. "Of course. I'm so sorry. I really didn't mean for that to sound selfish. Believe me, this is all we have wanted for a year, and I've done my homework on proper nutrition."

Dr. Love winked. "Good. As for your skin, yes, you can moisturize, but there are other factors that may or may not work in your favor." She took Becky's hand. "How big you get, obviously is one thing, and your ethnicity plays another."

"And am I a good ethnicity to not get them?"

She shook her head. "No, white girls need to make sure they moisturize."

"You said how big I get. How big can I get?"

"Well, who knows, maybe you'll have twins, or perhaps more."

Brent cut in. "Can we find that out now?"

She sighed. "You haven't done this before, clearly." She moved to the uterus poster, and pointed to the walls of the uterus. "Your fetus is about the size of a poppy seed right now. If you are carrying twins, and they are identical, that didn't happen until about two weeks in, and an ultra sound would never pick that up. In ten weeks, we can see the little bugger, and if he or she is sharing the hotel with a sibling." She motioned for Brent to take a seat. When he was eye level with Dr. Love, she closed the gap between them and stared him down. "Why are you asking about twins? Does it run in the family?"

Becky cut in. "No, Doctor. It's just that Brent and I shared a dream."

She smiled. "If I had a nickel for every couple who had a dream about twins, I'd retire."

"It's not that we had a dream, it's that we had the same dream."

She waved her off. "Been there, heard that." She reached for Brent's hand. "Here, I need you to take this to the nurse at the station." She handed him a sealed cup of urine. "Because, you are leaving so I can examine your wife's kooch. Okay?"

"Kooch?"

"Vagina, son."

"Oh, yeah, I'll be leaving."

"Close the door on your way out."

"Brent carried the cargo to the nurse station. "Dr. Love wanted me to give this to you. It's my wife's urine." He set it on the counter.

"Thank you, Mr. Smith." She turned and handed it to another nurse. "So, here is how we do lab runs."

Brent gathered the woman was new.

"You seal it in this container, write this security number on it, put it in the lock box, and Templeton Labs will pick it up."

Her words piqued Brent's curiosity. "Excuse me, what's the name of your lab?"

She came back to the counter. "Templeton. It's the same lab the hospital uses. Is there an issue?"

Brent hesitated. "No, as matter of fact, I suspect it's a great lab."

Chapter 20

A meal fit for a millionaire's club and not a loony bin.

"How was the meal?"

Carl nodded.

"Let's talk about the man who you say caused your stutter." Dr. Coldsnow leaned into Mr. Pearl. "Bring up file One."

Carl wrote: 'Abe Templeton.'

Mr. Pearl interrupted Mr. Coldsnow. "I sent it to your phone."

Dr. Coldsnow tapped his screen, remained on the material beyond familiarizing himself. Carl wondered what thoughts ran through the doctor's head.

Mrs. Wickmire scooted closer to her husband. "What is File One, Doctor?"

"My first case, Mrs. Wickmire. It's about a case of a Methodist preacher who meets a man who came to his church and convinced the congregation into believing he had special powers. It was similar to what Mr. Templeton did to your husband. He suggested cheaters to cheat each other, he suggested the vain to be more vain, he suggested followers of the wrong—to stutter."

Carl followed the wrong, he always had; it was his job.

Mrs Wickmire pressed Dr. Coldsnow, "He destroyed their church?"

"Yes."

"Everyone?"

"No. In that church were people of good hearts. Some not necessarily believers, some were, some weren't. But for them, good things seemed to happen."

"How could he do that?"

"I think he knew people. He singled those parishioners out and suggested good things would happen. He guided their path where he wanted them to go. Led them to people who he knew could help them." Dr. Coldsnow shook his head. "He took divine credit for it, and the parishioners ate it up."

"How did you solve the case?"

"I didn't."

"What became of the man who fooled all those people?"

Dr. Coldsnow slid his hands over his face and wiped his expression. "I don't know, but that was thirty years ago, and he was an old man, so I can only guess he's either passed away, or is well beyond his trickster years."

"How much did he take from the church?" Mrs. Wickmire positioned herself like a student in front of Dr. Coldsnow.

"He didn't take anything from the church, no money from anyone, unless you consider that the church shuttered its doors."

Carl wrote: 'What did the preacher do? Couldn't he stop him?'

The doctor read Carl's note and shrugged. "He might have been the one most greatly affected. This man rationalized apologetics to the point of rocking the preacher's faith."

Mrs. Wickmire tapped the table. "What became of him?"

"He changed professions."

Carl wrote: 'So you think Mr. Templeton has those same suggestive abilities?'

"Well, you're stuttering. So I guess they share something in common."

Mr. Pearl handed Dr. Coldsnow some papers.

Dr. Coldsnow slid them in front of Carl. "The police have stated that Mr. Templeton has done nothing threatening. There is no evidence that any food was tampered with, no drugs in your system. However, I'd like to speak with him, and the only way is for you to sign off on his records so I can track him down. You are the human resource manager, and you can allow it."

Carl signed the document. He took his pad: 'Whatever I can do to help.'

"I'll get this over to your company, and we will see if we can reach out to Mr. Templeton." He excused himself and stood. "As I said, I need you here until Monday, so enjoy the next two days here." He nodded to Mrs. Wickmire. "You too are welcome to stay with your husband. He'll be up top, and free to move about the grounds."

She smiled. "Thank you, Dr. Coldsnow."

He mentioned. "I understand you have two daughters. They are likewise welcome to come and stay. We have a pool and outdoor dining carts. This is truly designed for a club feel."

"Thank you, doctor. Our daughters are busy, but I'm sure they'd love to come see their father tomorrow."

The doctor turned and his assistants fell in line behind him.

Mrs. Wickmire rubbed Carl's shoulder. "Are you feeling better now?"

Carl buried his face into his hands and shook his head.

"Why?"

Carl sighed, grabbed his pad and wrote: 'I can't help but feel this is my fault. I brought this on myself.'

"Honey, it is your job. You are responsible for separation of employees."

He ground the ink into the page: 'That doesn't make it right.'

"But it doesn't make it wrong."

Carl frowned. He put the pen to the paper: 'It does when I'm following bad orders.'

"Was Mr. Templeton fired by a bad employee?"

Carl wrote: 'Not a bad employee, but a bad person.'

"Then why didn't he make that employee stutter."

Carl leaned in and smiled. He wrote: 'She never came to the separation. Although he did give me a directive to give to her.'

"What was it?"

He scribbled: 'One pound.'

"What does that mean?"

Carl shrugged.

"Do you want me to find out?"

He nodded.

"What's her name?"

He wrote: 'Mindy Docket.'

Chapter 21

Mindy's keys hit the hall table like the jangling of spurs.

"Is that you, Honey?" Her husband's voice sputtered from the other room.

She lowered her bag and found the nearest cushion and plunked down. "Ron, I need you." Mindy buried her face into a pillow and screamed.

Her husband's voice slid over the back of the couch and into her space. "What is it, Mindy?"

She sighed and sat up. "One-fourteen."

Ron came around the couch with a ladle in his hand.

"What are you wearing?"

"You like it?" He twirled. "It's your apron."

"Cute, but I'm bummed."

Ron pulled an ottoman up and planted himself in front of Mindy. "Have you considered pregnancy?"

She guffawed. "I'm not pregnant." She threw a cushion at her husband. "Do you realize I pissed a bucket today? I took two water pills, and I gained a fucking pound." She sneered. "I'm going to kill that old man."

"You seriously think he is making you gain a pound a day?"

"Damn straight. He poisoned me with something."

"Have the police been notified?"

"Yes, and they found nothing. Worthless half breeds."
She pointed at her husband. "But I'm taking care of it."

"What are you up to?"

"I have Hunter getting me his address and history. I'll
dig some dirt up on that shithead and threaten him if he
doesn't tell me how to fix this."

Ron sighed. "You have a high paying job. Don't fuck it
up. You start messing with old employees you fired, and
you are going to bring a ton of issues down on yourself."

"Like what?"

"Well, let's see, not leaving a fired employee alone,
invading the private information of an employee, and
perhaps worse, looking like a lunatic for accusing someone
of making you gain weight."

"Ron, you don't get it. This is more than my gaining
weight. I'm gaining weight when I am not eating, when I'm
taking diuretics, and exercising. This guy left and told our
HR man to stutter, and he's locked up right now in a
mental hospital."

"He's still there?"

"Yeah. He was supposed to get out today, but he had
some sort of breakdown, and they are keeping him there."

Ron stood. "Come here." He held his arms out and
Mindy pulled herself up and into his chest. "You are going
to be okay. Please rethink doing anything rash."

She rested her ear against his chest. "Have you ever known me to be anything but rash?"

"Nope."

"So, are you going to help me?"

"Nope."

"I thought so." Her phone buzzed. "Hold that thought." She retrieved her purse and dug for the call. "Hello."

"I got your info." Hunter's tone came across like a spy.

"Awesome."

"You want me to text it to you?"

"Hell no." She worked her way to the kitchen. If taking water pills didn't lose weight, who the fuck cared if she had a Coke. "Just give me the address over the phone. I don't want this traced back to either of us."

Hunter gave the address; Mindy scribbled it on the counter. "Thanks. Now, forget you ever found it."

"Found what?"

"Exactly." She disconnected. "Ron, we have a job."

Ron hollered from the front room. "No we don't."

"Yes we do." She transferred the address to her hand.

He came around the corner into the kitchen. "What is our job?"

"I want to see where this old man lives."

"Now?"

Mindy raised her hands in disgust. "Yes, now!"

She grabbed her purse and found her keys. Waiting at the door, she demanded Ron to hurry.

"I have to turn off the stove, honey. Jesus, can't we eat first?"

"No!" She started counting to ten. "So help me, don't let me get to ten."

Ron waved her on, and he followed. "Let's do this now." He stopped her before she exited. "Just remember, don't go postal."

"I'm four fucking pounds heavier, I'm might go super postal."

Ron's expression turned. "I mean it, Mindy."

"Fine. Let's just get there."

He opened the door and shook his head. "This is a bad idea."

They settled into the car, and Mindy directed her husband. "We are looking for Muerte Aisle."

"How about a number?"

"28672 Muerte Aisle."

"Look it up on GPS."

Mindy typed it into her phone. "Hmm."

"What?"

"It only lists 100 Muerte Aisle."

Ron Shrugged. "Maybe it's an apartment."

They passed the center of town, ran out the north end, out past old town and into the only rural part of their urban community.

Ron motioned. "Here's Muerte Aisle." They came to a cemetery.

"A cemetery? That old man put a cemetery down for his address?"

Ron turned off his headlights. "Let's go in."

"Are you serious?"

"Sure, who knows, maybe he's a sexton. I see a house in the distance."

"Yeah, well, I'm not so sure I'm ready to bark at the old man here in a cemetery."

Ron smiled. "I'll do the talking."

"What about a flashlight?"

"You don't pay attention do you?"

"Why?"

"Honey, I keep one in the trunk."

"You are a good man." She waited for him to exit, climbed over the console and exited out the driver's door with him. She locked an arm around him and ordered. "Lead the way."

Ron retrieved the flashlight and they followed a well paved road past tombstones and plaques. They rounded a corner and Ron noticed marker directions. "Hey, what did you say the number Hunter gave you was?"

She put her hand in front of the flashlight. "28672."

Ron whistled. "Look at that marker."

The sign read: 28500–28700.

"Let's see where that takes us."

"No, I don't want to walk through a cemetery at night."

"Honey, everyone here is dead."

"That's what worries me."

He took her hand and veered away from the house.

"Why are we going this way?"

"I want to see that number."

"Good Lord. I should have come alone."

"I can go home if you want. You want to call me when you're done?"

"Just keep going."

They passed 28600, and made it to a mausoleum wall. "Looks like your number is here."

"I bet that jackass has his name on one of these, and I bet it's this number."

They followed the rows. Ron aimed the beam, each number reflecting light back at them. Ron pulled his wife back.

"What?"

"Hunter's crafty." He pointed the beam at 28672. It read: M. Docket.

She pulled her phone out. Searched her directory, and hit enter.

"Hello?"

Mindy lit into the call, "Asshole."

"What?"

"Hunter?"

"Yeah."

"This is Mindy."

"Okay. Are you calling about the address?"

"Yeah. I'm calling about the address."

"I don't have it yet."

"So why give me a grave with my name on it?"

"What are you talking about?"

Mindy pulled the phone away and screamed into it. "That fucking address you gave me today."

"Address I gave you? What are you talking about?"

"You called me an hour ago with the address 28672 Muerte Aisle."

"Mindy, I didn't call you tonight."

"Yes, you did, Ron was right there when you called. You want to talk to him."

"I don't give a shit who was right there, I didn't call you."

"It sure as hell sounded like you."

"Well, it wasn't me. Helen has been here all night with me. Would you like to speak with her?"

"Swear you didn't call me."

"I swear to God I didn't call you."

Mindy's punch was gone. She wanted Hunter to say he did call, but he swore he didn't. "Okay, I'll talk about this tomorrow."

"And I'm sure tomorrow, I'll have your address."

"Yeah. Thanks." She disconnected.

Ron shrugged. "What happened?"

"Let's get home."

Chapter 22

Carl had a horrible dream, swirling smoke, summer heat, burning acid. He nudged his wife with urgency.

His wife turned; the speed of a caring parent on child patrol. "What is it?" The sheets damp, his hair soaked, trying to catch his breath. "Good Lord, you have a fever." His wife reached for the nightstand phone and dialed. "This is Becky Wickmire." Her words rolled like distant thunder, pitching in and out of control. "My husband is sick."

Carl reached for her leg, hugged her presence and tried to stop the room from spinning.

The night stand lamp flipped on, she wiggled from his grasp and sat. "Yes, He's writhing in pain though." A couple of affirmatives later and she hung up the phone. "I'll get a damp rag. They're coming with a doctor, just hang in there."

Someone pounded on the door and his wife spun into action. She leapt from the bed. "Hang on, baby."

Two orderlies and a doctor pushed past her with a gurney. Their faces wobbled in the mist of dizziness. Carl held on as they rolled him off the bed and onto the gurney. They belted him in, the constriction adding to his helplessness. "Whhhhhere are wwwwwe gggggoing?"

"The doctor administered a shot."

Carl's wife asked. "Shouldn't you know what's wrong before you start sticking my husband with drugs?"

"Just a sedative."

"A sedative? Are you crazy? He's sick, not delusional."

An orderly stood between Carl's wife and him. "Sit down and shut up. We know what we are doing."

Carl loved his wife. She put her arms akimbo. "Excuse me, what did you just say to me?"

"You want to be restrained too?"

Carl tried to defend her but sleep overwhelmed him, echoes of conversations drifted away.

He awoke in a sterile environment. The fever had dissipated, his thoughts cleared.

Where am I?

He was cuffed, and could only clank his wedding band against the gurney railing.

Dr. Coldsnow entered. "It was touch and go there, Carl." He leaned over and scanned his eyes with a small flashlight. "Nod your head if you're feeling okay."

Carl nodded. He wanted freed and motioned to his restraints, jangling the chain.

"Yeah, yeah, yeah. Let us get you to your room, and we will take those off." His two assistants entered. Mr. Pearl held his computer in one hand, and Ms. Ping did the same. "Take Carl to his room."

"You got it." Mr. Pearl rolled Carl out of the room into a dank hallway. He was down below. The place he first remembered, the worst part of the manor. They rolled toward the elevator but stopped two rooms shy. He yanked on his cuffs and grunted.

"Just relax, Carl, I'll have those off in a second." He opened a heavy steel door with a thunk of metal against metal. "One sec." Mr. Pearl hit a button and the sound of footsteps echoed from the hallway. Two orderlies entered and Mr. Pearl turned to greet them. "He might resist." They took position, strong arms, as Mr. Pearl released Carl's limbs from the gurney.

An orderly pressed his hand on Carl's chest. "Don't resist and this will go smoothly."

Mr. Pearl stepped out, and the orderlies helped Carl off the gurney. They backed out with the rolling bed and locked the door behind them.

Ten by ten, a bed, a toilet, a desk. No window, just a slot at the door to receive meals. It opened and Mr. Pearl's voice pushed through. "Get familiar with your surroundings. We'll be around at meal time."

Carl rushed to the door. The slot closed and Carl pounded out his fear.

Mr. Pearl's muffled voice warned him. "If you don't act civil, your food could be slow in coming."

What has Mr. Templeton done to me? Am I that bad a person?

Carl's anxiety rose, he circled the room trying to calm himself. Two cameras pointed down from above. He went to his desk, inside a pad and pen. He wrote: 'Where is my wife?'

He held it above his head in front of a camera.

"Your wife is fine. She went home yesterday." Dr. Coldsnow's voice piped through a speaker.

Yesterday? What the hell is he talking about?

He scribbled another note: 'What day is it?'

"It's Monday afternoon."

Carl had lost a day and a half. He wrote: 'Why am I here? I'm not mentally ill.'

"No, you aren't mentally ill, but you are very important to me."

Carl dug into the paper: '? ? ?'

"Chum, Carl. Chum."

Carl lifted his hands, the optic eye of the camera staring at him.

"You are going to prove my theory. If nothing else, everything I know is tied up with you."

Carl needed to know. He tried again: 'I don't understand.'

"You will."

Chapter 23

Hunter's head popped over the top of Brent's cubicle. "Hump day! I got your address and info."

Brent nodded and motioned for his co-worker to join him. Hunter rolled around his side of the wall and slid Brent's partition closed when he entered. "You might want to know, you aren't the only request for this." He held up a folder.

"Mindy or Stripling?"

"Hah! Good guess. Mindy."

"Don't tell her I asked."

Hunter waved him off. "Why even ask that. You know I wouldn't tell that woman anything. She's fucking going nuts. Came in this morning screaming she was up to one sixteen, and that Mr. Templeton was responsible."

Brent leaned back in his chair. "I'm leaning toward him being responsible."

"Yeah, it's looking more and more like he is, but that doesn't change the fact that she's going nuts. She's always been a little high strung, but this is ridiculous."

Brent nodded. "And her high strung notes are pretty damaging." Brent spun his chair to face Hunter. "This could wind up like Tiffany."

"What? You think Templeton could commit suicide?"

"Not that. Just the whole denying that she had anything to do with an ex-employee being unhappy, and that it was the employee who was making Mindy's life miserable. That job meant everything to Tiffany. You could see the look on her face when she left that things weren't good. Then after she jumps, Mindy stands in the middle of the floor and proclaims she knew the woman was unstable, and that's why she fired her."

Hunter shook his head. "Shit, she was jealous of that girl."

"I think most women were. She was good looking."

"Fired over being better looking than your boss." Hunter shrugged. "I can't believe she hasn't fired me for the same reason." He teased Brent. "You're safe though."

"Funny. Hey, is your man coming over to do the sweep of our house?"

"Yeah, yeah, yeah. Sorry we didn't make it in this weekend. I promise I'll get him over there tonight. Who knows, maybe we'll find the Secret Service spying on you."

"Just give me the information on Templeton."

Hunter pulled out a one sheet from the folder. "One for you, and now I'm headed over to Godzilla to give her one." He slipped out of the cubicle and left Brent to mull over what to do with the information.

What issues did Brent have? The old man may have done nothing bad to him, but what was he setting him up for. The dinner, the telephone call, the feeling he was being watched, perhaps listened in on.

He studied the document. The paper listed an address across town, where the city meets the country. He held a position with Life Choices Inc. before Longmont, and Clear Pathways before that, both positions listed as twenty year employments. He jotted down the numbers of both businesses and tucked the paper under a pile in a drawer. Brent stood and made sure everyone minded their own business. He tightened his partition, picked up the phone and dialed Life Choices.

"Coldsnow Manor, how can I help you?"

Fuck me.

He hung up.

Holy shit. What is it about Coldsnow Manor and Templeton.

He checked his cell phone to see if it matched the number he had called at the doctor's office. Different. Brent tried Clear Pathways.

"Coldsnow Manor…"

Brent hung up.

How many numbers do they have?

Hunter peered over his cubicle. "Well, how soon do you think until she explodes?"

"You give it to her?"

"Yep."

"You better come in here."

Hunter slid the partition open. "What is it this time?"

Brent relayed that all avenues led to a Coldsnow Manor.

"So the guy lied about his past employment. That's on HR, not us."

"Maybe, but it is odd that the last three numbers I've dialed have all been different, and yet, they all go to that place."

"It's a business, they might have fifty numbers."

Brent shrugged. "Just seems weird, as though any number I dial is going to that place."

"Here, let me see your cell phone."

Brent gave it up. "What are you going to do?"

"Random verification. Just want you to rest assure that you can get to another place." He called out. "Give me a number between one and ten."

"Three."

Hunter tapped Brent's phone. "Three it is. Give me another, and make it random."

"One."

Hunter tapped the number, along with eight more called out from Brent. He laid the phone on the table and put it on speaker.

"Coldsnow Manor, how may I help you?"

Brent grabbed the phone and disconnected.

Hunter stared at Brent. "Wow! You have got to be kidding me. That was like winning the lottery."

"No it wasn't." He held the phone up and dialed, 911.

"Coldsnow Manor, how may I help you?"

Hunter took his phone. "Your phone's been tampered with."

"No shit, but so is my desk phone."

"Why?"

"Hunter, the last two calls before this one came from my desk phone."

"Yep, someone's gotten to your desk phone as well."

"Oh my God, what is going on? Why me?"

"I will be at your house pronto after work with my cousin. We will find the bugs."

A voice pierced their conversation. From across the room, Mindy shrilled. "Brent, get in my office."

He sighed. "I gotta go." He stood and edged his way past Hunter and out of his cubicle. "Try those numbers on your phone."

"I plan on it."

Brent entered Mindy's office.

"Close the door behind you." Mindy sat at her desk and urged Brent to hurry.

"I called those numbers and guess what I got?"

"Coldsnow Manor?"

Mindy stiffened. "No, but how do you know about Coldsnow Manor?"

"Just a wrong number that called me a couple of times."

"Interesting, because that's where Carl is."

Brent's cell phone chirped. While he listened to Mindy, he took a peek at the message: *'The path is your own, but the light is lit where you should go.'*

"No, the numbers were both to some Methodist church back east. I asked if they knew of an Abe Templeton, and the lady said no, that the church was newly reopened after years of being closed. That little fucker lied his way into this company. I have my dirt on him. If he ever wants a job again, he's going to tell me what he did to me, or so help me God, I will bury him."

"Are you going to go talk to him?"

"Yeah, and this time I have his real address." She mentioned what happened earlier in the week. "He's not getting away with this."

Brent stood, jarred by the revelation of Carl's location. He waved Mindy off as he headed for the door. "Careful what you ask for. You might just get it."

Mindy's spit back. "I fucking plan on it."

Chapter 24

The door opened instead of the slot. "Good Wednesday morning to you, Carl." Dr. Coldsnow and his two assistants entered.

Carl pulled his knees to his chest, cornered at the far end of his bed.

Dr. Coldsnow took Carl's desk chair and squared it off facing him. He sat and crossed his legs. "I hope the last four days have calmed you." He waved his hand for Mr. Pearl to retrieve Carl's pad and pen. "I'm sure he wants to speak."

Carl scrambled for the pen and jotted: 'Where is my wife?'

"I assume at home." Dr. Coldsnow patted the edge of the bed. "Relax. I'm going to share how long you'll be here, and why. Believe me, I'm protecting you."

Carl wrote: 'You're keeping me here against my will. I have lost all track of time because you keep drugging me. How are you protecting me?'

"Think about the man who started this whole adventure. I want to ask you some questions about Mr. Templeton."

Carl knew all things led to there. He nodded.

"Did Mr. Templeton have scar on his lower arm? Pretty noticeable jagged line?"

Carl nodded.

"Did he have a gray beard?"

Carl nodded.

"Let me guess, it was gray, except for a dark streak," Dr. Coldsnow ran his finger from the corner of his mouth, down to his chin, "right here on the left side of his face?"

Carl nodded. He picked up his pad and wrote: 'How do you know that?'

"Because I believe you and I met the definition of an evil man. In fact, I'm sure of it."

Carl wrote: 'When did you meet him?'

Dr. Coldsnow leaned toward Carl. He put his hands on his knees and ground his teeth. "That Methodist church he destroyed was mine." He let that sink into Carl's thoughts. "I was the preacher he castigated. He made me stutter just like you, Carl."

Carl continued: 'But you don't stutter anymore.'

"Nope, no I don't." Dr. Coldsnow slapped his lap and stood. "He released me of my stutter for a price."

Carl listened.

"You see, he told me, write a speech for the congregation, one that admits to my duplicity in allowing the corrupt to steal from the other members of the church, for allowing a man guilty of rape to hide behind my word, for not shaming those who stood with me in allowing it all to happen, to all the atrocities he said my congregation was guilty of, and for not promoting a good environment. He said if I did that, he would allow me to give that speech with the fluidity of a carnival barker." Dr. Coldsnow exhaled. "I did, my stuttering stopped, everyone who he made stutter stopped, and everyone left my church—half in panic, the other half because I had betrayed their trust."

Dr. Coldsnow appeared to lose his confidence, an edge chipped away. "I don't know how he did it. What suggestive powers he had, but all these years, I swore I'd find him and discover how and get my retribution." He leaned on the chair. "I changed professions, started this institution looking for people like you, because I was sure it would lead me to him. Somehow, he would do this again. The day of Dr. Morehead's call, I'd resolved that the old man had died of old age, and I would never get my answers. Then you. As though he played with me, you get delivered to my doorstep." Dr. Coldsnow pointed at Carl. "You see, Carl, that's why you are here. You are bait. He is going to have to come to you to let you off the hook, and I have let everyone know you are here so that he will find out. One thing I remember about that old man, he feels the need to give options, and when he does, I'm going to exchange you from this room with him."

Carl wrote: 'What about his age? You said he was old.'

"Make up. I'm guessing he was probably a lot younger than I thought. Carl, you have to understand. This man ruined a lot of lives. I need your help to catch him. You can't believe he's a good man, do you?"

Carl jotted down: 'I don't know.'

"Look what he did to me?"

Carl wrote: 'He stopped your actions of duplicity, of protecting the guilty, and freed the parishioners of it.'

"There's more to it than that, Carl."

Carl wrote: 'Explain then.'

"He changed the fundamentals of what the congregation believed about God. He was blasphemous and led them to believe he was God. That's the thing about converts. They are impressionable. They can be led to bad things if they are convinced of it."

Carl went on: 'Did he claim to be God?'

"He let his parlor tricks do the talking."

Carl wrote: 'What parlor tricks?'

Dr. Coldsnow laughed. "Really? How about you and me stuttering?" The doctor circled his finger and rounded up his assistants. "Okay, we are done." He knocked on metal and an orderly keyed the lock to open the door. He turned back, Carl still tucked in the corner. "I still have faith in one thing. I have faith that your Mr. Templeton is going to show up at this place. He's narcissistic enough to try and dupe you into believing he's God." The door closed, the slat opened, and Dr. Coldsnow offered, "Until then, enjoy your stay."

Chapter 25

"I got the creep's address, let's go."

Ron craned his neck, a picture of comfort on the couch. "Why don't you go to the club and see if you gained a pound yet."

"I'm serious." She dropped her keys on the table. "Get your shit a packin' and let's go a trackin'."

Ron turned the volume down on the TV. "Where is it this time?"

"It's a house, thank you. Over in the Lake district."

"Well, at least it's not dark yet, so I guess we can cruise by there."

"That's the spirit." Mindy went to the kitchen and fetched a Coke.

Ron followed. "I thought you were swearing off those while you were gaining weight."

"This is all ending tonight. He's going to fess up, give me whatever antidote I need, and I will be back to one-ten in a day."

Ron tapped Mindy's nose. "Nothing stupid, okay?"

She pushed him aside and worked back to the door. "Yeah, whatever. Let's go." She hurried him out the door and they hopped in the car.

"What are you going to say to him when you see him?"

"Something about how my husband will beat the shit out of you if you don't come clean about what you did to me." She nodded. "That's where you come in."

"I don't come in anywhere near that conversation."

"Look at me." She pointed to a jowl. "You see that puffiness? That could get a lot worse if I keep gaining weight."

Ron pointed out, "You know, there's an old adage about stress and weight gain. Maybe all he planted was a suggestion that is causing you to stress, and you are feeding it by stressing more."

"Did you not hear me about what I did on Monday? I took two water pills. I should have lost five pounds, and instead, I gain one pound. So far, true to his threat, I have gained one pound a day."

"From what you said, he didn't threaten you. In fact, he never spoke to you."

"Thankfully, or I might be in the same loony bin as Carl."

"Please enlighten me what you think this guy has done?"

"He has infected me with something that has caused me to gain weight, and he did something to Carl to cause him to stutter, all because he was a jack-off employee who couldn't fit in with the group."

"Why does this strike me as really similar to Tiffany?"

Mindy twisted in her seat and faced her husband. "I have told you to never mention that woman's name again. She killed herself with the intent of hurting me."

Ron pulled over. He put the car in park, pulled the key out, and tossed it to her. "You are being a selfish, narcissistic bitch. Do this yourself. I'm done with your petty games. When you are done spying on this employee, please make sure you leave him alive." He exited and started walking north.

Mindy scooted out of the car and chased after him. "Come on, get back here."

Ron turned. "Go do your thing. The best you can do right now is leave me alone."

"Really? That's your attitude?"

He stepped toward her, and Mindy felt a line crossed. His gaze sent a wave of fear with it. "Go."

Mindy cowered. "Okay." She retreated to the car and drove to the Lake District. She brought up Templeton's address and drove around the descending order of numbers until she found the residence. On a corner, a well-maintained home reached skyward, and a young Asian woman tended to flowers.

Mindy pulled up and stepped out. "Excuse me."

A pretty woman, Mindy guessed twenty-five. Hell, she was Asian, maybe she was fifty. She looked young. She lifted her visor. "Yes?"

"I'm looking for Mr. Templeton, does he live here?"

She nodded.

"Is he home?"

She shook her head.

Mindy tried to get a word out of her.

Shit, does she speak English?

Mindy raised her voice and put her hand to her mouth. "Do you speak English?"

The woman stood. Her grammar flowed in fluid perfection. "Rather well, and you?"

"I'm sorry. I didn't mean to offend you."

"And yet, you did it quite well."

"Sorry."

"Now, how can I help you?"

"Do you know when Mr. Templeton will be coming back?"

"I do not. He lost a job he loved very much, and so he has had to go out and do what he can to make ends meet."

"And where might that be?"

The woman stepped closer. "You ask a lot of questions. Might I have your name?"

"Look, I'm not trying to cause trouble. I just wanted to have a conversation with your boss."

"My boss?"

"Mr. Templeton."

"I see, my boss?"

"Well, whatever arrangement you have for keeping up such a beautiful yard." Mindy wasn't getting answers from this woman. Clearly, she'd outstayed her welcome. "I'll check in tomorrow. Let him know that a woman came to see him about some business."

"Business?"

"Yeah, business."

The woman nodded, and pointed to the Lithodora beneath Mindy's feet. "Careful where you walk, if you are a pound over one-ten, you will crush the buds." She winked.

Mindy fixed on her gaze and twisted her foot into the plant. "I'll remember that." She had Templeton's address. She'd be back.

Chapter 26

Brent kissed his wife. "Honey, would you like to go for a drive?"

She squeezed him and rubbed her nose on his chin. "What did you have in mind?"

"I have Mr. Templeton's address."

His wife winced. "Are you sure you want to do this. I mean, he's not done anything to us."

"I'm not trying to start trouble. I just need to ask him honestly, how he is doing all the strange things happening."

"Can we go later?"

He shook his head. "No. We have to be back here by eight."

"Why?"

"Hunter and his cousin are coming by to sweep the house for listening devices."

Becky kissed Brent. "It is so Double-O-Seven." She released him and grabbed a hat. "So where does he live?"

"In the Lake District."

"Nice digs."

"Lot of nice houses."

"Must be nice."

"Guess we'll see." Brent opened the door and swept his hand for his wife to pass. "After you."

"Thank you, dear."

They pulled out and Becky ran the dial to jazz.

"No milquetoast love songs?"

She smiled. "I'm going to give birth to a more academic kid."

"I thought we were having triplets?"

"Then they will be three academic kids."

Brent rolled down the window, and a southern breeze swept gentle heat in the waning hours of daylight.

Becky scooted to the center and leaned her head on his shoulder. "I'm so happy right now. I can't explain it. Something makes me feel at peace."

Brent squeezed her knee. "Wish I felt the same thing." He exhaled. "Except there something eating at me about all of this."

She shook her head. "You are overthinking this."

"You should be happy. I mean, there is something pressing me to do more than accept my daily lot." He held a finger up. "I have a mystery I want to solve."

"Oh? Are you thinking about a new career as a detective? If so, please let me know before you quit your day job."

"I have a mystery to solve. Maybe I can explain it, but if I tell you, you can't freak out."

"What is it?"

"Take my phone." He pulled it out of his breast pocket and handed it to her.

"What do you want me to do?"

"I'm going to show you a trick." He leaned in and looked at the screen.

She scolded him. "Watch the road."

"Just trust me. Take it to phone."

His wife spun the screen. "Okay, what now?"

"We are going to play a game. Every time I see a car, I will give you the second number of the license plate, and you will punch in that number, okay?"

"And this is going where?"

"I will predict, before someone answers, who it is."

"Oh, this I like. Where did you learn this trick?"

"Honey, it's kind of why we are going to see Mr. Templeton." The first car passed and he called out "two." Another car passed and he called out "four." When he had ten numbers logged in, he nodded. "Okay, hit send."

"So who's going to answer?"

"A place called Coldsnow Manor."

She put it on speaker. "Coldsnow Manor, can I help you?" Becky giggled and disconnected.

"You want to try it again?"

Her eyes lit up. "Yeah."

He gave her ten numbers off house addresses. She put them in, and they did the same.

"Coldsnow Manor, can I help you?"

Becky finished it. "What's this all about?"

"My phone has been altered."

"By who?"

Brent grinned. "Who do you think?"

She shrugged, "It hurts to consider the options." She tilted her head, "An ex-girlfriend?"

"Very funny."

"So you think Mr. Templeton has something to do with this?"

"I don't know, but guess what Coldsnow Manor is? And guess who's there?"

"What is it? And who?"

"It's in a mental institution, and Carl is there."

"Get out!" Becky slapped Brent's shoulder.

He nodded. "Dead serious."

"So why does Mr. Templeton want you to know that?"

"Beats the shit out me, but whatever it is, it's important to him."

"Why?"

"Because I keep getting this message." He grabbed the phone and showed her the messages of a lit path.

"Maybe he wants you to get Carl out?"

Brent shrugged. "I don't know about that, but every time Coldsnow Manor comes up, that message is sent to me." As if their conversation was heard beyond the interior of their car, his phone pinged. "Ha! Is that my path message?"

"Holy shit. It says: 'The path is your own, but the light is lit where you should go'."

"Same thing it always says."

She shook her head. "It's got to be tied to every time Coldsnow answers your phone."

"You would think, except I got a message once when I was talking to Mindy about Coldsnow. I wasn't on my phone."

"Honey, we need to go to the police."

"Really, and tell them what?"

"All of this." She held the phone up.

"You want to have your baby in Coldsnow? You start telling the police what's going on here and they are going to think we are crazy." They made their way to the Lake District and Becky guided Brent down the lanes to their location. "Let me find out how he is doing this." Brent stopped.

"What?" Becky paid attention to what Brent focused on. "Is that Mindy?"

"Shit, yeah." Brent put the car in reverse and parked behind a vehicle. "Lower your head."

They peered over the dash and watched Mindy hop in her car and squeal away.

Becky offered, "That didn't look like it went too well."

"Nope." Brent turned the engine off and motioned to the door. "Let's walk."

They locked arms and made their way up an idyllic sidewalk. The sun hung low on the horizon, the breeze still kept them warm, and the two found themselves in front of a young woman placing flowers into the ground.

She never looked up, and spoke to the dirt she turned over. "Here I thought I was working with the most precious thing on the street, a flower in bloom, and you show my flowers up. They pale in comparison to your condition." She lifted herself off the ground, lifted her visor and showed her Asian descent. She bowed to Brent's wife.

Becky stopped. "I'm sorry, were you talking to me?"

She pulled her glove off and made it to the cement. With a hand, she reached out and put it on Becky's stomach. "Yes, I was." She turned to Brent. "You are here to see Mr. Templeton, no?"

"How did you know?"

She smiled. "You've been expected."

"Is he here?"

She shook her head. "You can see Abe later, He will know you came by."

"Do you know who I am?"

"I do."

"Well, I'm not one to be rude, so I'd like to introduce myself?"

"Very well, Brent." She smiled. "Introduce yourself."

"I'm sorry; you have me at a disadvantage. Who are you?"

She put her hand out. "Ms. Ping."

"It's a pleasure to meet you." Brent tilted in appreciation. "Will he be home soon?"

Her head toggled. "No."

Brent pressed her. "Where is he?"

She sighed and turned to a dozen flowers still in pots. "He's putting lights up right now."

She picked up a flower, dropped to her knees and put her glove back on.

Brent bent down. "Where is he putting lights up?"

She lowered her visor and unearthed some soil. "On a path for someone to see."

Chapter 27

The slot opened up, a tray slid in. The clock held fast at two, too early for dinner. He scooted off his bed and approached the door.

"Carl, do you remember when you were ten and your cousin was teased for her dental braces?" The voice didn't come from the speaker; it didn't come from the slot. Someone stood next to him. The room was empty.

Carl nodded.

"You know what I liked about that day?"

Carl shrugged.

"You took a sock in the nose. You had no way to defend a twelve-year-old against two fourteen-year-old boys, but you defended her anyway."

He stepped closer to the tray: a simple bowl, water filled, and a rag.

"Take the rag, dip it in the water and clean your face of the sweat you feel. Wipe it away, shed it."

He dipped the rag in the water. The cool release against his skin drew him years away, to virtue, to principles. He closed his eyes and from his lips came. "God, that feels good."

"Yes it does."

Carl smiled. He turned to a camera, waved. "Doctor, you did it." He waved harder. "Hey, you did it. Let me out."

He spun back to the door. The slot was closed, the tray was gone. He tried to speak but he stammered. "Whhhhhhhhere ddddddddddid you ggggggggo?" He held the rag. He brought it to his face, dry, warm, no relief.

I don't understand.

Dr. Coldsnow's voice piped in, "Carl, are you okay in there?"

He tried to speak, gurgles spit forward. He grabbed his pad: 'Did you hear me speak?'

"No."

He continued: 'Did you bring the tray to me?'

"What tray?"

He scribbled: 'What about this rag.'

He held it out to the camera.

"That's your sink rag."

Carl turned to the sink. It was the sink rag.

I'm hallucinating, maybe I am crazy.

"Did you eat your lunch today?"

Carl nodded.

"Let's get you out of your room and have a discussion. Would that work for you?"

Carl nodded.

Footsteps echoed from beyond the door. The door clanked and metal to metal tumbled the lock. It creaked open and two orderlies motioned for Carl to follow. No binds, no cuffs. He walked between them, the cat calls from moaning patients, chattering of conversations with imaginary friends. They walked opposite the elevator, deeper into the bowels of underground catacombs. From one hallway into another, more groans, sad reminders that crazy is merely a state of mind.

"This way, Mr. Wickmire." An orderly swept his hand through a bright room, another elevator, up top to a private office.

The doors opened and Dr. Coldsnow greeted him. "Carl, come in, have a seat."

Should he feel grateful? The sky outside opened up the universe.

Dr. Coldsnow held a brief conversation with the orderlies who remained. He pressed a button and spoke. "Lucy, send Pearl and Ping in."

The door clicked, unlocked, and Mr. Pearl and Ms. Ping entered. Mr. Pearl opened his computer and Ms. Ping did the same. She tapped in with each word spoken.

Mr. Pearl interrupted. "I've sent it to your phone."

Dr. Coldsnow pulled his device out and swept a screen. "Let's talk about your regrets." He walked to his desk and retrieved a pad and pen. "Here you go."

Carl wrote: 'What would you like to know?'

Dr. Coldsnow directed Carl to a couch. They sat opposite each other. "Tell me what makes you such a complicit person?"

Carl wrote: 'I'm not.'

"Bullshit. You are; you are as complicit as they come. Every day you go to work, open your e-mail, and when a manager says, 'We need to separate an employee,' you don't question it."

Carl stabbed his pen into the letters: 'Not true.'

"Oh, so you question separations?" Dr. Coldsnow formed the nuance of a smile.

Carl nodded.

"And yet you comply with orders. So noble of you."

Carl scribbled: 'It is my job.'

"Look, I was afflicted with stuttering just as you were, and the truth is, the man who did this to us was right. I was complicit." Dr. Coldsnow leaned back and smiled. "However, my issue isn't about whether he was right, but rather, what right he had to pass judgment."

That's not what ailed the doctor. Carl matched the doctor's intensity: 'I'm not here because you want to find out how he did it.'

"Really, and why then do I have you held out here as bait?"

Carl continued: 'Because God has forsaken you, and you want to have him in audience again.'

"God? Oh, Jesus you are delusional. Trust me, Mr. Templeton, or as I remember him, Mr. Goodman, is a charlatan, and I will prove it."

Carl tapped out a question: 'Will that get you back to your faith again?'

Dr. Coldsnow steeled. "My faith is fine."

Carl wrote: 'Let me ask you a question, Dr.'

"Go for it."

Carl took his time: 'When I've been right, it didn't defeat me when I've been beaten, it's empowered me. What happened to you?'

"I'm very empowered. Look at me, look at this place."

Carl pressed on: 'Are you sure?'

"Really? I'm empowered enough to put you in here."

Carl wrote on: 'You didn't put me in here.'

"Why are you here then?"

Carl shook his head: 'I'm here because I'm bait, but I'm not sure I'm your bait.' Carl hesitated. He drew a conclusion: 'The longer you keep me here, the more I realize Templeton might have had a point.'

Dr. Coldsnow nodded. "That's what I wanted to hear. You are complicit." He sighed. "Just as I was."

Carl wrote: 'And you think that's the work of a charlatan?'

Dr. Coldsnow paused. "A self-righteous man with a penchant for passing judgments on others, and then passing himself off as speaking for God."

Carl wrote: 'I don't know if he's speaking for God, but why can't he speak for God?'

"Because that's not how God works."

Carl directed the doctor to his pad: 'Then tell me, how does God work?'

"There's a book written how he works."

Carl wrote: 'Maybe he's here to set the record straight.'

Dr. Coldsnow pointed. "And that's why you are bait, because I haven't given up, and I will prove he's a charlatan."

Carl offered: 'Perhaps he'll prove otherwise.'

Chapter 28

Brent pulled into the driveway, and on the porch Hunter and another gentleman waited.

"I thought you guys said eight?" Brent and Becky climbed the steps.

Hunter nodded to Becky and gestured to the other gentleman. "This is Neal, my cousin. When I told him about what happened to you, he got all happy to try out his equipment and pushed me to come over immediately. Sorry I didn't call."

"It's fine."

He turned to Brent. "Where were you two? Baby shopping?"

"We stopped by Templeton's place."

"How'd that go?"

Brent unlocked the door and welcomed his friends in. "He wasn't home." He kept his voice down. "But the woman in the front yard knew who I was, and that Becky was pregnant."

"Well then," he turned to his cousin, "Neal, you better get started."

As Neal unpacked a backpack, Becky offered everyone a drink.

"I'll take a beer if you have one." Hunter turned to his cousin. "How about you?"

"Same."

Becky rubbed Brent's shoulder. "Honey?"

"Iced tea."

She smiled. "I'll take one too."

Brent did a double take. "Oh, I see you were taking orders for the host. I see how it is." He gave her a peck on the cheek and went to the kitchen. When he returned, Neal had a contraption on his head with a light, and a wand in his hand. "Um, let me guess, Harry Potter?"

Neal flipped a switch and the wand squealed with the charge of a runaway train. "Holy shit."

"Brent put the beers down. "What?"

"This thing is going off like you have a thousand of them in here."

"What do you mean?"

"I mean, I should have to get close to one to hear a frequency sound. Instead, I just turned it on, and it's like I'm on top of one."

Brent pulled Becky close. "Can you locate where they are?"

Neal swept the wand in every direction and the noise never lessened. "It would appear the house is one big bug."

"I don't get it."

"In other words," he raised it high, then low. He moved to the left and then the right, "It doesn't matter where you are, anything you say is heard by someone intimately."

"Can we find one?"

Neal exhaled. "Let's see." As he walked forward, the modulation didn't change; a steady squeal. "Fuck." He raised the wand to the ceiling. The pitch never changed. He redialed the handle, but it didn't change the frequency pitch. He laid the wand against a wall and spread it like putting frosting on a cake. The hum never changed. "This should have changed when I traipsed over the electrical grid of the house, but it's so constant that nothing is overpowering it."

"Could it be your equipment?"

Neal shrugged. "I guess." He turned the wand off and went out the front door. When he came back he shook his head. "No, it's working. There is something here."

"Can you try the kitchen?"

Neal turned on the wand and walked toward the kitchen. Nothing changed; the frequency continued one steady pitch.

Neal scanned the entire house; every room caused a constant squawk. "This is weird. The only way this could happen is if every square inch was a listening device."

Becky interrupted. "But we know where one of the devices is."

Neal spun around. "Where?"

She held up Brent's phone. "Here."

He put the wand to the phone and the squeal continued. "Excellent. Now we can find out what sort of technology this guy has." He took the phone and winced. "You don't mind if I smash it do you?"

Brent sighed. "Damn it. That's a new phone."

"Dude, this is all we have."

Hunter shrugged. "Just say you dropped it. You can get a new one tomorrow."

Brent waved him on. "Go ahead."

Brent didn't like the fact that Neal relished the destruction a little too much, but when he pried open the phone, and studied the guts, he came back with. "There's nothing in the phone."

"So what does that mean?"

Neal turned his wand off. "It means that whatever technology this guy has, it's beyond anything I've ever swept. This is like his ear is your house."

"So what do we do?"

Hunter offered. "Learn sign language."

"Seriously, Hunter."

"Go to a hotel."

Becky wedged herself into the conversation. "This feels like a violation. Call the police, Brent."

"And tell them what?" He waved his hand around the house. "They don't have the technology to investigate this."

"Call the FBI then."

"Well, that's a great idea, but at eight o'clock on a Wednesday night, we can't do anything."

Hunter pulled Brent out the front door. "Who the hell is Templeton? Are we being investigated at work for something illegal?"

Brent shook his head. "Not hardly."

"Then what?"

"If I told you what my wife thought, I'd be locked up like Carl. Let's just call the FBI tomorrow and let them figure this out."

Chapter 29

"Fourteen pounds!" Mindy plopped onto the couch and leaned into her husband. "Two weeks and I have gained fourteen pounds."

Her husband cupped her head with his hand. "Mindy, I'm concerned. I didn't think what you'd said made much sense, but now I have to admit, there is something going on."

"Does that mean you'll go with me to that man's house?"

He sighed. "You've gone over there every day for a week and he hasn't been there. Why do you keep going?"

Mindy sat up. "It's my only option. You and I both know if I went to the police and told them a man is making me gain a pound a day, they'd laugh at me." She turned to her husband. "We need to camp out there and wait for him to come home, and I can't do this alone."

Her husband jumped in further, "What about Carl? Any word on his situation?"

"Stripling said his wife came in, in a panic, and wanted the company to help get him out. Apparently, she hasn't seen him in over a week."

"It seems like his situation, combined with yours, is evidence enough to sway the police that something is going on."

"You would think, but according to Stripling, the police have checked out Mr. Templeton and cleared him." She pointed at her husband. "That little bastard has everyone fooled but me."

"So what's the plan?"

"Tomorrow's Friday. I'm going to call in sick, and we can wait in the car outside his home until he arrives."

"And then what?"

Mindy inched closer to her husband. "And then you threaten him with his life."

He closed his eyes and rubbed the creases in his forehead. "Mindy, as much as I enjoy being your heavy, making a man who is at least thirty years older than me, and from what I gather kind of frail, shake in his boots isn't really my idea of a good plan. It has only one direction and that's me in jail for threatening someone."

Mindy stiffened. "Threatening someone? Seriously? Have you taken a look at me?" She stood and spun in a circle. "Check my ass, it now rolls over those panties you find so sexy. There is a layer of love hanging off my belly, and I swear to God, this chin now has a twin just below it."

He laughed. "That's a bit of an exaggeration. You've put on fourteen pounds, it's not like you're obese."

She tilted her head. "It will be fifteen tomorrow, and by the time I go back to work, it will be eighteen."

Her husband stood and pulled Mindy close to him. "I'll tell you what, we'll go and wait for Mr. Templeton, and if he doesn't show up, we'll go to that nuthouse and see Carl. Maybe he's coherent enough to tell us what he remembers about his meeting with the old man."

Mindy smiled. "Thanks, Ron." She pushed away and reached for her purse. "I have something to help us out." She pulled out a gun. "Here."

"What the fuck?" He grabbed it and held it like a used diaper. "What are you doing with this?"

"It's licensed and I bought it."

"Why?"

Mindy shrugged. "Protection."

"And what do you want me to do with this?"

"I want us to take it with us—to persuade Mr. Templeton."

"No, no, no, no, no. We protect our home with a weapon. We don't take one out with us to force someone to do something, or to settle a score." He swept around Mindy and warned her. "I'm going to hide this, and you better not find it." He turned and faced her. "Are we clear?"

She crossed her arms. "You better hide it good."

Her husband disappeared from sight, and she eliminated half the house.

I'll find that.

When he returned, he smiled. "Don't worry, if you think you know roughly where it is, it'll be removed before tomorrow and put in a place I know you won't find it."

Mindy sighed. "Can we pack up and get over to that creep's house, please?"

Her husband waved his hand. "Lead the way."

She gathered some food, Cokes, a pair of binoculars, and a pillow.

"Why a pillow?"

"We might be there awhile."

"Very well." He grabbed a coat and they locked up the house.

By the time they made it across town, over to the Lake District, nightfall had settled in, and daytime noises turned into nighttime haunts. They parked across the street, the object of their desire had a single light on, the front room, and the Asian woman sat with a book in hand, drapes open, in plain view.

"Shall we see if he's home?" Mindy's husband put the car in park.

"No, let's wait. I want to make sure he is. If he's not, she'll call him and tell him. I think that's why he's never home when I come. She's always here, and he never is."

"Who is she?"

"I don't know. She's Asian so she isn't his granddaughter."

"Maybe she's his wife."

Mindy laughed. "Yeah, right. That old man is probably married to Rosy Palm."

Her husband shook his head. "Well, she's someone to him, because it appears she is pretty comfortable in his home. Sitting in a chair reading a book isn't really the position of hired help."

One hour turned into two, and two into three. The woman never moved, and Mr. Templeton never made an appearance.

"Honey, it's after ten, how much longer are we going to stay?"

Mindy threw her pillow at her husband. "Until he gets home."

The Asian woman stood from her chair and reached wide across the window.

Mindy rushed her husband. "Give me the binoculars. I think she's closing the drapes." Mindy focused the lens to a sharp view. The woman hesitated. Her head lifted and she leaned into the window. Her gaze peered out and followed the line of binocular. As Mindy watched her, she smiled and winked before closing the drapes.

"Oh, shit!"

"What?"

"She knows we're here."

Mindy's husband chuckled. "How? She's never looked up, and we are pretty well camouflaged, Honey."

"She looked right through my lens. She knows." Mindy, opened her door. "Come on, let's go."

"Where?"

"To the door."

"And do what?"

"I want her to know we aren't leaving until we speak to her boss."

"Her boss? Isn't that a bit presumptuous, and kind of racist. You think she's a maid because she's Asian?"

"That would be Mexican. Maybe she does his laundry."

"Oh, and that's not a racist thing to say at all."

"Ron, just get your ass out of the car and come on." Mindy held the door open on the passenger side.

Her husband glanced. "I think I'll exit my side. I'm a bit big to go over the console."

"Hurry up. I want to get to that door before she plays possum and turns out all the lights." Mindy crossed the street without her husband. "Don't let me get to that door without you."

Her husband caught up as she rang the doorbell. "Let me do the talking."

The porch light snapped on, and the sound of a door chain slid across the wood. The door opened a crack, and a caruncle-less almond shaped eye peered out. "Can I help you, Ms. Docket?"

Mindy stepped around her husband and squared off with the eye. "How did you know it was me, and how do you know my name?"

"We've met, remember?"

"I never introduced myself."

"One doesn't always need introductions to know who someone is."

"Is that something that shitty little boss of yours told you?" She tried to push on the door, but the chain had no give. "Huh? Where is that little freak?"

The door closed, the chain rattled, and the door opened wide. "I'm very sorry you are upset. Your plight is known and Abe will be in touch with you when available."

Mindy's husband pulled her back and put himself in the space between them. "If I may?"

"Please, Ron. How can I help you?"

165

Mindy's husband toggled his expression from the woman to his wife and back again. "How do you know my name?"

"You look like a Ron."

"That's cute, but it would appear you've been checking up on us, and that's not cute."

The woman stepped aside. "Would you like to come in?"

Mindy's husband hesitated, but Mindy marched past him and into the home. "Yes, yes we would."

Her husband followed. "We just have some questions to ask Mr. Templeton." He stopped and held his hand out. "What may I call you?"

"Ms. Ping."

The three entered the living room and Mindy, with her husband, sat on the couch. Ms. Ping took a chair opposite and offered, "Would you like something to drink?" She focused on Mindy. "Perhaps a Coke?"

Mindy steeled her resolve. "Keep it up and you will find yourself in jail, which is where Mr. Templeton is going."

Ms. Ping smiled. "May I tell you a story?"

Mindy leaned forward but her husband caught her from standing. He nodded. "Please, do."

"This is the story of, sài wēng shī mǎ, yān zhī fēi fú."

Mindy's husband shook his head. "I'm sorry, I don't understand whatever that language is."

The woman smiled. "It's okay; I wasn't going to tell you the story in Chinese." She continued. "It means a bad thing may become a good thing under the right circumstances." She bowed to Mindy and her husband. "This story is about twins, twins who were very bad boys, who had waited until the spring's end and still hadn't planted the fall's harvest. Their father had had enough and he put them to task. He told them, they would work the fields until they met each other in the middle, having sowed all the seeds for harvest. They would not be allowed to sleep, to eat, or to stand until they finished—"

"Good Lord, is this going to be some stupid parable?" Mindy tugged on her husband's arm. "There is nothing to see here, let's go."

Her husband squeezed her hand. "Just let the woman speak." He turned to Ms. Ping. "Please, continue."

"When they finished, they were hungry, they were tired, and they wanted to come inside. Their father asked, 'Have you learned anything?' The first twin said, 'Yes, father, I have learned that my actions have consequences, and for that I'm very sorry.' The father smiled and said, 'Please come in and prepare for dinner.' The father turned to the second twin, 'And you?' The second boy said, 'I learned I hate you.' The father smiled and pointed away from him. 'Your dinner is in the fields.' He closed the door on him."

Mindy stood. "Not very forgiving on the father's part."

Ms. Ping rose with her. "Life isn't always about forgiveness, Ms. Docket, it can be about consequences."

Mindy pulled her husband up. "Ron, this was a wasted trip." She turned to the door and her voice echoed through the foyer as she stepped out of the front room. "Please tell Mr. Templeton I'll be back."

The woman met her at the door and opened it. As they stepped through the proscenium arch of the stage she'd offered them, she accepted. "Of that, I'm sure."

Mindy huffed as they stepped off the porch. "Okay, let's go see Carl."

Chapter 30

Carl etched on his pad: 'What makes you think anyone will come for me?' He held it up to the camera.

Dr. Coldsnow's voice rang out, "He isn't going to leave you here. He delights in discovering if you learned a lesson."

He wrote: 'It's been two weeks.' He waved it over his head.

"Relax, Mr. Wickmire; I'm not going to hurt the bait."

Carl lifted himself off his chair and took refuge on the bed. Minutes felt like hours, day in and day out. No word from his wife, just a daily stream of reassurances from Dr. Coldsnow that he'd be released as soon as a trade could be made with Mr. Templeton. He should feel good about swapping places, but a side of him gnawed at the thought. Somehow this wasn't the old man's doing. A responsibility to his own actions overwhelmed him. If he could get out of that place, he'd make it up to Mr. Templeton. Trading places with him wasn't the right answer.

His door meal slot opened.

What time is it? It shouldn't be meal time.

A tray slid in. Carl hurried off the bed and made his way to the door. On the tray a flat piece of painted glass rested on the tray.

A voice said, "These walls are not what bind you to imprisonment."

Without stutter, Carl asked, "Then what does?" He didn't turn to the camera.

"Your answer lies in the tray."

Carl lifted a piece of glass and turned it over—a mirror, his reflection giving him a view he hadn't seen in days. "I see." He returned the mirror. "Can I ask a question?"

"If you will get out of here?"

Carl bowed his head. "Yes."

"You tell me."

"I'm not a strong person. I know that. I have done things because it was my job. There were times that I knew I should have stood up for someone, and I opted to remain quiet. I followed the leaders. It was my job." Carl stepped closer, put his cheek to the door and echoed into the metal, "I can't be strong. I have a family that expects me to buy things, to make life better." A tear raced over cheek and chin. "Why is that wrong?"

"You must oil the machine, you must tighten the bolts. That is your job."

Carl buried his forehead into the cool touch of metal. "What does that mean?"

"It means you are not a follower."

"But I am a follower."

"No, Carl. You were a follower, were a follower, were." The tray slid out and the opening closed.

"Wait. Come back, come back." Carl didn't want to stutter into the camera. He couldn't go back to struggling with his voice. "Please, come back." He crouched to the slot and tried to slide it up. "Are you there? Please help me."

Dr. Coldsnow's voice boomed through a speaker. "Carl, what are you doing?"

Carl slumped to his rear, turned and rested against the door. Both cameras blipped red and moved in his direction. "Nothing." His voice came out with the smoothness of lacquer, rich, full, and complete.

"Say that again."

"I said, nothing."

Building alarms kicked in, patients howled, lock-down as tumblers throughout the hall echoed tight. Rows of exit doors clicked shut. Dr. Coldsnow's voice urged orderlies to secure the building and sweep the rooms.

Carl stood and went to a camera. "What's going on?"

"You've been visited, haven't you?"

Carl understood. "I've been freed."

"I need to know, how long ago were you visited."

Carl smiled. His fork had arrived. "You have cameras throughout this building, you tell me."

"Our cameras went down for two minutes. When we went back on, you were at a closed door. What did you see?"

Carl shook his head. "Aren't you more curious why I'm not stuttering anymore?"

"Carl, this is a very dangerous man. If he can manipulate our cameras, he may cause serious harm to patients. Please tell me, when were you visited?"

"Do I look harmed to you?"

"Remember why you are here. Remember what he did to you?"

"You mean straightening the curvature of my spine?"

Dr. Coldsnow's voice softened. "Please, Carl. I've waited all these years. I need that man."

"More than you realize." Carl pulled his desk chair out and sat. "Even if you accomplished locking him inside the facility, it isn't going to hold him."

"You are delusional. This is what happens to all his subjects. They think he's other worldly. He's not, Carl. He's just a man, a very crafty man with knowledge about a lot of things. He can hypnotize, he has electronic skills, and he has money to buy a circus of people to help him. He has an agenda, but he is just a man, Carl. Of that I can assure you."

"Well, he has un-hypnotized me, and I wish to go home."

Dr. Coldsnow's voice darkened. "I'll get back to you on that."

****

"Carl, wake up."

Carl's eyes snapped open. Dr. Coldsnow and two orderlies stood over him. Dr. Coldsnow shined a pen light in one of Carl's eyes. Carl felt relief. The nightmare was over. He smiled and attempted to say something. He strained to push the words out. He couldn't.

This can't be. He freed me.

"We saw you in distress. Are you okay, Carl? It appears you had a bad dream."

Carl shook his head.

"What happened?"

Carl motioned to his mouth and shrugged.

"Did you dream you could talk?"

Carl nodded. Tears welled.

No fucking way. I could talk. I could talk and he knows it. What did Dr. Coldsnow do to me?

Carl pulled away from the doctor's probing and tightened himself against the wall. He pulled his blanket up around his neck.

"It's okay, Carl." Dr. Coldsnow reached for Carl's pad and handed it to him. "Here, tell me what you experienced."

Pearl and Ping entered; both their computers on.

Carl scribbled: 'I could talk. Mr. Templeton visited me.'

"That was just a subliminal suggestion he planted in you before he left." Dr. Coldsnow ordered his muscle to leave. When the room emptied to the four of them, he reached out to Carl. "Here, don't panic. This is about over. We need to find out what triggered this."

Carl wrote: 'Why?'

Dr. Coldsnow assisted Carl to standing. "Because I need to understand how he hypnotized you. If we can do that, we may be able to unlock what he's done."

Carl turned to Pearl and Ping. They were buried in their work, tapping out what they were programmed to do. He shook his head. That was not a dream. Dr. Coldsnow kept a chiseled gaze. Templeton promised he was free. It was real. Carl wrote: 'I don't believe you.'

Dr. Coldsnow shrugged. "Don't believe what?"

Carl continued: 'Why don't I remember going to sleep?'

Doctor Coldsnow sighed. "Carl, that's the power of this man. I'm not the bad guy here. I'm trying to help you. You may not like my tactics, but I've gone through a few of these, and I have seen this happen before. It happened to half my congregation." He raised his hands. "Just explain to me why you think you could speak. Let's see if we can backtrack and unwind what's happened to you."

Carl grabbed his chair and composed the whole story on paper. He handed it to the doctor, who read it and gave it to Pearl to view. Pearl handed the note to Ping who typed away. Dr. Coldsnow crossed his arms and lowered his view to Carl. "Let me ask you a question."

Carl nodded.

"Your story said someone brought a tray to your door. Is that right?"

Carl nodded.

"And you said that we admitted that our cameras were down for several minutes, right?"

Carl nodded.

"What do you think happens when the cameras go down?"

Carl shrugged.

"The place automatically goes into lockdown, and it doesn't unlock until the cameras come back on and all patients are accounted for." His demeanor apologized. "Carl, the cameras never went down. You fell asleep about two hours ago, and we noticed you thrashing in your bed. That's why we are here."

Carl dropped his head. It couldn't be. It was real. He resigned and wrote: 'Two weeks and I'm still here.'

Dr. Coldsnow stiffened. "Two weeks?"

Carl canvassed the faces of Mr. Pearl and Ms. Ping. They stared with surprise.

"Carl, you've been here three weeks."

Carl wrote: 'No I haven't.'

"Carl, you most certainly have."

Carl sped the ink across the page: 'You have film of me over the last week?'

Dr. Coldsnow turned to Ping. "Bring it up."

Ms. Ping stepped forward and placed her laptop on Carl's desk. She hit play, pushed fast forward, and Carl watched time elapse. She went through the first fourteen days, then day fifteen, day sixteen, day seventeen.... Nothing extraordinary: food, writing, contemplating, talking to the camera, no visitors. Carl waved the laptop away. He stood and moved to the bed. He lay down and pulled the blanket to his shoulders.

It's not fear, my spine is straight.

Dr. Coldsnow kept him awake. "Let's discuss what may have triggered the dream."

Carl shook his head and waved them away. If that was a dream, he wanted to go back to it. He had no desire to find out that his imprisonment was real.

Chapter 31

Brent held his wife's phone close to his face, as though he feared his whispers could be deciphered. "Yes," he paused, "I've been referred to your office by the joint task force on homeland security."

"How can we help you?"

Brent wasn't sure they could. "Well, I don't know how to say this."

His interviewer chuckled. "How about just saying it? We can make sense of it, I promise."

"Someone has my home under surveillance."

"What is your name?" The question came across with the force of an interrogation.

"Brent Smith," Brent worried this had been a huge mistake. "I promise you, I'm not wanted for anything, nor do I have any ties to anyone outside the country. Maybe I am overreacting, and perhaps I shouldn't have called."

"You've already called, so let's discuss this."

Shit, what have I done to us?

"I had an issue at work, and a co-worker we let go appears to have bugged my home."

"Was he released for behavior that appeared to threaten our sovereignty?"

"What? No, nothing like that." Brent pulled the phone away as though contagious.

"Then why are you calling us?"

"Because the man knew things that I'd discussed with my wife in the privacy of my home. I called a buddy who does work with bugging devices, and he scanned our home. Our home is emitting some sort of frequency to his equipment that he can't figure out. He said it's high tech. High tech like government high tech."

"Homeland security sent you to us?"

"Yes. I explained everything I just explained to you. I gave them the employee's name, and they checked it out. They called me back and said your office was more suited to handle this."

Brent could hear the prancing of keys of a typewriter.

"I see. Abraham Templeton, I take it that's the man in question?"

"Yes, how did you know?"

"I'm looking at your conversation with Homeland."

"What can you tell me about him?"

"Sorry, Mr. Smith, but I'm not at liberty to tell you anything."

"Am I in danger?"

The gentleman laughed. "Okay, I can tell you a little. He isn't on any sort of watch list. I don't think you have anything to worry about in that regards, but we will send out a few field agents to confirm your allegations on the bugging."

"Thank you; and I'm not saying Mr. Templeton is responsible, just that the whole situation is a mystery." Brent disconnected and waited. Silent glances at Becky, not willing to have conversations others could hear.

Minutes felt like hours, and when the knock came, Brent nodded. "Well, I guess the day of reckoning is here."

He answered the door and two gentlemen waited. He'd thought they'd have suits and sunglasses, but one had equipment like Neal's and looked like a beach comber, the other as if he'd been called off the golf course. "Are you with the FBI?"

"No, we are with the Secret Service."

"Secret Service?"

"We are the ones you called, and we are responsible for this sort of targeting."

"Targeting?"

"Web based fraud, digital spying, things like that."

"Okay. Come in."

"Agent Dale Michaels," he took Brent's hand as he passed, "And this is Agent Paul Gabriel." Gabriel bowed and pulled his equipment in. "So, you have a bug in your home somewhere?"

Brent followed them. "According to my guy, the whole house is bugged."

"You mean like every lamp shade in the joint?"

"I mean like the entire house is one big bug."

Becky stood. "Can I interest you gentlemen in some coffee?"

Michaels shook his head. "No, ma'am." He continued, "Let's see what our equipment picks up."

Brent cleared space for the other agent.

Agent Gabriel flipped a switch and his wand had an eerie silence. He adjusted the dial and pulled his headphones on. Brent watched as the agent swept across the room, his box never chirping. He slid the phones off. "Your guy said this room was filled with bugs?"

"Yeah, I was there. His machine screamed the entire time it was on."

"Have you been here since it was last swept? I mean, did you leave and could someone have come in and removed the bugs?"

"We've been here. This was done last night, and we haven't left."

Agent Gabriel put the headphones back on. He tried more furniture, the walls, another room. Nothing, the box never squawked. He came out of the hallway. "Mr. Smith. There is nothing in your house."

"That can't be. The person we suspect knows things that only someone listening here could know."

He shrugged. "I don't know what to tell you, but he didn't get it from anything planted in here." He circled around and brought the wand into contact with Brent. The box whined. Everyone hesitated. Becky looked at Brent, and Michaels stared at Gabriel. Agent Gabriel scanned Brent's body, the box screamed over every inch. "Wow." He motioned. "Take your shirt off."

Brent slid it over his shoulders and handed it to Agent Gabriel.

The agent scanned the fabric, nothing. He turned the wand onto Brent's chest. It screamed. "Holy shit. Give me your hand." Brent held it out and the wand tapped it. It screamed. "Mr. Smith, you are the bug."

"What do you mean?"

"It would appear that someone has planted the bug, or bugs, inside you."

Brent toggled his head. "But I don't understand. Last night it was this house. Now you are saying it's me?" He held his arms out. "Is that even possible?"

Agent Michaels took his wand and headphones. He swept it across Brent's body a second time. "It would appear so." He eyed Brent. "The question is, why are you important enough to bug?"

Becky interrupted. "He's not. We are just two regular people, officers."

Agent Michaels turned to Becky. "We aren't officers, and relax; we aren't accusing you of anything."

Brent worried more about the obvious. "Is this dangerous having electronic devices inside me?"

Michaels craned his neck. "Don't know until we get you x-rayed."

"X-rayed? Are you serious?"

"You are a human bug. How else are we supposed to know, Mr. Smith?" Michaels added, "It could be in your GI tract, who knows, maybe you will shit it out."

Agent Gabriel disagreed. "It's not in his GI tract. His hand, his face, his legs all chirp. In fact, I don't think an x-ray is going to find one bug. I think it's going to find hundreds of them."

Becky's face dropped. "Hundreds? Oh my God. Is my husband going to be okay?"

Agent Michaels pulled his phone out. "Let's get you to a hospital."

Chapter 32

Mindy stepped on the scale and it teetered up another pound. "Shit, God damn it! Ron, get your ass in here."

Her husband dragged his tired body into the bathroom. "Five a.m.; Really?"

"Look! I told you one more pound."

"And this couldn't wait until eight or nine?"

"Grab the keys; we are going to surprise them this morning. He might have hid out last night, but he's got to be there now, and he will eventually want to leave his house. Today, we get our revenge."

Ron warned her. "You better not have found the gun."

"I didn't look."

"Well, I need to shower before we go."

Mindy hugged her husband. "Wow, you are awfully compliant this morning. You aren't going to insist we not go?"

"No, I think you're right, we really do need to find out what's going on."

"I like your attitude. Still wish you'd bring the gun."

"No." Ron scooted her out.

She echoed through the door. "Hurry up before I find the gun."

He shouted back, "Seriously, don't go looking for it."

She worked her way to the kitchen and found a nearly full Coke on the countertop. Flat but still good. She sat and had a second while she waited for her husband to finish.

They made it out the door by five-twenty.

"I see you brought your pillow again."

"I didn't sleep much last night."

Her husband nodded. "I know; you kicked me several times while tossing and turning."

She winked. "I did those on purpose."

They crossed over to the Lake District. The morning birds began their cycle of day-break calls. They pulled to a sliver's view of Mr. Templeton's house. "We'll get the jump on him if he leaves the house. If we are going to spot him, we are going to have to employ some stealth."

"Damn, Honey, you are so cool this morning." Mindy leaned across and kissed his cheek.

"Grab your pillow and I'll take the first watch."

Mindy was way ahead of him. She tucked the pillow between the door and seat and leaned into a fetal position. "Wake me when that dickhead leaves the house."

When Mindy woke, her husband had a glued portrait. "Anything?"

He shook his head. "Not a peep."

"What time is it?"

"Seven-ten."

"Can we knock?"

Ron shrugged. "Why not?"

They exited and double-stepped to the house, morning dew fading from the rising sun. Mindy banged on the door and shouted, "Open up!"

She waited long enough to catch her breath and breathe more anger. "Open the fuck up!" She rapped harder on the door. From inside, she could hear steps approaching. "I'm going to punch that old man."

Ron pulled his wife away from her nearness to the door. "Relax. We'll get to the bottom of this."

"This is seriously evil what he's done to me. There is no getting to the bottom of this, I will shake the life from him and he will fix whatever fucked up thing he did to me." She clenched her teeth. "There better be a cure to whatever he gave me."

The door sprang open, void of any chain. Inside, Ms. Ping, dressed and ready for the day, smiled. "I've prepared breakfast for us all." She stepped aside and swept her hand wide.

"Where is Mr. Templeton?" Mindy stepped in and leveled herself at Ms. Ping. She stepped closer but the Asian woman didn't move.

"Not here, but please come in."

Ron pulled his wife away.

Mindy insisted. "Can I check?"

"Mrs. Docket, you are more than welcome to inspect the premises."

Ron interfered. "Did you say you have breakfast for us?"

"Yes, I've been expecting you." She smiled, "You could have come in when you got here."

"You saw us?"

She shook her head. "One doesn't have to see someone to know they are here."

"And how is that?"

She leaned into Mindy's husband and whispered, "shān yǔ yù lái fēng mǎn lóu"

"Ms. Ping, I said last night I don't speak Chinese."

She winked, "You actually said you don't speak that language."

"Fair enough, but I still haven't learned it in the ten hours since we last saw you."

She nodded. "Coming events cast their shadows before them." She guided Mindy and her husband into a dining hall, eclectic in decorations.

Ron whistled. "Wow, look at the masks on the wall, Mindy."

"I don't care about some dumb wooden masks."

Ms. Ping corrected her. "They were gifts from leaders. She pointed to the closest mask. This one came from the Kenyan leader. He felt it a need to pay."

Ron pressed her. "What did Mr. Templeton do for him?"

"He was given peace."

"How did he do that?"

She tilted her head. "He was helped finding his soul." Her smile gave way to a precocious snicker.

Mindy didn't find her funny. "You said I can search the premises for him. I'd like to look now."

Ms. Ping spread her arms wide. "Please, feel free. I'll keep the food warm while you hunt."

Mindy gathered her surroundings. Three plates, food served. A wine glass with a Coke in front of one plate. She huffed but grabbed the can and hurried out of the room and up the stairs. Ron followed.

One room after the other in rapid succession. When they hit the master bedroom, Ron stopped her. "Do you notice anything odd?"

"Like what?"

"Look." He pointed to an open closet. They stepped in a room, large and wide, with nothing but female clothing. "This isn't his room." He turned to Mindy. "Maybe Mr.

Templeton works for her, and if that's the case, maybe she needs a little interrogating."

"Check all the rooms and find which room is his." Mindy pushed her husband out of the room. They retraced their steps but none of the rooms had any other clothing in them.

"Are you sure this is his official address?"

"That's what Hunter sent, and said it was on his official hiring form, and the police seemed to have interviewed him from here."

They met Ms. Ping at the base of the stairs. "Did that rest your suspicions, Mrs. Docket?"

Mindy leaned in. "Does he even live here?"

"Every day."

"And what does he wear?" Mindy crossed her arms.

"He has a closet full of clothing, did you not see it?"

Ron tilted his head. "Which room?"

"The master of course."

"No, we didn't see any men's clothing in there."

She bowed. "I can assure you he has all his clothing in his room."

"Show us." Mindy pointed the way back up the stairs.

Ms. Ping led them to the master bedroom, and when she pushed open the walk-in closet, where they'd seen nothing but women's clothing, there were rows and racks of nothing but men's clothing.

Ron twisted around, gathering in the entirety of the room. "This was all women's clothing before."

Ms. Ping shrugged. "I can assure you that this is Abraham's room, and that his clothes have always been here."

Mindy and her husband pounded on the walls for hollow knocks of trapdoors.

"Are you looking for something, Mr. Docket?"

"This was your clothing before."

"I suspect hunger has the best of you. bú shàn shǐ zhě bù shàn zhōng."

Ron raised a hand. "Translation?"

"A bad beginning makes a bad ending."

"Meaning?"

She smiled. "You're hungry." She guided them back to the dining hall. "I hope you know how to use chopsticks."

Chapter 33

Doctor Coldsnow's Entry

"Give him shock therapy."

"Sir?" Mr. Pearl leaned in. "We haven't used shock therapy for twenty years."

"We still have the equipment in this facility; in fact, the room where we once conducted therapy is still down there."

"Why would we perform a practice that is no longer sanctioned by the APA?"

"Because it is cruel and unusual punishment, and I need a fly in the spider web." Coldsnow turned and tapped the screen to Carl's room. "I am this close to discovering the secrets of the universe, and the mere imposition of such a strategy will smoke him out."

Mr. Pearl questioned, "Excuse me?"

"Mr. Pearl, if I do not believe in far reaching technology or in alien equipment, then what would be the alternative to what we are witnessing?"

"Psychosomatic conditioning."

"Fair enough, but do you believe someone has that kind of ability, with or without drugs, to maintain that kind of grip over someone?"

"Why not?"

"Fair enough, again. If that's the case, I want to know how, and that would be an incredible understanding of the human mind."

"But that's not what you mean, is it?"

"No, it is not."

"Do you believe that Mr. Templeton is something more than an old man?"

Dr. Coldsnow took a seat, pushed grey hair from his forehead and rested his skull between pinched temples. "We believe in God because we are conditioned to do so. More than just experience but in the nature of all we know. How can there be time before time without something all powerful mixing the crucible of life. Then again, the paradox of what is before that. It is overwhelming, and the ability of the mind to overcome doubt with explanations that foster comfort lead us to accept far flung notions that God is out there and that he is the pilot of our ship. I preached it, I believed it, but let's be real, it was bullshit."

"And how does Mr. Templeton fit into all this?"

"Because for the first time in my life, including my sectarian life, I am having doubt about the randomness of life."

"Are you suggesting Mr. Templeton to be more than human?"

Dr. Coldsnow sat straight, spun in his seat and faced Mr. Pearl. "I don't know, but I aim to find out."

Someone tapped on the door.

"Enter."

Ms. Ping stepped in and smiled. "Did I miss anything?"

"A moment of self-doubt, Ms. Ping," Dr. Coldsnow rose, straightened his tie and nodded, "Mr. Templeton was here, and we didn't get him, but I am as resolute as ever to ensnare one little old man."

"And how are you going to go about doing that?" Ms. Ping trained her gaze at Dr. Coldsnow.

"I am going to put our newest patient in a position to see if Mr. Templeton is a Good Samaritan, and will come get the person he put in here."

She had a queer expression. "Why?"

"Our Mr. Templeton, who I'm positive is Mr. Goodman, will have to seek out Mr. Wickmire."

"And why do you think that?"

"Because he gets his rocks off undoing his hypnotism and making his subjects believe he's magical."

"And you believe he'd go to such lengths, even though this place is a trap to him, to undo Mr. Wickmire's affliction?"

Dr. Coldsnow spun around and gathered in the rays of a beautiful day. He tapped on the window. "You see a cloud out there?"

"No."

"When I was a child, I didn't have a propensity toward believing God created clouds." He shied away and sat at his desk, "I didn't think in terms like that. I knew a physical answer existed out there. I still do." He locked his fingers in a steeple, "Don't get me wrong. I wanted to believe that there was something out there that was unexplainable, something that could compel me to believe in God." He raised a finger and pointed with clenched teeth. "Even when I preached I preached with one eye on the obvious."

Ms. Ping clasped her hands and stood, taking in Dr. Coldsnow's words. "And what was that?"

"That it was all bullshit, every God damned bit of it."

"Is that why you gave up the ministry?"

"Maybe, because clearly I was the charlatan, so right or wrong, I had to give it up." Dr. Coldsnow slapped his desk. "Our Mr. Templeton is—" Coldsnow hesitated.

"Is—?"

"Is going to prove to me one way or the other, everything I ever wanted to know." The doctor bowed his head, a defeat in his voice that hid a finish line he felt shame for finding.

"Maybe that's all he ever wanted from you. Do you think you are going about this the right way?"

The doctor came out of his thoughts. "Excuse me?"

"Perhaps you don't need to bait him into coming, perhaps he'd come if you let Mr. Wickmire go. According to your reports and your summations, he'll come to those who learn a lesson."

Dr. Coldsnow sighed. "He is like a thief in the night. If I let Wickmire go, he'll come to him and vanish before I can capture him."

Ms. Ping stepped closer. "Why try to catch him, why not just give a message to him via Mr. Wickmire?"

"Too risky. There is no guarantee he'd put himself in my company."

Ms. Ping faced the doctor. "So let me get this straight. We had a waiter who you think came from him. We've had suspect communication events with Mr. Wickmire that are unexplainable, and there have been strange calls attributed to us, from what appears to be him, and you don't think he's already put himself in your company?" Ms. Ping pulled a chair forward and sat opposite the doctor. "Who knows, he may be in this building as we speak."

The doctor weighed the words. "No, I can't believe that. If I believed that he was all those things, all those mysterious things that have happened to us since Mr.

Wickmire has been here, I'd have to lay credence to all that I don't believe in."

"What do you believe in, Dr. Coldsnow?"

He leaned in. "The truth, Ms. Ping, the truth."

"Shuǐ jìnghuà hòu, shítou huì lùchū lái." Ms. Ping smiled.

"And what might that mean, Ms. Ping?"

"When the water is purified, the stones are revealed."

The doctor collected her revelation and a mulled it over. "The truth isn't that fantastic. It's simple. We are born, we exist, and we die."

"Perhaps."

"Perhaps? Perhaps it doesn't matter one way or the other. Maybe our actions have no consequences on what comes next, because maybe dirt over your head is all there is."

Ms. Ping cautioned him, "Again, perhaps, but that would imply that our actions are only about the hereafter, when it might be more germane to the here-right-now."

Dr. Coldsnow caught Ms. Ping's penetrating stare. "You are wiser than your years."

"Just food for thought, Dr. Coldsnow."

"Speaking of which, has our mystery man shown up at his home?"

"Not yet."

"We haven't had any lapses in coverage?"

"No, it is watched every hour."

"Very good." Coldsnow noted the time. "Aren't you off shift?"

Ms. Ping turned to the doctor's grandfather clock. "That I am." She stood. "I have some housecleaning to do, so my day still has motion."

"Where is home, Ms. Ping?"

"The Lake District."

Dr. Coldsnow grinned. "You are a neighbor of Mr. Templeton?"

"Part of the reasons I have taken the most shifts."

"How close?"

"Very."

Chapter 34

"Right this way, Mr. Smith." A tech held the door open to a room of medical technology.

"Wow, this seems rather futuristic."

"Just a computerized axial tomography machine."

"A what?"

"A CAT scan."

"Ah. Yes, you'd think I'd have figured that one out."

The tech motioned for Brent to take his place on a table. "Hop up and lie back." He attached a sensor to Brent's head, chest, and arms.

His head rested just outside a large ringed tube, his arms lay out flat to his sides.

"Now, I understand that we are going to start at your feet and if we find what—" the tech studied a paper, "What the hell. Is this correct, we are looking for hundreds of electronic devices?"

"That's what I'm told."

"Wow, well, let's get started."

Brent exhaled. The silence overpowered the sterility of white. His table moved and he slid into a cove of cameras and clicks.

A voice from outside the machine cautioned him, "Stay still throughout the scan, please."

"Yes, sir."

"Oh, and you know you don't need this, right?"

"Excuse me?"

"Go down your own path, and go down it unknown."

Brent called out. "What did you say?"

"Please remain still, Mr. Smith, we are about to start taking images."

"What did you say before that?"

"This brings attention to yourself, and it's not your path."

"That's it." Brent pulled a sensor from an arm, "Get me out of here."

The tech rushed through the door. "What's the matter?"

The table moved him out. "You tell me."

"What are you talking about?"

"You keep giving me mixed signals."

"All I've said is stay still."

"And then you tell me that I don't need to do this."

"Mr. Smith, I haven't said anything like that."

"I could have sworn," Brent considered the commotion he'd brought to the moment. "Yeah, I'm sorry, just a little tired, that's all." He held his arm up to let the tech reattach the sensor.

"We'll get you out of here in fifteen minutes, I promise."

"Sure, thanks." He settled back into the chamber. As Brent waited, the emptiness of white and silence returned. Alone in his thoughts, seconds felt like minutes.

The door opened and the tech returned with another man. The man approached Brent as the table pulled out again. "Hello, Mr. Smith, how are you?"

Brent tilted his head so he could get a better glimpse of the person talking to him. "Fine, and you are?"

"I'm Dr. Moorehead. I read your report and from your work response, I see you worked with one of my former patients, a Carl Wickmire?"

"Yes, he was our Human Resource Director."

"I've asked the tech to send you to my office after you are done with these tests. Would that be okay with you?"

"Sure."

This has trouble written all over it.

"Good, I'll see you soon. And I hope you don't keep hearing voices; that's a bad sign."

"Just an overreaction. I think it was just the whirring of the machine."

"Really? I wasn't aware the tech had started with the test." He patted the cover, "Well, anyway, good luck and I'll see you in a few."

The door closed. Brent lay back down and the table repositioned him. The tech called out, "Alright, let's finally get this thing started." In a steady stream, Brent also heard, "Oh, and by the way, what did I say about going down your path unknown?"

Brent spoke back, "Yeah, I was thinking about that as the doctor was talking."

The tech laughed over the intercom, "You were thinking about getting started when the doc was talking?"

"Let's go." Brent turned his thumb up.

"Remember, perfectly still."

"Gotcha."

The voice silenced, it'd made its point. When they finished, the tech came out from another room holding a scan image.

"I don't know what they thought they would find, but you don't have anything foreign in you, but I do see you have a pinched nerve in your sixth vertebrae. Does that give you any pain?"

"Not really, should it?"

"Not necessarily." He helped Brent out of the chamber and to a sitting position. "Just something you should be aware of if you ever have any issues."

"What kind of issues?"

"I don't know, I'm just a tech. I can tell you what kind of patients we have who come in with those though."

"What kind?"

"Syndromes like palsies."

"Well that sucks."

"If you don't have it now, you probably aren't going to get it, so I wouldn't worry too much."

Brent pulled off the sensors as they spoke. "That's good to know."

The tech handed him the image. "Here, you need to take this to the agents who ordered it, and after that, I understand that Dr. Moorehead wanted you to swing by there."

"Thanks."

Brent took his hospital gown off and put his clothes on, gathered his new phone and wallet and found his way to the hall where the agents waited. "Here, this is it, and they found nothing."

Agent Gabriel put his arms akimbo, "Really?"

"That's what this image shows."

Agent Michaels held it up. "Son of a bitch." He slapped it down. "We'll be back over at your house this afternoon. Let's see what happens this time."

"Thanks, thanks for everything." He continued, "Did you see my wife?"

"Last I saw, she got a message on her phone and hurried out to the car."

From the other direction, he saw Dr. Moorehead coming his way. "Thanks again, I need to go." Brent turned away from the doctor and walked toward a side exit.

Dr. Moorehead called from down the hall, "Mr. Smith, my office is this way."

Brent hit the door and turned, "I'll be right back; I need to get something from the car."

The doctor tilted his head, frozen in his position. "It can't wait?"

"Nope." With that, Brent exited.

The car idled at the base of the steps, Becky in the driver's seat.

Brent jumped in. "How did you know to be here?"

"You texted me."

"I did?" Brent took Becky's phone. The last message came from him: *'Be at the exit on the Northeast corner with the door that reads 'labs' on it. Keep the car running.'*

"You sent that, didn't you?"

"Not exactly, but I think it was for my benefit."

The lab door swung open and Dr. Moorehead walked down the steps toward the car.

"Put it in gear and let's go."

"Who is that?"

"Just go."

Becky drove off to the doctor hollering for them to stop. "Who is that?"

"That's an unlit path that I don't want to go down."

Chapter 35

Carl woke to the clanking of keys. The door swung open and two orderlies entered with a gurney. Carl scurried to the corner of his bed, to the crux of two walls. He grabbed his pad and pen: 'What do you want?'

He held the paper up at the two men.

"Doc wants you pronto in his therapy room."

Carl scribbled: 'For what?'

One of the orderlies shrugged. "Therapy I'd say."

Carl continued: 'I can walk.'

"I don't give a shit. We were told to deliver you hogtied. You can either do this the easy way or you can do it the fun way." He leaned in and tapped Carl on the forehead. "Which one?"

Carl froze.

"Outstanding, I was hoping to get some cardio in this morning."

Carl went to the paper to write one last note but there was already one written. He fixed on the words: 'This isn't the battle you should fight.'

He raised his hands and gave in peacefully.

"Well, shit. He came to his senses a little too easy. I was hoping for a fight."

Dr. Coldsnow called out over the speaker. "That's enough. Don't be thugs, boys."

The orderly grunted. "Sorry, Boss." He winked at Carl.

Carl accepted the bindings. His feet and arms, along with his waist and neck were secured to the gurney. They coasted him out into the hallway to the hoots of screaming patients hidden behind metal doors. One eyed him from his food portal, "Oh, aren't you tied down. They gonna torture you, boy."

The orderlies rolled him past the elevator and to the farthest reaches of the underground dungeon. "Hey Mick, what's down here at this end. I don't think we've ever gone down here."

"Don't know; I've not been down here either."

"Kind of spooky."

"Seriously? I find it peaceful being away from all that fucking screaming."

They were met by Dr. Coldsnow. He swung open the end door and nodded. "In here."

They rolled Carl into a quiet room with soft blue walls and medical equipment. "Looks like an operating room, Doc."

"Kind of is, Ben." Dr. Coldsnow took control of the gurney. "You and Mick can go."

As they left, Mr. Pearl entered. Mr. Pearl closed the door behind him and approached Carl's gurney. "You can't do this, Dr. Coldsnow."

"Oh, but I can. If you see these signatures, they've signed off on what I think's best."

Carl had little movement, but he had enough to realize Dr. Coldsnow planned something horrible. He struggled with words, he wanted to scream, and scream was his only option.

"Enough, Carl. If I'm right, you won't have to worry."

Mr. Pearl interrupted, "Are you insane? Listen to yourself. You think that at any moment some white knight is going to come in here and save the day. We are in the belly of this building, even if your mystery man was here, he wouldn't know where this is."

Dr. Coldsnow cornered Mr. Pearl. "One of two things is going to be proved here today, and you and I know which one it is, don't we, Mr. Pearl?"

"Yes we do, and for that reason, you are going to shock a patient into a rabid broken man just to prove a point."

"And how else is he going to be cured from whatever Mr. Templeton did to him?" He continued with his preparations and put a rubber mouthpiece in Carl's mouth. "If you don't like what I'm about to do, you can go topside."

Carl choked on the piece in his mouth.

"At least let him see if you have scared him into talking." Mr. Pearl reached out and removed the mouthpiece from Carl's mouth. "Come on, buddy, speak to me with eloquence."

Tears welled in Carl's eyes. He wanted to, they were right there on the end of his tongue, but as he pushed, they scrambled into a guttural expression of maddening nonsense.

"See, you see what he's become? You think this has been a wasted four weeks?"

Four weeks? Carl had lost another week's time? How could that be? He struggled, he wanted to write something.

Dr. Coldsnow patted his shoulder. "Stop struggling, Carl."

"He looks like he wants to write something. Can't you give him his right arm so he can write something to you?"

"We are past this nonsense. It's time to either prove Mr. Templeton's greatness or his fraudulence."

Mr. Pearl exhaled. "Please, Dr. Coldsnow. No matter how you feel, I beg of you, this isn't the way to go about it. Mr. Templeton hasn't come here to get Carl, and he isn't going to, and you can't just zap this man because you are upset."

"Upset? You think this is about me being upset?" He grinned. "Mr. Pearl, I'm not upset. I'm focused, and I know

what I'm doing. None of this is going to be bad for Carl."
Dr. Coldsnow stepped to a panel and flipped a switch, a
hum picked up pace in the room. "This process may very
well reset Mr. Wickmire's cognitive abilities. Dare I say he
may very well stop stuttering after one quick zap."

"You are committing a criminal act, and I can't allow
you to do that."

"They signed the papers."

"Where in that agreement does it say anything about
shock therapy?"

Dr. Coldsnow tapped the final line. "Any and all…"

"Any and all, yet you haven't done a tenth of the
processes available to you. You've done nothing more than
keep him locked away hoping some man will come to you
and give himself up for this man's salvation."

"It wouldn't have mattered if we'd tried any and all
treatments, trust me."

"How do you know?"

Dr. Coldsnow spun around. "Have you forgotten, I was
fucking patient Number One!" He held his hand aloft. "This
is on him. Whatever happens today, this is on Mr.
Goodman, Mr. Templeton, or whatever he calls himself
today." Dr. Coldsnow returned the rubber piece to Carl's
mouth and pulled up two cloth-ended electrodes. He
tapped them, sparks arched across. "Let's do this." He

stepped around the gurney and looked down into Carl's eyes. "This will be over in a minute and you will be cured."

Carl closed his eyes as Dr. Coldsnow brought the pads to Carl's temples.

Chapter 36

"Not going to work isn't going to help matters, Mindy."

"Look at me, Ron. I'm almost thirty pounds heavier." She wore sweats. "I can't even fit into my clothes."

Ron pulled Mindy close. We can't procrastinate on things. Last week we were going to go to visit Carl, remember?"

"Yeah, I just am too depressed right now."

Her husband took her by the shoulders and forced her to pay attention. "Snap out of it. We go today to see Carl."

"What if they do the same thing to me that they did to Carl? What if they lock me up?"

"For what?"

Mindy cried. "Why did they lock up Carl? They don't have to have a reason. We've seen the doctor five times this month, and he swears this is my fault, that there is nothing physically wrong with me, and the last time I checked, they put people away who can't figure out what is mentally wrong with them."

Ron huffed. "Mindy, there is nothing mentally wrong with you," he smiled, "At least not anything that wasn't already wrong with you before you started gaining weight."

"Ron, I can't take jokes right now, okay."

Her husband nodded. "I understand, but just know this, I am still in your corner and I still love you."

Mindy called in sick, everyone knew why. She couldn't wear her clothes so the sweats stayed in place. "Okay, I'm ready, let's go see Carl."

Her husband patted her back, "It's going to be okay." He guided her out the door and to the car.

"I hope you're right. I really thought this would be over by now."

The gravity of her life weighed upon her. She took stock in her own behavior. "Ron?"

"What, sweetheart?"

"Am I a bitch?"

"You're a tough minded woman."

She wiped a crease forming on her brow. "That's not what I asked."

"Well, people perceive women who are tough as bitches."

"Yeah, but being tough doesn't mean you have to be rude."

"Mindy," her husband patted her knee, "You aren't always as fair as you can be."

Mindy's shoulders sagged. "So that means I am a bitch?"

Her husband exhaled and kept his vision to the road. "Yeah, yeah you really are."

"Why have you never told me?"

He laughed. "You're kidding, right?"

"No, why have you never told me I'm a bitch?"

"I tell you all the time, but as a bitch, you don't listen."

"You have never told me I'm a bitch."

"I just told you a few weeks ago when I got out and walked home."

"You did?"

"So you haven't figured out when I'm upset it's because you are being unreasonable?"

Mindy sighed. "You are too passive."

Her husband smiled. "There's only room for one aggressive spouse in this relationship.

She shook off her pity. "I'm pretty good at being who I am."

Her husband nodded. "That you are."

Through thick trees, a manor filled a clearing. They passed the gate and pulled into a sparsely-filled parking lot. Mindy pointed. "Jeez, Carl is probably playing hooky. This place looks relaxing."

"Looks can be deceiving."

Mindy took her husband's arm. "Well. Let's go see Carl."

They came in from the side and the power flickered off.

"I hope that's not an omen?" They stood still, just inside the door."

Ron held her hand. "Um, perhaps we should come back."

Mindy squeezed his hand. "They must have some sort of generator. We can wait."

Ron whispered, "We are in a mental facility. What if a patient did that?"

A door opened and the lights flickered back on. Coming out of the hallway, behind the front office, two suits with lab coats on, chatted with annoyance. One took notice. "Can I help you?"

Mindy stepped up to the counter. "Yes, we are here to see Carl Whitmire."

"And who might you be?"

"A friend."

The gentleman straightened and apologized, "This facility is by appointment only."

"May we speak to your superior?"

He smiled. "Well, I'm the Chief Operating Officer, Chief Physician, and second largest donor to Eastern State. The wing you are in is named after me. I doubt you'll find anyone higher up that is going to let you evade the rules." He bowed, "Dr. Coldsnow, at your service."

Behind him the younger gentleman joined them. He whispered something that put distress in the words the doctor exchanged with him. He nodded, turned a smile toward Mindy, and stepped back the way he came.

The doctor turned his attention back to Mindy as well. He paused, closed his eyes, and mouthed something.

Her husband joined her at the counter's edge.

The doctor's eyes opened and he smiled. "Now, where were we?"

"Would it matter that I also work with him?"

He chuckled. "No."

Mindy shrugged. "You can't blame a girl for trying."

He reversed himself. "Wait. You say you work with him? What's your name?"

Mindy's husband stopped her from answering, dropping her first name for her middle, "Catherine, we should go." He nodded to Dr. Coldsnow. "We'll set up an appointment."

The doctor remained fixed. "You do that." When Mindy and her husband turned he muttered. "How many days do you think a person could live gaining a pound a day?"

Neither turned, Mindy engaged in a conversation about nothing with her husband. "Should we drop by the store on the way home?"

The doctor gave it one last shot. "Don't you want to find Templeton?"

Her husband whispered, "Don't get my ass kicked trying to get you out of here."

She whispered back, "I have a plan."

Ron countered, "That's what worries me."

Outside the twin doors, birds sang of spring's bliss. Mindy ordered, "Drive us around this circular driveway, and park right here."

"Why would I want to do that?"

"Because I said so."

"And I said, don't get my ass kicked getting you out."

"I'm only going to the door."

He shook his head. "Get in the car."

Ron pulled forward and went left instead of right, opting to grant Mindy her request. He pulled up in front of the main doors. "You better leave the door open in case they chase you."

Mindy popped the door open and climbed the steps. She yanked both doors open like a butterfly's wings. She stood akimbo. The doctor turned and they faced off at fifty feet. "I find out you are with that fucknuts and I will bury you along with him."

The doctor laughed.

"I will have you arrested for whatever he's doing to me."

"You're a new one for me, and I'd love to study you."

"Is that what you are doing to our employee?"

An orderly came up behind him.

Dr. Coldsnow pointed toward Mindy. "Bring her to me."

Mindy backed away and tapped down the steps, the motor running. She jumped in the car. "Go!"

Her husband leaned across her, a large man hurrying down the steps. He put it in gear and they left the premises.

"Whew." Mindy exhaled.

"Are we going to get visitors?"

She twisted her head and watched the orderly diminish to a white dot in the distance. "I told them I would have them arrested."

"I'm not sure that's going to be much of a deterrence."

"Maybe you should tell me where that gun is."

"Nope, and this needs to stop. We're going to the police station."

"When?"

"Now."

Mindy thought about it and shrugged. "Probably best."

Chapter 37

Brent's wife twisted in her seat. "I know this sounds weird, but I think we need to go to see Carl."

"Why?"

"Because I think you are being led there."

"And do you know when they want me there?"

She smiled. "Right now."

"Didn't I just run from one hospital?"

"Well, if this one is the wrong one, maybe you'll get another message."

"Do you want to go with me?" Brent considered his options. "With the possibility of the house being bugged, you could stay in the car."

She shook her head. "Nope, if you go in to that place, I'm going with you. You've already said his wife hasn't spoken to him in four weeks. I don't want you disappearing, and since I'm the one making you go, I should share the responsibility."

"I wouldn't worry about me disappearing; I'm not stuttering."

"Well, you do seem to have other issues, like wondering what is in our home, besides; I'm trusting whatever is in your corner. If we are being bugged and I'm telling you to

217

go see Carl, I'm sure our mysterious person will let us know with some pithy parable."

"You think that is the path the person, whoever it is, wants me to take?"

"Let's find out."

Brent reversed course and headed the other direction.

"You know where it is?"

"Yeah, it's out there in the South Hills. Eastern State Hospital. He's in a special wing." Brent had other concerns. "I hope you are right about not getting sucked in. I don't want you to have to fight to get me out."

As if in the car, the mysterious source texted Brent.

Becky grinned. "That was your text ping."

Brent nodded. "Yep. Can you read it?"

She scanned his phone. "Take the path of least resistance."

"That's it? We already knew that. Maybe it means don't do this?"

Becky shook her head. "I don't think it is."

"Why?"

"Because it didn't give you a negative.

"Didn't sound like a raging endorsement."

"Doesn't read like a 'don't go' message."

"Really?"

Becky smiled. "I'm sure you'll get more texts if we're in danger."

Brent huffed. "I hope you're right."

She smiled. "So do I."

They came through a canopy of trees to the gates of the hospital. Brent hit the button to raise the gate and nothing happened. "Damn."

"What?"

"The gate isn't opening."

Brent stepped out of the car and approached the gate. It had no give. It lifted but fell back down. He turned to Becky staring at him through the front windshield. "Looks like you'll have to hold it open while I go through."

Her voice deadened by the glass. "Okay."

Brent took in the facility, and to the south he saw a service entrance wide open.

Becky came up beside him and lifted the crossbar. "Drive it through."

"No."

"What? You changed your mind?"

"You said I should find the path of least resistance, right?" He motioned to the south.

His wife toggled between the open gate and Brent. "That's why you are here, you're brilliant."

"Well, if we go by the clues, that's the way in." He motioned to the south

She dropped the crossbar and turned back to the car. "Let's do it by the book."

Brent turned the car around and they made their way to the service entrance. It put them opposite the front side of the building, and as he made it around the structure, a construction project closed off the road.

Becky noticed, "That's clearly a sign that there would have been resistance."

Brent put the car in reverse and went back to the rear of the hospital.

Becky pointed to a service entrance. "I guess we go in through there."

"You want to enter a mental facility through the backdoor. You don't think that could be a lot of resistance?" Brent motioned for Becky to step out of the car with him. They met around the car, and he took her hand.

Becky had ease written on her face. "Let's find out."

Brent pulled her close. "Why do you have a smile on your face?"

"I don't know. I feel like you're being guided."

Brent brought her down to Earth. "Oh brother, you know a lot of men have gone to their grave believing they were guided."

Becky winked. "I bet just as many have gone to their grave not realizing they were being guided."

"You sure you want to do this?" They stepped closer to the building.

"I told you earlier, I felt like we need to be here?"

"That's because I think we're being played and clues are leading us here. I just don't think we are as indestructible as you seem to think we are."

Becky swung their clasped hands. "Let's find out."

"You aren't scared?"

She pulled a hand away and placed her palm on Brent's cheek. "I came because I don't ever want to leave you, and something feels like this is right. Trust me."

"If you feel someone is leading us here, I trust you." Brent pulled her to the service door.

Becky pointed. "That's a keycard door."

Brent reached for the door and before he could test it, it swung at him and a woman carried trash.

She spun and held the door. She searched for her keycard. "Damn." She eyed Brent. "Are you a distributor?"

Becky spoke in his place. "Yes, can we help you?"

"Hold this door, and I'll get you to the service office."

Brent bowed his head. "Thank you."

As she spun to the trash bin, Becky whispered. "Path of least resistance, hmm."

Brent grinned. "Don't get too ahead of yourself. If this text is right and this is the path of least resistance, then the front door was a bad thing, which must mean us being identified is a bad thing."

Our hospital worker came back. "The power just went out and the generator hasn't kicked back on."

Brent quizzed her. "What happened?"

"No idea we had a power surge, and everything in the place went." She guided them in. When they hit the kitchen, she pointed to the east. "This is the last room for a while with an outer window, so it will be dark. She handed Brent and his wife a flashlight. Go down that hall, and turn left. It will take you to the Service offices."

Brent noted another direction. "What happens if a person accidentally goes right up there?"

"That's the stairwell to the basement. You don't want to go down there. That's the crazies."

"Crazies?"

"Where all the departments keep their worst patients."

"How many are down there."

"Normally the same eight from the Bedford wing, but for the last month, Coldsnow Manor has had a patient in there."

Brent gave Becky a glance. "I see." He turned to their path of least resistance. "Thanks, and we'll make sure not to veer off."

She sneered. "It can get freaky when they are all howling."

Becky asked, "What about left?"

"Takes you to our newest wing. Nice dining hall and the front of our hospital."

"What's the name of the newest wing?"

"Coldsnow Manor." She paid them good day and turned back to the kitchen.

When she'd disappeared, Brent flicked the switch to his flashlight and Becky did the same. "Path of least resistance. Pretty sure it isn't toward Coldsnow Manor, let's go right."

Becky sighed. "I hope it isn't to the right again when we get to the end of the hall."

In the claustrophobia of darkness, she kept their concentric circles of light trained in front of them. When they hit the T, to the left was a servant cleaning a spill in the faint light of a lantern.

"You can't come down here just yet. I have a mess."

Becky whispered, "Fuck."

Brent shrugged. "Choices, both are kind of eerie." He turned her around. "That door."

Becky shook her head. "I don't like that idea."

"You said something was calling us here. If everything is a clue, then that spill says this way." Brent offered, "Make you a deal. If that door is locked we go to Coldsnow Manor."

Becky poked a finger into Brent's chest. "Fine, but I'm not good with this and am lodging my protest now."

"Duly noted. Do you want to stay with the service department?"

She spit her irritation at Brent. "Just go, and don't worry about it being locked, you and I both know that this is the path."

Brent reminded her, "You better hope that it isn't the doctor who is sending us those texts. Remember, all things came from Coldsnow Manor?"

Becky bowed his head. "Catch twenty-two."

"Yeah, it's either one hundred percent the best place, or one hundred percent the worst place." Brent reached out and the door creaked open. A stairwell to the bowels of the facility. "Well, we aren't getting any younger."

Becky peered over the railing and shined her flashlight. "That's three floors. Which one do we want?"

"Play it by ear, I guess."

Chapter 38

The power snapped and Carl lay bound by restraints, a smell of ozone around him, and Dr. Coldsnow screaming expletives. In the darkness, a match lit. Before it could burn to dry, Dr. Coldsnow leaned over Carl. "Proof."

Mr. Pearl echoed. "So, you got what you want. Now what? The power is off and we are in the dark."

The doctor rejected Mr. Pearl. "Please, we are in a box, with halls that go east and west, and north and south. Pretty sure we can make it topside without any issues."

"Are we taking Mr. Wickmire?"

Dr. Coldsnow lit another match. The glow of restraints dancing against the flame. "No, I'd say he's shackled enough. I'll get the orderlies to watch him."

"Why not take him back; it doesn't sound like we went into lockdown."

"We didn't. He can stay in there while we get the electricity back on."

"Then what?"

"We do it again." Doctor Coldsnow backed out the room and locked it behind him.

They left Carl to think about things. Quiet, dark, alone.

If I can get out, I'll go to Stripling. Mindy has to go.

A key entered the door, the clank of metal on metal an echo in the small room. The door creaked open, but Carl could neither talk nor turn his head. Afraid the orderlies would do what they wanted, he wept.

A woman's voice soothed him. "Don't cry. You will be out soon." Steps in the dark circled him, "Just remember to do what's right." A voice so lithe it floated on gentle rafters of kindness, but with a hint of persuasion.

Carl tried to speak.

"Shh," her voice kissed his ears, "You'll speak soon. I'm here so you won't be alone."

He wanted to see this person. Who was helping him?

Is this the reckoning that Dr. Coldsnow spoke of?

She answered his thought. "No, your reckoning unlocked the door. I am merely a light along the pathway."

A cool breeze circled him.

"When you find your center, you will be whole. Take the lit path."

What do you mean?

She swam through his thoughts. "There are only two paths, pick."

The electricity flickered and the lights came on. The cruel reminder that Dr. Coldsnow would return soon.

Please tell me you are still here, and that you can still read my thoughts.

"Of course I'm still here. I told you, you are going home."

"Can I see your face?"

"Sure." The door creaked more and footsteps approached. "Carl?" Becky leaned over him, Brent alongside her.

Brent whispered, "We'll get you out of here."

"Where is she?" He spoke.

"Who?"

"I'm speaking, oh blessed wonder. Thank you." Carl's breath heaved. "Where is the woman who was standing next to me? I need to see her."

"There was no woman. The lights came on and we were standing in front of a door slightly ajar. We peeked in, and there you were."

"He did it."

"Who?"

"Doctor Coldsnow. I heard him tell his assistant that he could scare me back to speaking, and he did."

Brent locked eyes with Carl. "I wouldn't give that man that much credit, Carl. Becky had a premonition to follow some really weird things, and they all led me here. I don't think it's to celebrate. I think it's to extricate."

"No. I think once I'm speaking, he and his assistant will let me go."

Becky ran her hand over Carl's forehead. "Carl, you're a grown man, and if you think you should wait for him, and that is your lit path, you should take it."

"What did you say?"

"Just a text that Brent has been getting and it's proved to be good advice. However, we can't stay. We snuck in because Brent had more instructions to follow the path of least resistance, and that led us to that door, which was the last path of least resistance to you. We are here illegally."

"I change my mind."

Brent's wife tilted her gaze. "Why?"

"Because that line is the same line I was given, and if you have it, then you are lit path."

Brent reminded them, "We don't know the way out, we have a man shackled to a gurney, and a car too small to accommodate a gurney."

Becky grabbed Carl's gurney and spun his body right. "Let's do this, Brent."

"Where are we doing this to, Becky?"

"Anywhere but here."

"Let me do it, you are with child."

Carl laughed.

Brent nodded. "It's true, Carl. We're going to have a kid."

"Do you know what sex?"

"Not yet."

"Triplet girls if you ask me."

"What did you say?"

"I had a dream about you; you became a father of three girls."

Becky stopped the conversation, "Okay, Honey, creepy that he had that dream but we can all laugh about it another day. Let's hurry."

Carl offered, "You don't want to go to your right, that's the direction of my cell."

"Cell?"

"Worse, an iron box with no windows, just a slot for food and cameras to watch me."

"Was there a way out from there?"

"No, just the crazies."

"Yeah, we heard about them. Okay, how about elevators?"

"I wasn't awake when they brought me down here, and the only elevator I have been in awake was to Dr. Coldsnow's office, and I don't think that's the path of least resistance for you."

"There has to be a service elevator down here somewhere. We know the Coldsnow wing would be toward the Doctor's elevator, so let's take a few of those halls ahead of us."

Carl rolled along; rows of argon lighting gave a pale hue to the walls.

Brent called out, "Well, the service elevator is out of the question. It's broken. Looks like that's been awhile too."

Carl observed, "No wonder we were fed at different times, they had to bring it down the stairwell."

Brent came into view. "I need to get these shackles off you. We have no way to get you out of here."

"Then take me back." He revealed a peace in his voice. "I made a mistake in life, not just the day Mindy fired Mr. Templeton, but I lied to him about why we were meeting, and that I did stand up for employees. If that's the lesson I had to learn then I am sure something will work out."

Brent's wife joined her husband in an aerial view. "Carl, as noble as that is, if our task is to get you out of here, of which my husband believes me when I say it is, then my husband has to help with getting you out of here."

Above Carl, two faces debated.

Brent faced his wife. "You have some plan I don't know about?"

Chapter 39

Mindy and Ron pulled up to the police station, Mindy unsure what she should tell the officers. It wasn't as if they hadn't spoken to her before. For the last month, she made several calls a week to find out if they knew how Mr. Templeton was making her gain weight.

"Honey, what am I going to say? They think I'm the crazy lady," she gathered in her weight, "The crazy fat lady."

"I'll do the talking." He took her hand and they stepped up to the precinct.

The desk cop clicked the door and they entered. He stood, tilted his head. "Mrs. Docket?"

Mindy sighed. "Yes."

He hit a com. "Sarg, you need to come in here."

Mindy held a hand up. "I'm not here about my calls."

"I'm aware of what your calls are about, and I think the Sarg should see you."

A door between them opened and out stepped a burly Sargent. "Mrs. Docket, are you out jogging tonight?"

She held her hands wide. "Sweats are all I can wear. Twenty-eight pounds and counting. Of course, you jacka—
"

"That's not why we are here, Officer. My wife is lodging a complaint on behalf of a co-worker of hers."

"And who might that be?"

"Dr. Coldsnow. He is holding an employee against his will."

"You are talking about Mr. Wickmire out at Eastern?"

"Yes."

"We've been out there. He's being treated."

Mindy butted in, "No he isn't. He is being tortured, and Mr. Templeton is together with Dr. Coldsnow."

"You are accusing Dr. Coldsnow of causing your affliction along with Mr. Templeton? Why don't you go home and rest on it, maybe you will have a third person by the morning."

"Unfucking believable."

"Mindy! Shut up." Her husband put his hand out. "Thank you for speaking to us. The only thing I'll say is that I took my wife to see Carl today, and some of the things the doctor said would imply he understood the exact nature of my wife's issue without ever being told."

The Sargent crossed his arms and studied Mindy's husband. "Okay. I'll make a run out there myself, and I'll personally seek a conversation with Mr. Wickmire."

"Why the change of heart?"

"You. I don't know what kind of man could handle that woman. I bleed for you; also, you aren't the first call about Dr. Coldsnow. Mr. Wickmire's wife has called a lot more than your wife."

Mindy cried as her husband led her out. "I can't keep gaining weight. Why can't they believe me?"

"Let's just hope the officer can speak to Carl." He turned to the Sargent. "May I call you tomorrow?"

He nodded. "After noon though. If you call before then, I won't speak to either of you again."

"Yes, sir."

Mindy took Ron's hand and let him pull her to the car. "Can we go for a drive?"

"Where to?"

"Lake District."

Ron nodded. "Yeah, let's do that."

They drove to Mr. Templeton's home, the Asian woman working in the front yard.

Ron noted. "That's not like a servant."

"What is she doing?"

"She putting flowers around those lights leading up to the door."

"Well, let's go see. She probably already knows we are here."

They came up the walkway and Ms. Ping raised her visor. "Ms. Docket, how are you?"

"Fat, and your bos—housemate is responsible. I've been nice and begged to meet with him, and yet whenever I come over here, you tell me he isn't home, but that he isn't away either. So, how about we come stay with you until he arrives?"

Ms. Ping's smile broadened. "You have no idea how soon he will be here."

Mindy crossed her arms. "Let me guess, tomorrow sometime?"

"Only if it takes me longer to get these last lights decorated. I am making the path beautiful, for beautiful people. Care to be one of them?"

"No, I care not to be one of them. I just want your old decrepit boyfriend to face me with the truth."

Ms. Ping raised a tray to Mindy. "Here, go plant this."

"What?"

"The Lithodora you stepped on has to be replaced, and since you did the damage, you should pay the price of putting in the labor to fix it."

"I don't do labor, I hire people like you to do that."

"Very well, I thought as much."

"You have two trays of that plant?"

"I do not."

Mindy stepped to the other side of the walkway. "This is the same one as the one I squished?"

"Yes, Ms. Docket, it is."

Mindy stepped into another grouping of Lithodora and ground her foot. "Looks like you will need two trays." She motioned to her husband. "I think we can wait in the car, since this woman has said he will be here before tomorrow." Mindy turned to Ms. Ping. "You seem like you aren't a liar, so I will assume you are telling the truth that he will be back soon, and before tomorrow."

"I wouldn't lie, and you are welcome to wait inside."

"Not a chance."

Ms. Ping bowed. "Fair enough."

Ron took Mindy's hand. They crossed the street, all the while Ron offering advice, "It is a really bad move to piss that woman off. She can call your man and have him not come home, or worse, call the police."

"I'm sitting across the street waiting for someone to come home. I'm doing nothing wrong."

"You caused damage to her flowers. That's probably a misdemeanor."

"No, it's Civil."

"Are you sure?"

"Yeah."

"How do you know?"

"The company legal advisor—oh shit, Mr. Templeton himself told me."

"How ironic."

They made it to the car. Across the street, the woman had gone back into the house.

Mindy asked, "Are you taking the first watch?"

"Uh, it's just past noon. I think we can safely not worry about it."

"Yeah, I guess."

Mindy's husband gave a queer expression, his head turned to his side mirror.

"What's wrong?"

"You said your guy is a little old man, right?"

Mindy craned her neck and joined her husband in watching a figure walking up the street, holding a briefcase and treating his cane like a baton in the marching band. As he neared, Mindy's heart jumped. "Oh my God, that's him."

Chapter 40

After finding Carl, Brent knew his job. "Becky, we have to get these restraints off Carl."

She responded, "Those are shackles, and unless you have the time to cut them off, I think we're stuck with the gurney."

"We can't be stuck with the gurney. The service elevator is inoperable, and that leaves us with the director of this ward's office." They gave Carl an aerial view as they discussed their predicament over the top of his shackled body. Brent leaned in and the gurney railing rocked. "Wait." He bent and studied the metal. "The weld is cracked."

Becky joined him. Can we find something to hit it with?"

Brent tilted his head, mouth agape. "Seriously?"

"Yeah, why not?"

"We are three floors below the person who could put us in jail for trespassing, kidnapping, destruction of property. If I hit that with something it would sound like a dinner bell, and all those crazies at the other end would start howling." He brought in Carl. "Is that about right?"

Carl spoke out to the ceiling. "He's right."

"Then what do you suggest we do?"

Brent wondered.

His wife closed her eyes and whispered, "Path of least resistance, path of least resistance." She hesitated. "Lit path."

Brent followed along. "Do we have a lit path?"

"If he's not in his office, then that is the most lit and least resistant way to go."

Brent hesitated, "First off, I do not believe that is the path of least resistance, and second, I would think that elevator is by invite only."

Carl spoke out to the ceiling. "He's right."

Brent's wife patted Carl's wrist. "Wish the woman you were speaking to was here to help."

Brent offered, "She might be." He asked Carl, "You just heard the woman's voice, right?"

"Yes."

"I've had that same experience." He continued, "What did her voice bring up in your thoughts about what she looked like?"

Becky lowered her voice. "Really?"

"Let him think about it." Brent tiptoed to the hall's edge, "Keep going." He scanned both directions. It was not only clear, it was empty. "What is down here?"

"Just the crazies and apparently a couple of lobotomy rooms. The orderlies said no one ever ventures into these rooms down here. The other said it's used like a storage unit."

Brent backtracked. "So, anyone at this hospital sound like the woman you heard?"

"No, but she did sound like what I thought an associate of Dr. Coldsnow's would sound like if she'd ever spoken."

"Why?"

"You know how kids with parents from another language develop a certain tone to their English?"

"So who is his assistant?"

"An Asian woman." He continued, "Ms. Ping."

Becky stiffened. "Coincidence?"

Brent leaned into Carl. "What'd she look like?"

"Mid to late thirties, can't tell you the length of her black hair because she always wore it up in a bun with two bone hair sticks."

"Hair sticks?"

"Yeah, two long ones that crossed through her bun."

"How tall?"

"Not tiny, not tall. Maybe five-six."

Becky eyed Brent. "Could be a coincidence.

Brent surmised, "Age is close, height is close. Hair's a little off; two out of three isn't bad."

Becky objected, "That fits her hair exactly."

"Oh yeah, our Ms. Ping's hair is pretty long, and she doesn't wear it in a bun."

"We've seen her at home, and her hair is about the length it has to be to be able to use two hair rods."

"This does seem really fishy, Becky. This would change everything about what's going on?"

"How?"

"More and more people colluding on things."

Becky suggested, "I doubt Mr. Templeton's Ms. Ping is the assistant of the director here."

Brent pushed out sarcasm, "Huh, who would have figured that we'd both have a Ms. Ping who talks about lit paths."

Becky took control. "Carl, do you know where his office is situated in respect to a way out?"

"The front desk has a big two-door opening to the side of the building. There is a room to the left of the office. That's his office, and then there's a door directly behind that orderlies come from. To your immediate right is the hall to the dining room, and Five-Star restaurant, exclusively for Coldsnow Manor patients, his donors, and whoever else he's friends with."

"So if a donor wanted to see him in the dining area, he wouldn't be in his office?" Becky nodded to Brent. "You don't want me straining myself because I'm pregnant, so I have an idea. I'm going to meet with the doctor as a financial donor."

Brent reminded her, "You do realize you will be meeting with the man who did this to my co-worker?"

"I haven't signed my rights away."

"I'd say they don't much care about signatures." Brent stepped around the gurney and placed a hand on her stomach.

"I think I'm being protected." She kissed Brent. "I'll go, but you better be as fierce as I was going to be if I had to get you out."

"Just make sure that you vacate if Carl is discovered missing. I suspect our good doctor would be wise to know that you are less a donor and more a meddler." Brent kept his worry off his face.

His wife took the corridor back to the flight of stairs, and Brent phone buzzed a text. He smiled thinking his wife wished him luck. He pulled up the phone and someone else had texted him. From the facility, a text came back: 'Your path is in front of you, come to the lights.'

Lights? What do they mean?

Brent eased Carl back the way they came. "Carl, I have a feeling I need to follow."

Carl whispered, "Voices been talking to you?"

"No, I'm being texted by someone." He leaned over the gurney and wink, "I suspect he has the same voice as the one you are hearing."

"Wouldn't be a he then, because the last person who I spoke to was definitely a woman."

"Well, then she is directing me to the lion's den."

Carl sighed. "Can't you find a way to get these binds off? I'm sure there has to be keys around here."

"Trust me, Carl, please." Brent swung the gurney left as they reached the T; a row of lights lined the hall.

Please let this be the lights.

Over linoleum the wheels squeaked out their presence. The crazies knew, they came alive, a low burble of varied ailments crescendo'ed. "Shit, Carl. You had to listen to this?"

"Every time meal trays arrived."

"They could raise the dead." The voices had reached a fevered pitch.

Brent stopped the gurney short of the cells, in front of the Doctor's personal elevator. He pulled his phone out and texted: 'here'

They waited.

Carl asked, "How do you think this elevator is opening; and what makes you think we will like what we see?"

"I don't, but what other options do we have?"

The elevator gears turned and the movement inside the shaft quieted the crazies. As though listening for peeps, the titular noise that brought them their food, served as precedence to any concerns they may have had.

Brent drew in a deep breath and held out hope. "Well, either I have a ton of explaining to do, or my wife's beautiful face will be on this elevator."

"She is in the Doctor's office. Where do you think he is?"

The bell rang, the elevator had arrived. "Guess we are about to find out."

No one stood inside, but a key lay on the floor.

"Carl, not sure, but I think my wife found the key to the restraints." Brent retrieved it, and shoved the gurney half way in. "Let's stop this from going back up." He tested the key. The first restraint released. Brent unlocked the neck restraint, followed by Carl's wrist.

Carl grabbed the key. "I got the rest." He released his waist, his other leg, and rolled off gurney. "Okay, what now?"

"Let's leave this here. We can get topside before they go around the building to those stairs."

"Where do the stairs lead us to?"

"The kitchen." His phone chirped. Brent checked his text: 'They seem to be in a hurry to get to his office.'

"Let's go, Carl, the jig is up."

"I go up there these scrubs are going to give me away."

"We won't be sticking around to make friends, let's go."

Chapter 41

Dr. Coldsnow's entry

"Mr. Pearl, please find out why those patients are screaming."

Mr. Pearl brought up his phone. "The monitors are down."

"Why isn't the place on lockdown?" Dr. Coldsnow cornered his assistant.

"It appears they are turned off, not down."

"Shit." He ordered, "Get to my office while I deal with this woman."

"Yes, sir." Mr. Pearl stepped away, leaving for Dr. Coldsnow's office.

Dr. Coldsnow turned to the woman, whose husband held her tight. "May I help you?"

The woman stepped up to the counter. "Yes, we are here to see Carl Whitmire."

"And who might you be?"

"A friend."

Dr. Coldsnow straightened and apologized, "This facility is by appointment only."

The woman pointed a finger. "May we speak to your superior?"

Dr. Coldsnow smiled. "Well, I'm the Chief Operating Officer, Chief Physician, and second largest donor to Eastern State. The wing you are in is named after me. I doubt you'll find anyone higher up that is going to let you evade the rules." He bowed, "Dr. Coldsnow, at your service."

Behind him, Mr. Pearl came back. He whispered "They don't see Mr. Wickmire."

Mr. Pearl nodded, turned a smile toward the woman, and stepped back the way he came.

Dr. Coldsnow turned his attention back to woman. He paused, closed his eyes, and mouthed 'shit'.

The woman's husband joined her at the counter's edge.

Dr. Coldsnow's eyes opened and he smiled. "Now, where were we?" His visitor had persistence he found Lilliputian. He smiled.

"Would it matter that I also work with him?"

Dr. Coldsnow chuckled. "No."

She shrugged. "You can't blame a girl for trying."

He reversed himself. "Wait. You say you work with him? What's your name?"

The woman's husband stopped her from answering. "Catherine, we should go." He nodded to Dr. Coldsnow. "We'll set up an appointment."

Dr. Coldsnow remained fixed. "You do that." When the couple turned he muttered. "How many days do you think a person could live gaining a pound a day?"

Neither turned; she gave a nonsensical response to the gentleman. "Should we drop by the store on the way home?"

Dr. Coldsnow gave it one last shot. "Don't you want to find Templeton?"

They continued their private conversation, ignoring Dr. Coldsnow's words.

They exited and Dr. Coldsnow lifted his phone. "Get me an orderly."

While the doctor riffled through papers on the front desk, the woman returned with a grand entrance, whisking both doors wide and standing akimbo. She shouted, "I find out you are with that fucknuts and I will bury you along with him."

Dr. Coldsnow laughed.

"I will have you arrested for whatever he's doing to me."

Dr. Coldsnow listened and surmised, "You're a new one for me, and I'd love to study you."

"Is that what you are doing to our employee?"

An orderly came up behind him.

Dr. Coldsnow pointed toward her. "Bring her to me."

The woman turned back the way she came.

At the door, Dr. Coldsnow watched his orderly chase a car that sped out of the place. He shook his head. "Okay, Mr. Goodman, Templeton, whatever you are parading as, let's find out what you next move is."

"Excuse me," another woman approached. "Hello, I'm Rebecca Smith."

Dr. Coldsnow tried to clear his plate. "How can I help you, Ms. Smith?"

She stepped up; both viewing the front steps. "Perhaps you're busy. I wished to find out to whom I'd speak about charitable donations."

Dr. Coldsnow stopped. "You don't say." He turned and smiled. "For whom do you work that you have money to donate?"

"Excuse me?" She stared at the doctor.

"What company are you representing?"

"None. I'm a legacy child and housewife. My grandmother had spent time at a facility across the state, and since I live here, I thought my charitable donation would best be served in the community I live in."

"Can I tell you what I think, Ms. Smith?"

The woman nodded.

"I think nothing is a coincidence."

She smiled. "I don't think anyone would find a charitable donation to a facility a coincidence, but rather a common occurrence."

"Things are always so layered, Ms. Smith. That man has a way of weaving in narratives from everywhere, even distracting me with what should have been." He nodded to her, "If you are not here because of some providence, of which if you are, you understand my point, then I'd turn and walk away. If you are, then I wish to meet with you in my office."

Her voice dripped annoyance, "I haven't any idea what you are talking about, Dr. Coldsnow. I merely found my way from the dining hall and sought information. However, it would appear you have far different things on your mind."

He bowed. "I reserve the right to not apologize, and I hope you are what should have been. Perhaps another day would be best, I'm in the middle of some important business, and I need to take my leave. Should you not do the same, I will assume you aren't a coincidence."

She backed away, her direction the way she came. "I think I should seek another administrator, Dr. Coldsnow. You clearly are busy."

"That I am." He nodded and turned toward his office. Mr. Pearl exited and approached him. "Power is back on down there, and the natives are screaming."

Dr. Coldsnow huffed. "Guess it's my move, Mr. Pearl."

"We have another issue."

"Of course we do. What might that be?"

"The elevator is stuck on the bottom floor."

"Stuck?"

"It appears something is blocking the door."

"Why do I suspect he has others doing his bidding?"

"Who?"

"Pieces on a board, young man, pieces on a board."

"So you think your mysterious man orchestrated this? That woman who barged in here didn't appear to be on Mr. Templeton's side."

Dr. Coldsnow caught his reflection in the hall mirror. "You don't have to be on his side to do what he wants you to do. That's his whole point." He motioned to the door, "Let's get down there."

Chapter 42

Carl rubbed life back into his wrists. It felt good to be freed. The elevator door opened and closed against the gurney.

Brent nodded. "That should keep them from coming here by elevator. Let's get to the service stairs and get up top."

"If anyone sees me dressed like this, they'll stop us."

Brent asked, "You trust my wife, Carl?"

Carl nodded. "I don't have much choice, and if Mr. Templeton sent you, then maybe I should."

"I don't know who sent me."

"Yes you do. We both do."

"Let's not speculate before we know everything."

They hurried to the darkest parts of the underground hallways. "Speculate? You have no idea what things have happened to me in here. Things that defy logic."

Luminescence from the flashlight found the stairs. "Of that we share. I'll tell you all about it when we are out of this place." They cracked the door ajar. Silence in the well. "Let's go."

They tiptoed up to the first floor. Carl let Brent lead the way. Around a corner they met Brent's wife holding a long coat. She put it around Carl. She faced her husband. "By your expression I can assume you didn't text me to grab a long coat?"

Carl whispered, "Let me guess, that kind of weird stuff?"

Brent nodded. "Yeah, like that."

Carl put the coat on. "Now what?"

Brent's wife led, Brent followed Carl and they filed into the kitchen.

A suited man shouted from an open office. "Do you have your supplier's badge?"

The kitchen worker they'd met interrupted, "Dr. Coldsnow's assistant dropped these by." She handed Brent's wife three badges.

The gentleman held his hand out the door. "Let me see those."

Brent's wife nodded and stepped away, passing them on to an open hand.

"Please remember to sign in before you come."

She answered, "Yes, sir."

The door swung close, and they continued on to the backdoor.

His co-worker and his wife rushed him to their car. From the far end of the building a woman walked away, toward a side exit. "That looks like Dr. Coldsnow's assistant."

His co-worker joined him in observing her. "That looks like that could be Ms. Ping."

Carl nodded. "Exactly."

Brent's wife snapped her fingers. "No time to dally, boys. Let's go."

Carl insisted, "To the police station, now."

Brent nodded. "I agree." He jumped into the car and they exited the service entrance.

Through the outskirts of the city, and into town, they pulled up front of the police station. Carl noticed someone leaving. "Is that Mindy?"

His co-worker cringed. "Holy shit, she's gotten big."

Carl pressed his face to the window. "What happened to her?"

"One pound."

"That looks like a lot more than one pound."

"Apparently, it's per day."

"That's what Templeton meant by one pound?"

Brent shrugged. "Remember, we don't know what Mr. Templeton did."

Carl regained himself. "Really? Are we still at odds with that?"

Brent's wife turned and leaned against the rest. "Carl, I also am part of this argument, and I have to come to terms with how a man who didn't know us," she squinted, "granted he knew we were trying, arranging for a high-end restaurant reservation for a birth announcement."

Carl went to cut in, but she hushed him.

"Before you say that's not a big deal, might I remind you that we picked the restaurant at random on that day. The reservation was set a week before at that exact time." She whispered, "My husband is the kind of guy who is going to get to the bottom of this. It's just who he is."

Carl turned his attention to Brent. "What's the bottom to you, Brent?"

"If I knew the bottom I'd tell you, but in truth, neither of us knows anything. So finding out from the source is important, and to be honest, I don't know who the source is."

Brent's wife joined Carl. "You don't think all these things lead to Mr. Templeton?"

"They appear to, but that also appears to be impossible." He shared his view between the two and the road, "And you two are both analytical enough to grant me that."

Carl sat back. "Well, then. Let me add to your mystery. Dr. Coldsnow was Mr. Templeton's first victim."

Brent adjusted his mirror, and Carl locked on to his gaze.

"Oh yeah? What did he inflict him with?"

Carl uttered, "Stuttering."

Brent debated Carl. "Says who?"

"Dr. Coldsnow himself."

"What if Dr. Coldsnow is the one who is pulling the strings? Wouldn't it help him to say he was a victim?"

"What purpose would he have with you? I assume you would agree all these events are tied to something, or someone, and Mr. Templeton is the only one who knew all of us."

Brent smiled. "With regards to those two men, but many people know all three of us."

His wife sighed. "He'll figure it out, Carl."

Brent nodded. "Thank you."

She gazed out the window. "It wasn't a compliment."

Carl's co-worker shrugged. "So you are ready to attach something more than science to this?"

She nodded. "Yes. Yes I am."

Carl shook his head. "I can't." He brought in his doubts. "I can't go back to blaming someone else for this. Something inside me has changed, and if I believe this was something other than more than ordinary, I might become cynical and slip back to what I did."

Brent reminded him. "You did nothing wrong."

"I lied."

"You did what any HR does. You got him away from our work environment."

"When he asked if there was something wrong, I should have said 'yes' and I did just the opposite."

Brent offered. "If you think you were given a chance to change, and you're good with that, awesome, but until I know how all the weird stuff was pulled off, I'm not giving anyone any credit for doing it with suggestions."

Brent's phone chirped. He turned to his wife. "Is that a text?'

She held his phone to her face. "Says your path is lit."

Chapter 43

Mindy rifled through her purse.

"What are you looking for?" Ron kept his head turned toward Mr. Templeton.

"Looking for this." She held up her phone. "I'm going to record whatever he says." She pushed her door open and approached Mr. Templeton.

"Ms. Docket. To what do I owe the pleasure?"

Mindy pointed a finger. "Fuck you."

"Such ire."

"Over three weeks I've waited for you to show up."

"If you had wanted to see me, you should have not fired me." He leaned in. "Also, I told Mr. Wickmire I'd return to the office in one month. You can rehire me at a substantial raise."

Mindy eased into the dig. "Oh, I see, so you weren't man enough to accept you didn't do a very good job, and now you think you can blackmail me into rehiring you?"

Mindy stiffened when Mr. Templeton smiled.

He eyed his house. "See, she did have cause." He turned to Mindy and held his elbow out. "Are you here to find your lit path?"

Mindy slapped his elbow. "Fuck you. Whatever fucking game you're playing, whatever drugs you have me on, it's over. I want my life back."

He leaned around Mindy. "You must be Ron."

Mindy's husband stepped forward "Yeah, and how'd you know my name?"

Mr. Templeton motioned to house. "Ms. Ping told me your name."

"Yeah, well, it's just as creepy hearing you call me that as it was the first time she said it, especially since she was guessing when she said I looked like a Ron."

The little old man chuckled. "She does a lot of things, but guessing isn't one of them." He bowed. "Perhaps you are looking for a lit path?"

Ron sighed. "As much as I am here to keep my wife from going postal, I am concerned about what you did to her. At the rate this is happening, she will be dead before the year is up."

Mr. Templeton adjusted his glasses. "Oh, I don't know about that. The human body can support a lot of weight."

"I don't think that's the point, Mr. Templeton."

"No, I suppose it isn't."

"So what did you do to my wife?" He held Mindy.

"In the game of chess, there are forces of light, and forces of dark. The forces of dark are merely those that oppose you. So regardless of the chess piece color, the opposite of the one you are will always be a force of darkness to you. In other words, we are all heroes in our own journeys."

Mindy broke free. "What nonsense are you spewing? My husband asked you a simple question. What did you do to me?" Mindy felt misted. She patted her chest and turned back to her husband. "I can't stay like this."

Mr. Templeton asked Mindy, "Why do you think I did something to you?"

She spun back. "Because I keep gaining a pound a day, and that's what Carl said you told him to tell me."

"Ms. Docket, I did not ask what you think I did to you, of that we seem to be in agreement. My question was, and still is, 'why do you think I did something to you?'"

"Because you are a bitter, vindictive, old asshole. Any other reason satisfy you?"

"I see. Do you think Mr. Wickmire agrees with you?"

Mindy balled her fist. "Of course, what you've done to both of us is a crime."

"If you say so."

"If I say so? Don't get cute with me, Mr. Templeton. My husband and I will crush you."

"Much like those poor flowers." He pointed to the Lithodora. Whoever would crush them? Do you have any idea?"

"I just want to stop gaining weight. Now, cough it up."

"I'll be in this week, as I promised."

"My husband has heard everything you've just said."

Mr. Templeton smiled. "You're husband agrees with you. That's a good mate."

"I also have this." Mindy pulled out the phone. "I've recorded everything." She grabbed her husband's arm. "That should be enough to get the police over here."

Mr. Templeton held a hand out. "So you aren't going to stay and sit with us?"

Mindy huffed. "You are unbelievable. The police will be here as soon as they hear this." She pulled back with a winner's grin. "See you soon."

Mr. Templeton shrugged. "Okay, see you soon."

Mindy and her husband took their leave. They headed toward their car. "This should get them to take me seriously."

Ron smiled. "I would agree, Honey."

They exited with an aggressive turn in the street, heading to the police station.

As they reached the station, Mindy noticed a car crossing the intersection. "That's Brent and his wife." She tilted her head, "Who's that in the back seat?" They'd passed too quickly.

"Honey, let's get this in there. I'm sure whatever they were doing here; it too, probably had something to do with your fired employee."

She turned back to her husband. "Let's do this." Mindy jumped out of the car and hurried to the police door.

A speaker squawked, "State your business."

"I'm here to see your boss."

"My boss?" His voice dripped annoyance. "How about you tell me what you want and I'll make that decision."

Mindy gritted her teeth.

"Honey, let me." He stepped around her, "Hi. We were here earlier."

"I'm aware you were. Didn't Sarg tell you to give it a day and not bother anyone until late tomorrow?"

"Yes, but that was about Dr. Coldsnow. We haven't gone back there. However, we have more evidence."

The speaker clicked back, "And where did you get that evidence?"

"We recorded Mr. Templeton."

"Where?"

"His home."

The buzzer rang and the door clicked.

As they entered the desk officer called his superior, who whisked his door open. "Mrs. Docket, I told you I would deal with this tomorrow; going to Mr. Templeton's house was not something you should have done."

"What? Did he call you?"

"Call me? No, you just said, on camera, that you were at his home."

"Just listen to our conversation."

He put his arms akimbo. "Play it."

"Here?"

"Why not. This way I can decide to kick you out of here or arrest you."

"Oh, no, not with this information." Mindy hit 'play': *"Excuse me."*

A woman's voice, Ms. Ping's said, *"Yes?"*

"I'm looking for Mr. Templeton, does he live here?"

Mindy tried to turn the recording off.

"I want to hear that Ms. Docket."

"It's not the right recording."

"That sounded like the woman who was at that home when we first went over there."

"I think it is." Mindy pleaded, "He really is over there right now. Please help me."

"Let me hear the rest of that recording."

Mindy closed her eyes and started the recording.

Mindy's voice requested, *"Is he home?"*

A moment of silence before Mindy came on again, *"Do you speak English?"*

In perfect grammar, a reply, *"Rather well, and you?"*

"I'm sorry. I didn't mean to offend you."

"And yet, you did it quite well."

"Sorry."

"Now, how can I help you?"

"Do you know when Mr. Templeton will be coming back?"

"I do not. He lost a job he loved very much, and so he has had to go out and do what he can to make ends meet."

"And where might that be?"

You ask a lot of questions. Might I have your name?"

"Look, I'm not trying to cause trouble. I just wanted to have a conversation with your boss."

"My boss?"

"Mr. Templeton."

"I see, my boss?"

"Well, whatever arrangement you have for keeping up such a beautiful yard." Mindy's voice came off annoyed, *"I'll check in tomorrow. Let him know that a woman came to see him about some business."*

"Business?"

"Yeah, business."

"Careful where you walk, if you are a pound over one-ten, you will crush the buds."

The sound of plants being stepped on. *"I'll remember that."*

The Sarg crossed his arms. "You are lucky no one has called, that doesn't sound like anyone admitted to anything." He hesitated, "Other than you were trespassing."

Mindy's husband offered, "I was with my wife. Mr. Templeton talked about knowing what he did to her. I didn't know my wife had recorded her conversation with that woman, but we both were standing there and I'd vouch for what he said."

"Great, the husband of the harasser would verify it." He shook his head. "I am going to see Dr. Coldsnow tomorrow. As for Mr. Templeton, I have no reason to visit him—"

Mindy blurted, "But—"

The Sarg raised his hand, "But, I'll make an exception."

Mindy asked, "Can we go with you."

He sighed. "Did you not just hear me? Go home. Do not go to Eastern; do not go to Mr. Templeton's. I was going to tell you that your co-worker was just here."

"I saw them driving away."

"I don't mean the husband and wife he came with, I mean the one that was at the institution."

"Carl?"

"Yes, and he claims he was being held against his wishes, and yet, the doctor hasn't called the police about a missing patient, so we let him go home."

"Why would you do that? They may come after him."

"Not likely, since when we called Coldsnow Manor, they said Carl Wickmire was discharged."

Chapter 44

Becky turned in her seat. "Why would Dr. Coldsnow say you were released?"

Carl shrugged. "I'm not sure."

Brent pulled into Carl's driveway. Carl's wife waited on the porch. He'd barely stopped before Carl rushed out to greet his family.

Becky and Brent waited for Carl to share a moment before they intruded. "Carl, what would you like to do? Whatever it is, we're here to help."

"If you'd follow me over to Mr. Templeton's house, I'd appreciate that."

Mrs. Wickmire objected. "What? You have to be kidding me, Darling. That man just caused you to be institutionalized for nearly a month."

"No, I did that, or maybe Dr. Coldsnow did, but I'm free. Freer than I've been in a long time."

Brent warned him. "Don't assume you're free. The hospital could arrive here and want you back."

Carl shook his head. "Not without a fight."

"Well, that's not really what I had in mind, but I think all of us heading over to the Lake District would be a good idea."

Mrs. Wickmire called for their daughters, and Carl hustled his crew into the family car.

Brent and Becky led the procession across town. Into the Lake District, the two cars settled on parking across the street from Mr. Templeton's house; the woman who'd tended the yard earlier sat legs crossed on the steps to the door, sunglasses shading her view, a bonnet shading her face, the lit path glowing as the sun set in the west.

Becky nodded. "There's your lit path, Sweetheart." In front of them, the lights kicked on, a runway to the front door.

The Wickmires, daughters in tow, filed in next to Brent. Carl joined Brent in the view. "Do you still doubt the origins?"

"It has never been about doubt. It's about proof."

"And you expect to find something logical about all of this?"

"I expect to find something explainable."

Crossing the street, the six of them came into range of glowing lanterns. Ms. Ping removed her hat, lowered her sunglasses and smiled. "They are most beautiful at night."

"Is this the end of the journey?" Brent winked and grinned. Somewhere a thread of understanding had to be visible.

Ms. Ping stood, discarding her day shadings, she faced Brent. "You were invited on this journey, but this one is for who you brought. You have been employed, and I hope your triplets are worthy pay."

Becky cut in, "Triplets?"

Brent spoke over her, "Employed?"

Mrs. Wickmire stopped them all, "The one they brought is my husband. Is this some cult thing?"

Carl slowed her down. "It's fine, Darling. This is where I'm supposed to go. I know it."

Brent shook his head. "Maybe I'm supposed to go to find the proof."

Ms. Ping smiled. "Ever the logical one. You are loved for that."

"Is Mr. Templeton here?"

"Inside." She extended her hand. "Please go in. I have some things to pick up, I'll be back." She walked us to the door, opened it and turned the way she'd come.

"You aren't coming in?"

"I cannot. I have to go to work." She stepped away, made it to her car and backed out the driveway.

Inside the house, a voice caught Brent by surprise. "Carl, Brent! Bring your families in." Mr. Templeton stood in the foyer. He stepped up to Carl and put a hand on each shoulder. "Did you find out who you are?"

"Yes, sir."

Mrs. Wickmire pulled her husband away. She pointed at Mr. Templeton. "Did you have something to do with my husband's stuttering?"

Mr. Templeton took her in. "If predictability of a situation happening as you believe it will is what you mean, then I am guilty as charged."

Before Mrs. Wickmire could rebut, Mr. Templeton spun around to Brent's wife. "Good things happen to good people, and I promise you, you were never in danger."

"Danger?"

"None of your steps had consequence."

She tilted her head. "A literal path of no resistance."

He winked. "Young Mr. Smith has married a sharp woman." He turned his attention to her stomach. "Faith, Hope, and Charity."

Carl cut in. "I had that dream."

Mr. Templeton nodded. "Of course you did. I wanted you to know who the players were."

Brent joined them. "Players?"

He pulled them in, one family, one family in the making. "Yes."

"Players in what?"

Mr. Templeton took Brent in. "Would it give you peace of mind to know how this all came about?"

Brent cautioned Mr. Templeton, "As long as it is the truth."

Mr. Templeton volleyed back, "A truth you'll accept?"

"Factual."

He burst out in laughter. "Young Mr. Smith. You are fun. You are what make this life worth participating in." He raised a hand to his mouth and whispered, "If you have triplets will you cut me some slack?"

Brent shook his head. "Let's not field that question until we're there."

Mr. Templeton settled them into the front room. "May I get you something to drink?" A round of waters for the adults and juice for the girls, and Mr. Templeton sat. He directed himself to Carl, "So, how did your experience with Dr. Coldsnow go?"

Carl offered, "Not good. Did you know what they were doing to me?"

Mr. Templeton crossed his legs, reached to a lamp table and lifted a pipe. "I don't smoke this, but gosh, it sure makes me look sophisticated." He turned to Brent, "I mean, if this is so elaborate, I better look like a Moriarty, no?"

Brent proposed, "How about I ask twenty questions and you answer them with one hundred percent accuracy?"

"Son, I would never do anything other than that; however, you've already set the rules, and Rule One in the

Brent Smith rule book is it has to jive with your belief structure."

"Try me."

"First, let me answer the Guest of Honor." He stayed on topic with Carl, "You were in a controlled environment."

Brent seized on his admission. "So you do have control of what took place."

The little old man tilted his head. "Of course. I believe I've held that position quite consistently."

"So then how did you do it?"

"I am at a loss on how to answer your question, other than to say I told Dr. Coldsnow that it had to be a controlled environment."

Carl reminded him. "I was almost lobotomized."

Mr. Templeton's mouth dropped. "I know, right? However, the power went out, and it failed to happen."

"So Dr. Coldsnow planned that?"

Mr. Templeton's head shook off Carl's remark. "No, I did that."

Brent asked, "Did you have the hospital place bugged so you knew what was happening?"

Mr. Templeton raised his pipe to his lips. "Define bugged."

"Like you did at my house with listening devices."

"Did they find any? What did you call them, bugs? Did they find those at your home?"

"No, but something was there."

Mr. Templeton squared off with Brent. "That's illogical. If you believe there was something there, but have no proof, then how do you rationalize anything?" He finished with, "No, I don't believe bugs were involved with my understanding of Carl's position."

Brent's wife added, "What about the restaurants?"

Mr. Templeton's eyes widened. "Wasn't that the best? Getting the crow's nest, and that food, was that not divine?"

"How did you know I was pregnant?"

"How do I know you are having triplets?"

Brent joined his wife. "You don't." He locked gazes with the old man.

Mr. Templeton lost his smile. "I do, and so do you."

Brent broke off the confrontation and smiled. "Again, if my wife has triplets, that doesn't mean there isn't a logical explanation."

Mr. Templeton agreed. "I have been saying the same thing, only you don't see logic in the same fashion that I do."

"And how is that Mr. Templeton?"

He deadened his tone. "As the player and not the piece."

"Carl is no piece, Mr. Templeton."

"Of course not, he's the Guest of Honor. You are a piece." He picked up his pipe, "And a damn fine one. You have proven to be an amazing man, both as a husband and a friend. You also followed my bread crumbs."

Mrs. Wickmire sat between her two daughters. "I'm confused. Who are you, Mr. Templeton?"

"Just a concerned citizen of this world."

"And you decided to involve my husband in a month-long kidnapping where if you don't turn off the power his brain is shocked?"

Mr. Templeton held a stiff upper lip. "Um, yes."

"On whose authority do you have to do that, Mr. Templeton?"

He leaned out of his seat, directing his dialogue to her, "Mine."

"Then I will ask again, who are you to have that ability?"

"A concerned citizen of this world."

Brent held his hand up. "Can we just get on with the whole lit path thing? If I'm just a piece in your game, is there something you want to tell Carl, since he's your supposed Guest of Honor?"

"Brent, you will one day run a company. Mark my words. You are direct and I like that." He clapped his hands together and turned to Carl. "Carl, you have a huge future ahead of you. You may choose door Number One or you may choose door Number Two, but whichever you take, you will be a wonderful citizen of this world."

"And what are my two doors?"

Before he could answer, the doorbell rang.

Chapter 45

Carl's curiosity followed Mr. Templeton as the old man winked at the doorbell.

Mr. Templeton sighed, "With the winds come the verdict, and with the verdict comes the score." He lifted himself from his chair and nodded to Carl. "Stay in lit paths."

Everyone turned as Mr. Templeton walked to the foyer as though finding his mark to stand on. His voice perked. "Ms. Docket, please come in."

From around the corner, Mindy came to a full stop. "Carl? How did you get out?"

Carl stood. "I owe Brent and his wife. They came and got me."

"We came to get you as well. How did he get you?"

"Apparently, thanks to Mr. Templeton."

Mr. Templeton grinned. "Oh, I can't take all the credit."

Mindy spun back to Mr. Templeton. "Credit?" She tugged on her sweats. "I'm nearly thirty pounds heavier."

He held his arms wide. "But that's okay, you only had to follow the lit path, and you did."

Carl's co-worker pointed behind her. "The lights? I crushed them. Fuck you. Everyone here thinks you are some kind of God. You are a criminal."

Mr. Templeton rounded Mindy and disappeared. His voice called out from an open door. "You shouldn't have done that." He reappeared. "Now, anyone can just come in."

"Good, because the police will be here soon."

Mr. Templeton sighed. "So will others." He swept his arm. "Mr. and Mrs. Docket, you might as well come all the way in." He shrugged to the room. "Well, I guess you can't win them all."

Mr. Docket joined the conversation. "What's that supposed to mean, sir?"

"Sir? Such a fine young man. Have a seat and I'll explain."

"No, how about you just explain, Mr. Templeton."

"Her answer was following the lit path; she did not. Now, she must re-hire me." He shrugged.

Mindy cut in. "What the fuck?"

His eyes brightened and he winked to Carl. "I was two for three."

Carl shook his head. "Why?"

Mr. Templeton isolated Carl, approached him, his purpose a confidence between just the two of them. He leaned into Carl's position. "The board is open, and I'm good, but not that good."

Something opened the front door.

Mr. Templeton raised his voice. "Whoever has come in, please come all the way in."

Hunter, from work, made his way in.

Mr. Templeton greeted him. "Hunter, to what do I owe the pleasure?"

Mindy twirled around. "Why are you here?"

"I said I go out on my own terms, you bitch."

Carl's co-worker took front and center, pointed her finger and cursed. "Who the hell do you think you are?" She snapped her fingers toward Carl. "Carl! Escort this man out of here."

"This isn't work, Mindy."

"No it isn't, because if it was, he'd not be here." She turned back to Hunter. "Scram, I fired you yesterday."

Before Carl could offer a solution, Hunter pulled a gun from his jacket and aimed it at Mindy, his intent written on his face. Behind him, Dr. Coldsnow entered the house. He reached around Hunter and redirected his arm away from his intent. The gun discharged and struck Mr. Templeton. Dr. Coldsnow yanked the gun from Hunter and ran to his adversary. Carl couldn't tell if he said a prayer or if he told him something, but whatever it was, he had a smile on his face.

Mr. Pearl came through the foyer. "Dr. Coldsnow, was that a gun?"

The doctor waved Mr. Pearl over. "See if this clown has a pulse."

Carl nodded to his wife. "Let me have your phone."

He called 911. "There's been an accident." He gave them Mr. Templeton's address.

The dispatch had an air of expectation. 'Why does that address seem familiar?'

Carl admitted, "I'm sure you've run across it a few times today."

"Nobody leave. Was a weapon involved?"

"Yes, sir, but it has been removed and is secured."

"What condition is the victim in?"

"It appears to be bad."

"An ambulance is on the way. Everyone will be required to surrender immediately."

"We have the assailant."

"Doesn't matter. We need to determine that."

"Yes, sir."

Carl handed his wife's phone back and his wife stayed on the line. Mr. Pearl offered, "I think he has expired."

Mindy stiffened. "Wait, what?"

Mr. Pearl repeated. "He's dead."

Mindy didn't care about stains. She kneeled next to Mr. Templeton. "You said I have to rehire you." She pumped his chest and continued, "Let's get enough oxygen in that pea brain of yours to hear me hire you. Fuck your little games, curse, whatever the fuck it is. I'm in, I'm buying; you are rehired." Blood pooled around her fingers with each compression of the old man's chest.

Carl leaned over her and pulled her up. "Mindy, he's gone."

"I better start fucking losing weight, Carl."

"Dr. Coldsnow joined them. "Ms. Docket, right?"

"Yeah, why?"

"Just that you never introduced yourself last time." He held his hand out.

Carl pulled her away. "You need to leave, Dr. Coldsnow. You imprisoned me and you are not welcomed here."

The doctor shook his head. "You signed off on everything. However, you are in fact speaking again, so you have no reason to come back. As for my welcoming here, I am most welcomed here; it's why I'm not stuttering. Ms. Docket here, I'm sure has tried everything, and if she buys into his voodoo, then perhaps allowing me to get inside your head would work."

Mindy backed up. "No thanks. If it's all the same to you, I'll try other avenues first."

"Suit yourself, but you will be out to the Manor before too long." He winked.

Sirens in the distance spelled the chaos about to happen. Hunter was crying that he didn't mean to kill Mr. Templeton.

Dr. Coldsnow offered his assistance to Hunter as well. "I was here. I saw the insanity; I'm an expert on insanity. I will get your stay in our institution."

Carl did what he could. He left Mindy to her husband and tended to the door. The path lights had been crushed, and darkness led the authorities over Ms. Ping's flowers.

They came in; they sat the room down and went to each one for answers. The paramedics set Mr. Templeton in a body bag and placed him on a gurney. They exited to their ambulance, and with it, the police finished up.

As the ambulance left Ms. Ping made an appearance.

She stopped and nodded to Carl. "It's nice to see you unbound."

"It was you?"

An officer on the way out stopped her. "Who are you?"

"I am the woman of this house."

Carl and Dr. Coldsnow sang together, "You live here?"

"Of course." She turned her attention to the doctor. "Well played."

The officer gave her the news of Mr. Templeton. "Was he your husband?"

She leaned around the officer.

"I am not married."

"But you live here?"

"We both did. It's a big house."

They corralled Hunter, cuffed him, and with that, it was over.

Ms. Ping held center stage. "I hope you all found what you came looking for, but if you don't mind, I wish to be alone."

Carl understood. He wanted to go home. Too much had happened to absorb anything. Dr. Coldsnow followed behind him, and as he left, he asked Ms. Ping, "Can we talk tomorrow?"

Carl found it odd that she passed it off with "Sure, I'll stop by tomorrow."

Outside, on the porch, Dr. Coldsnow tipped his hat to Carl. "I suspect you'll be seen again." He winked. "Good job."

Mr. Pearl accompanied him and left Carl on the porch, Carl's wife waiting to go home.

Chapter 46

Mindy panicked. "Ron, what does all this mean? Am I going to continue gaining weight?" She felt tears leveling her lids. "You heard me hire him back, right?"

"Look, Honey. Whatever he did, he can't do it anymore, so relax. Tomorrow you will be a pound lighter, and every day after that, you will lose a pound. I know it."

Mindy leaned against her husband as he drove. "I hope you're right. I need to get back to my old self."

"You do realize that your co-worker they arrested is going to tie you up in court, right?"

"You heard the doc; he said he'd be fine."

"He said he would testify to insanity. Not sure after your co-worker's stay there that it will be a picnic." Her husband frowned. "You fired him? Wasn't he the one who gave you Mr. Templeton's address?"

"He also gave me the cemetery."

"You fired him for that?"

"I fired him for lying. He lied about sending me the text. He thought it would be funny to send me out there."

Her husband pointed out, "If he'd not shown up, you wouldn't be wondering about your weight coming off. Just remember that."

Mindy pulled away and faced her husband.

Before she could say a word he pulled over. "I want to be fully engaged before you tell me that you had nothing to do with this."

Mindy put her hand to her chest. "I didn't bring a weapon, and I didn't pull a trigger."

"No, but everything that has transpired over the last month has been from something you started, and you started it because it 'annoyed' you. Not because of work productivity, which should be your only concern."

"Life is more than work, Ron. I have slaved over making my team a family. I cultivated it."

"Nice job, Mindy. You ultimately led to the destruction of two men, and the third spent a month in a mental institution, and I'd bet is not coming back to the company."

"He isn't part of my team. He's HR."

Her husband put the car in drive. "Tomorrow is going to be hectic. I can promise you that after that man tells them about his firing, and about your request to find Mr. Templeton, the man he shot, that you are about to need a lawyer."

"For what?"

"For what? Seriously? How about the man you were stalking getting shot by someone you secretly got information from. You better consider finding another job,

Mindy. You can't hide what that man tells the investigators."

"I won't go to jail for anything."

"No, but you will probably be fired, and a good chance you get civilly charged by a half dozen complainants."

"My life was at risk. Look at me, Ron. I'm twenty-five percent bigger than I was a month ago. My urgency dictated my actions. No court of law would deny me that."

They pulled into their driveway. Her husband hesitated. "As much as I think we are in for trouble, I do agree. I hope this one pound thing is over."

Mindy's smile flattened. "Thanks." She opened her door, the night air quieted by her phone. She pulled it from her pocket. "Oh shit."

Ron pulled up alongside her. "Who is it?"

"Mr. Stripling."

"Better face the music now."

"Fuck no!" She continued to the house, holding the screen out until it went to voicemail. That was followed by a text. She read it. "Fuck."

"What does he want?"

"He said I need to meet him in HR tomorrow." She wept. "You think they are firing me?"

Ron squeezed her. "Yeah, I do. We will be fine, but you might need to learn bookkeeping. I'll just hire you keep records for me."

"What about your bookkeeper?"

"Her husband's been transferred so she's been driving two hours a day." He eyed her. "You'd know that if you ever listened to me." He cautioned her. "Getting fired might be the best thing for you, because that's the least of your problems. I mean it when I say this is going to be big news. This could go national."

"National?"

"Yeah, 'Lady found at home of man killed who she claimed made her gain a pound a day.' I can see talk shows trying to get you to go to their show."

"You're funny."

"I'm serious."

"No you aren't."

"Mindy!" He stopped her. "This went from crazy to murder. This—" he circled his hand around her, "is about to become a shit show. By tomorrow afternoon, local television will be here, and by tomorrow night, national news will be here."

"What are we going to do?"

"We?" He shook his head. "You are going to call your family and tell them that they might get questions about you."

"Like what?"

"Like, 'Did she ever practice witchcraft, had delusions that she was possessed,' you name it. The more sensational, the more they'll be asking."

From inside the house, the home phone rang. Mindy hurried to the hallway phone. "Hello?"

"Mrs. Docket. This is Sargent Mandel; I need you to be at our station at your earliest convenience. If you make it later than tomorrow at eight o'clock, we will come to your home."

"Am I being charged with something?"

"If you were, we'd be there now." He softened his voice. "Everything our suspect has told us, leads us to believe you may have corroborating information."

Mindy suggested. "Perhaps it would be wise to seek counsel?"

The Sargent agreed, "I'd say that'd be very wise."

She thanked him and hung up.

Ron stepped up. "And so it begins."

They slept on it. Mindy didn't sleep much, Mr. Templeton's words stuck in her head. She whispered, "I hired you back."

The sun peeked over the east and she scurried to the bathroom. She checked the calendar. The thirtieth day. Each square an additional pound, the last read one-thirty-nine. She stripped and exhaled. "Please say one-thirty-eight."

Mindy nodded. "Remember, I hired you back." She stepped up onto the weight plate. The digital numbers rose, before settling on a slow crawl starting at one-thirty-five. It rolled over to one-thirty-six, it inched to one-thirty-seven, it rocked to one-thirty-eight. "Stop right there, please."

It hovered, a light rock. Mindy stilled herself. "Stay there." The number flickered, and with a creep that jumped like a spider, landed on one-forty.

Ron's voice caught her by surprise. "Good or bad?"

She shook her head.

Chapter 47

Becky rolled toward Brent.

He'd been awake since they made it home, his thoughts swirling about curious conversations. He noticed her. "About time you woke up."

She put a hand on his chest and snuggled close. "I know that look. That's Rodin, and you haven't been to sleep yet, have you?"

"I've been trying to figure out how Dr. Coldsnow was caught by surprise when he heard Ms. Ping say she lived there to the police."

His wife deadpanned, "That's the thing that kept you awake all night? And not the fact that the puppeteer died?"

"That's just it. He almost had me convinced he was special, but look at that, his plan didn't go as planned."

"So you're okay not knowing how he did all those other things?"

Brent put an arm behind his head. "I don't know, not all of them have come true yet."

"Like?"

"Aren't we supposed to have triplets?"

"And if we do?"

"Then I guess I'll have to dig to find out how he called that, but mark my words, it wasn't magic."

"What about Carl's stuttering?"

"I can only speak for myself, and what has been done to me. For all I know, Carl might have been in on all of this. I never heard him stutter, and neither did you. This might be the most elaborate game of 'ruse' ever."

"And that must apply to a woman gaining a pound a day? She too might be faking it to trick you?"

"I'm just saying, I can only qualify the truth by that which I experience, and what have I experienced: listening devices heard from a novice with a detector, and then a completely different reading from the government, both noises of which disappeared the next day. Did it ever exist?"

"The texts?"

"Oh please. If I bought into that one, that means I buy into any text coming in to me."

"Didn't you say you heard voices when you were in the CAT scan?"

"Yes, and I never saw who was speaking."

"Didn't you say it was in the empty room?"

"Was it?"

"That's it? You're good with everything that happened as plausible under some sort of deception?"

"All but the expression on Dr. Coldsnow's face when he saw Ms. Ping." He confided, "Dr. Coldsnow had an expression when he leaned over Mr. Templeton. He was confused. Something happened that wasn't supposed to. I think he was in with the old man on everything."

"If that were the case, why was he surprised by Ms. Ping?"

"Exactly. Why? That creates the mystery I need to find out."

"Well, that should be easy to figure out because I'm guessing a room full of people will be spending time together at the courthouse."

"If that's the case, I owe Hunter the courtesy to at least snoop around."

"Why?"

"Because Hunter wasn't the only one holding that gun."

"If you mean Dr. Coldsnow, he was trying to take it."

"Okay, but what actually happened that we could see?"

"It went off before he could take it."

Brent shook his head. "That's not what we know."

"What do we know, Brent?"

"We know the gun was moved from Mindy to Mr. Templeton, all the while Dr. Coldsnow had a hold of Hunter's hand." He pointed out, "The one holding the gun. What we know is that the direction it went was done by the doctor."

"Maybe Hunter too was in on it."

"That much I believe I can answer. I am friends with Hunter, I had conversations with him about this, I know what he believed. I don't think he guided that gun anywhere but at Mindy."

"Are you accusing the doctor of killing Mr. Templeton?"

"No, just not accusing Hunter."

His wife propped her head on her hand. "So what are your thoughts?"

"I can't explain Ms. Ping."

"In what way?"

"The doctor knew where Mr. Templeton lived, and I'm sure it was surveillance by him; how would he never have known his assistant lived there?"

"What are you going to do?"

"I'm going to go visit someone."

"Ms. Ping?"

"No, Dr. Coldsnow."

His wife shook her head. "Really? He locks people up in a nuthouse. Why don't we go to Ms. Ping?"

"Carl said Dr. Coldsnow was once a stutter victim, and that he's been chasing Mr. Templeton for decades. He has to know something, and if pressed, maybe he'd care to share it with me."

She rolled away and stared at the ceiling. "I'm not going this time. You're on your own."

"Okay."

She grimaced. "Damn it. Fine, I'll go."

"I told you, you don't have to go."

"Did you forget? My path is super safe."

"Did you forget? The guy who told you that is dead?"

She shrugged. "I think I'm still safe."

His phone vibrated to the edge of the end table. "Catch that."

His wife reached out and grabbed the dancing phone. She swiped to a text. "You better look at this."

"What's it say?"

She read the text. '*Seek the truth and understand how to spell it.*' She sighed, "Guess we can write off Mr. Templeton as your texter."

"Call the number. I bet it's Coldsnow Manor."

His wife dialed it in, held it to her ear. Brent waited for her to speak. She pulled away. "It went to voicemail."

"Coldsnow Manor?"

"Mr. Templeton's cellphone."

Brent sat up. "Huh, Ms. Ping's mystery deepens."

"Why her?"

"She had to have sent this."

"That's not like you. You said you can't make assertions without seeing it yourself."

"Without rationally understanding it. We see things all the time that aren't real."

"Still, you can't assume it's her."

"I suppose not, but she's my first suspect of that post."

"So you want to go there instead?"

"No, I feel like I need to see the doctor."

"And that feeling doesn't seem given to you?"

Brent smiled. "Okay, maybe the powers-to-be know I'm an inquisitive guy, and maybe they knew I'd choose this. Either way, I am going to go see the doctor, especially since I am sure there are a bunch of forensic investigators at Mr. Templeton's house."

Becky rolled away and out of bed. "Breakfast before we go?"

"I told you to take it easy."

"I think after millions of years, females have figured out how to work and carry a child at the same time."

"And accidents happen. Why don't we have breakfast out?"

"Because there are things I want for the nursery. We need to cut corners, Brent."

"Fine, then I'll make breakfast." He shooed her to the bathroom. "Go shower, I'll get it ready."

Brent got out of bed behind her, grabbed his phone and hit reply: *'Who is this?'*

'You once said you needed the truth, and I said "truth as you see it." I want you to see it.'

Brent grinned, started to type before it dawned on him. He re-read the text.

How did Ms. Ping know that? Mr. Templeton said that after she'd left.

He typed: *'Who is this?'*

'I said you'd lead a company one day.'

He played along: *'Dead men tell no tales.'*

'Correct, dead ones do not.'

That annoyed Brent; it annoyed him long enough for his wife to make it out and ask, "Breakfast?"

Brent held a carton of eggs. "Sorry. Just trying to put things together."

His wife took the eggs. "Don't let it kill your reality, Sweetheart."

He stopped her. "My reality?" He pointed. "You're right; perhaps I need to know what my reality is." He motioned to the clock. "Let's get out of this house before eight. I don't want to be here if the police come by to question us. I want to figure something out first."

"I can't get breakfast done that fast."

"I'll jump in the shower and we'll pick-up breakfast. Time wins out."

Chapter 48

"Honey, I need to go somewhere."

Carl's wife looked up from the table. "Do we need to go to the police station?"

"No, I need to go somewhere else."

"Work?" She stood, worry spread across her face.

"No."

She faced him. "If not those two places, I can only think of one other, and do you think going back to the Lake District is smart? They probably have the place taped up."

"There is one other place."

His wife squinted. "Mindy's or the Smith's?"

Carl stared at his wife.

"No! You don't mean the sanitarium?"

"I need to go."

"I won't let you. I'll call the police as soon as you leave."

"You do what you think is best. Mr. Templeton said I was the Guest of Honor because I'd succeeded. The test is over for me."

Mrs. Wickmire tilted her head. "Are you listening to yourself? Do you realize that Dr. Coldsnow attempted to commit a felony on you, and you disappearing would greatly benefit him?"

"There is work to be done. Door Number Two is my choice."

His wife reeled. "Wait. Honey, what are you talking about?"

He grinned. "Did I stutter?"

"Why do you have to go back there? I need to know."

"I heard a calling. It's been calling me since I saw my reflection in a mirror while in my cage. Someone delivered a tray and told me who I had to look at. I picked up the mirror and looked."

"Didn't we determine that Mr. Templeton protected you, and Dr. Coldsnow didn't? Honey, Mr. Templeton isn't here anymore. I just don't see this as a good idea."

"It's not an idea. It's a calling."

His wife cried. "Am I losing you to some cult?"

Carl tucked his chin over her shoulder. "Shhh; you aren't losing me. My relationship to you will never be better. My fatherhood will never be better."

"Why do you feel so certain?"

"I understand what Mr. Templeton was saying to me."

"Do you want to take a gun with you?"

Carl reminded her. "First off, we don't have a gun, and second, no. I don't want to take a gun with me, and after last night I'd think that would be the last thing you'd want me to do."

"I just want you to protect yourself."

"I'm fine." Carl pecked his wife's forehead. "Pick a restaurant. I'll take you and the girls to dinner when I get back."

"Pinkie promise me, Mr. Wickmire."

He stuck his fist up and rolled out his pinkie. They locked and he called out, "Pinkie promise."

Carl grabbed his keys and called out goodbyes to his daughters.

In the car, it felt good to be alone. He sat and realized not another person could see him. No one was crowding him, and no one spied. He had passed the finish line.

Through town he drove, finding himself into the bucolic countryside and the grand entrance to Eastern State, home of Coldsnow Manor.

Without fear or fright, he parked and made his way up the steps. When he pushed the doors open, Dr. Coldsnow leaned over the front desk secretary.

The doctor looked up and shook his head. "Let me guess, I'm collecting my bet here and not at the house?"

"Bet?"

"Did you get a calling to come here?"

"No, I came because I fel—yes because of a calling."

The doctor straightened himself; shook his head, and motioned to Carl. "Can you believe I got fooled by Ms. Ping?"

Carl shrugged. "Perhaps you didn't get fooled. Perhaps you didn't ask the right questions."

"Well, I guess I'll never get to ask those questions because I killed him."

"What do you mean by collecting a bet?"

"Abe and I had a bet on three people."

"Is that what he meant by two out of three?"

"It is, but since Mindy didn't get to rehire Abe, and since she opened the path for anyone, he wound up losing that bet."

Carl shrugged. "Losing for what?"

"He couldn't save her from her own curse."

"And Brent and I were the wins?"

"You were his only win. Brent was never a bet."

"What about his wife's pregnancy?"

"Payment for being a piece."

"So who is the third?"

Dr. Coldsnow held his hand out to his office. "I was."

"You?"

"Yeah, but he lost that one too." He turned as he allowed Carl in, "So he was one for three."

"How did he lose you?"

"He said I wouldn't kill either of you. I was more than willing to end your life, and if Mindy had opted to stick around I would have done the same thing, but since I killed him, I won."

"How? You didn't do what you said you would. Just because you killed him, doesn't change your bet."

He grinned. "Carl, it wasn't about the act, it was about the desire."

"How much was the bet for?"

"One pound. One English Pound."

Carl clarified. "An English buck? You two played with our lives for one dollar?"

"A pound is worth more than a dollar."

"Barely. So this was a game?"

He nodded.

Carl continued. "I noticed something last night." Carl took a seat. Plush red leather, high bookshelf walls, a psychiatrist feel. "You had an odd conversation with Ms. Ping before you left last night."

"Yeah. Over the years, he has resorted to allies, and that's fair game. I just didn't see her being one. She fed me good intel. She had a shift where she watched his house. Never deceived me, or so I thought."

"Over the years? You've done this with him before?"

Dr. Coldsnow eyed Carl. "The world is not what you think it is, Mr. Wickmire, and we are targets, pieces, players, or gamblers. Some of us are more than one."

"And what was Mr. Templeton?"

He smiled. "A good citizen of the world." He winked.

Someone knocked and Dr. Coldsnow called out. "Come in."

Mr. Pearl stepped in.

"Good Morning, Mr. Pearl."

He nodded. "Ms. Ping is here."

Dr. Coldsnow nodded. "Figures she'd be the one paying me. Like she said, she lived with him."

A second knock.

"Come in."

Without fear or fright, Ms. Ping walked in as though nothing was amiss.

"Ms. Ping, or should I say, Mata Hari?"

"I am here to settle your bet."

"Settle the bet? Does his loss transfer to you?"

Ms. Ping smiled. "Oh, Dr. Coldsnow. You did not win."

"On the contrary. Mindy is a loss, and so am I."

"I accept Mindy as a loss. However, you were a win."

He faced Ms. Ping. "How am I a loss, as I told this gentleman, I was willing to kill either of them."

"Although it is true you had plans to end Mr. Wickmire's life, you had no such desire for Ms. Docket. You favored her, you saw you in her when she made her own mistake with Hunter; you knew you had to prevent that, you didn't want to lose her as an ally; someone like you, someone who wouldn't follow the lit path. You lose. You showed favor for her." She approached Dr. Coldsnow. "Give me my pound."

"You?"

She whispered, "Would you like double or nothing on Ms. Docket."

"Delivered here?"

"Yes."

"I want Hunter too."

Ms. Ping asked, "For what purpose?"

"Mr. Templeton put him in a murder situation, and he's just an innocent citizen, right?"

"No need."

Dr. Coldsnow held his arms out. "Why?"

"The body has disappeared."

Dr. Coldsnow showed contempt. "How?"

"There was no body in the morgue this morning. They called and said they've misplaced the body."

"Really, I guess you have other players. A few in high places."

"If you say so; however, without a body, there isn't much they can do to Hunter."

Dr. Coldsnow rose from his seat with force. "Fine! I'll take Ms. Docket. What will determine the bet?"

"See if you can make her yours. I welcome taking your brand of happiness away from you."

He changed the subject, "Are you taking over for Abe?"

"Taking over?"

"Well, who am I paying for this round?"

She held her hand out, "One Pound, please." Ms. Ping shook her head as she accepted a crisp clean pound. She nodded "Ms. Docket will be here to check in today."

"Is that the only game?"

"It is."

"Now that I know you work for him, not sure how you will keep eyes on your newest charge."

"Work for him?"

Carl interrupted. "Who was he?"

Dr. Coldsnow stayed on topic. "Let's not get too full of yourself, Ms. Ping. I've dealt with the old man quite a few times, and unless you were in the shadows all these years, of which at your age, I find that hard to believe, then yes, you worked for him."

Ms. Ping bowed her head. "If you say so."

He demanded. "Carl asked you, who was he? I want to know too. He came and went, he was as mysterious yesterday as he was forty years ago, but still he'd come to me with one pound bets. How did he do all this? Please tell me, you have nothing to fear from me now that he's gone." He pleaded. "I just want to know who he was."

Ms. Ping turned. "Was?"

She stood. "If you try to leave this place uninvited you will still stutter."

"You are telling me that know that Mr. Templeton is dead that I am still tied to this place?"

"Did you follow a lit path?"

"He's dead, I'll take my chances."

She shrugged. "Suit yourself." She motioned for Carl to follow. "Dr. Coldsnow, I will be taking him."

Dr. Coldsnow stayed with Carl's question, "Answer him, who was he?" Dr. Coldsnow bowed. "I thought he was all knowing and either extra-terrestrial or a God. Turns out he was just a man."

Ms. Ping smiled. "Just a citizen of the world."

"Yeah, yeah, yeah, that's the line I've been giving Guests of Honor for years."

"That because it is true."

Carl corrected her. "Was true."

She bowed, took Carl by the arm, and walked him out of the office. "I'm leaving my car here. Care to drive me home, Mr. Wickmire?"

Chapter 49

Mindy grabbed her husband's arm. "Ron, I want to go see Dr. Coldsnow."

"Are you out of your mind?"

"He wasn't with Mr. Templeton. Did you see the glee on his face when he bent over his corpse?"

"He did seem to have a 'beat you' look."

Mindy pulled her husband into the bedroom. "Get dressed. If he got what he wanted and he let Carl go without a fight, then maybe he can get this," she grabbed her waistline," curse off me."

Ron stopped her. "And if it isn't a curse?"

"All the better, then it is some psycho-babble that the doctor should be able to cut through."

He kept her attention. "You realize what he did to Carl? From the conversation I had with him before we left last night, Dr. Coldsnow caged him."

"And he said it was to smoke out Mr. Templeton. Now that the old man is dead, and I'm still gaining weight, I have to go to the one person who studied the old man. Look what he did for Carl. Carl isn't stuttering anymore. I have no choice."

"Why this route? If it isn't a drug doing this to you, and it is the power of suggestion, why not a different professional?"

"Carl said Dr. Coldsnow was Mr. Templeton's first victim, seems to me that's the best expert around." She pulled a sweatshirt over her head. "Besides, something feels right about this."

Her husband shook his head but followed her out. "I hope you know what you're doing. After all you've done, I don't think the police will bail you out of there."

Mindy winked. "They will if they need me to appear in court. You said that yourself. The way I see it, they will hold precedence over anyone else."

Ron opened Mindy's door. "Just be careful."

"Let's go." Mindy rushed Ron.

"Stop. We will get there obeying the speed limit."

She sighed and turned her attention to the houses passing by.

When they came to the tree-lined entrance, a familiar face caught Mindy's attention. "Ron, that's Carl in that car?"

Ron's head turned with hers, "And that's the Asian lady from Templeton's place."

"Why is he with her, and why here?"

As they crossed paths, Ms. Ping's gaze locked onto Mindy. She smiled and nodded.

"She's creepy, Ron."

Ron drove on, turned into the parking lot and settled nearest the exit. "Let's see what the warden can do for you."

"Stop it. If he can't do anything for me, I'm dead in half a year."

"No, you can survive—"

"Shut up, Ron. You're sounding like Mr. Templeton."

"Sorry." He retreated out his door and came around to hers. "Here, let's go see Dr. Coldsnow."

At the entrance to Coldsnow Manor, Dr. Coldsnow greeted them. "Mrs. Docket. So good to see you."

She still disliked him. "Oh yeah? Well, you're seeing me with one more pound."

"Sorry to hear that. I lost a pound today."

"Is that supposed to be funny?" Mindy held her arms akimbo.

"No, merely referring to a bet I lost. However, I was told I can double down."

Mindy came clean. "I need help."

"I know you do."

"What do you know about what Mr. Templeton did to me?"

"This one is new to me. However, the principle has to be the same. He conditioned you over the months he worked with you, and you were already hypnotized when he gave the key words to you." He escorted her to his office, her husband in tow. "I was able to unlock Carl's affliction by fear. "With you, who knows, but clearly we have different issues. With Carl, I could create the atmosphere slowly, more terrifying each day. You need this treated within a much shorter time period."

"I'll do whatever it takes."

"I like hearing that, Mrs. Docket."

Mr. Pearl entered the room. "You need me?"

Dr. Coldsnow turned Mindy to his assistant. "Mrs. Docket is going to be staying with us. Prepare the hospitality room for her and her husband."

Mindy cut in, "Hospitality room?"

"Yes, you will be staying up here, not down below." He offered, "Go home, get clothes, and come back here for orientation, a little paperwork, and a really nice dinner."

Mindy exhaled. "Oh good. I was worried you'd have me locked up like Carl."

"That's one form of therapy. I don't see any reason why you'd need that."

"Thank you."

Ron interrupted. "Does that mean I can see my wife whenever I want?"

"Well, provided we aren't in a session. Also, the first week, I need to evaluate her away from anyone she knows. So you will be away from her for the first week. You can call here, and I can give you reports, but just for that first week, no communication."

Ron shook his head. "I'm not sure I'm good with that, Doc."

"Then perhaps a better option would be to go to an outside professional. They might be better suited anyway."

Mindy stepped between them. "Ron, this is fine. I need to do this, and if that's the procedure, then fine."

Her husband pulled her away from the doctor. He whispered. "One week without knowing what's going on means he could seriously do damage to you."

Mindy whispered back. "It's one fucking week, Ron. Grow a pair and deal with it."

Ron raised his hands. "Fine. But just remember who you shouldn't piss off, because I'm the one who has to come get you if this goes sideways."

She kissed his cheek and whispered, "I'll sneak a phone inside, don't worry." She turned to the doctor. "He's fine and I accept."

The doctor crossed his arms. "You really didn't like the old man, did you?"

"Did you?"

"I was intrigued. I never figured out how he did it."

"How did you overcome his hypnosis, or poison, or whatever he did?"

"Dr. Templeton, actually Mr. Goodman back then, gave me and my congregation two choices; take the lit path or admit what we'd done was wrong."

"You took the lit path?"

"No, I chose to confess."

"So why still hold a grudge?"

He smiled. "Mrs. Docket." He tilted his head, "May I call you Mindy?"

"Feel free."

"Well, Mindy, much like you, I don't like to be told what to do, and my desire was to say nothing, but nothing wasn't working, and the only time I didn't stutter was when he came around. He ruined my career. He made me out to be a charlatan. My grudge is about his two choices."

Chapter 50

"Look at that?" Becky sat with Brent in the Pig's Blanket café, her finger extended.

Brent followed Becky's point. "That's Carl. Fast recovery."

"No, look who is in the passenger seat."

Brent took in the rider. "What the hell, that's Mr. Templeton, alive and well."

"How can that be? We saw him shot, zipped up, and taken away."

"It can't be." Brent stood. "Change of plans."

"Are we going to Carl's?"

"We are going wherever that car is going. By the looks of it, I'd say we are going to Mr. Templeton's house."

Brent paid the bill and Becky grabbed the leftovers.

"Really? I don't think we're that needy."

"Hey, I'm hungry, and if you haven't forgotten I'm eating for two."

"I thought you were having triplets?"

"Four then." She winked. "I hope it is triplets." She winked and chided him, "Then you have some real explainin' to do, Lucy!"

Brent ushered them out and to the car. "We aren't too far behind."

When they arrived, Carl's car was empty and the front door to Mr. Templeton's house rocked open."

Brent pulled in behind Carl. The two jumped out and hurried up the walkway.

As they reached the steps, Ms. Ping greeted them. "Was that you I saw eating at the diner?"

Brent squinted. "Where were you?"

"I was sitting in the passenger side of Mr. Wickmire's car."

Brent smiled. "I didn't see you. I did see an old man though."

"Old man?"

"That's who was sitting in that seat."

Ms. Ping shrugged. "You can ask Mr. Wickmire."

"I don't need to ask Carl what my wife and I saw. I am pretty sure I can distinguish the difference between you and Mr. Templeton."

Ms. Ping approached Brent. She toggled between him and his wife. "Are you sure?"

"I'll tell you the same thing I told Mr. Templeton. Everything has a logical answer."

Ms. Ping nodded. "Agreed, but define logical."

"Anything that the scientific world can verify."

"What if your understanding of logic is superseded by the illogical, only because your knowledge of logic is infantile?"

"Insult me all you want, but I know what I saw, and my wife can verify it."

"I see." She twirled around, "Tell me when you see an old man."

Brent moved past her. "May I?" He headed toward the door."

"Be my guest."

"Of honor?"

"No, that was already given."

"To Carl?"

"Not anymore. Now it is someone else."

"Who?"

"Mindy Docket."

Brent hesitated. "What's that supposed to mean?"

"Just that she needs our help."

"What about Hunter? Seems like he needs someone's help."

"Already done."

"What did you do, get him a lawyer, or did you have him committed?"

"One better. No charges."

"What did you tell the police, Ms. Ping that would have them drop a shooting death case?"

"I did not tell the police anything; the police told me."

Becky joined Brent. "What did the police tell you?"

"They can't find his body. They came and apologized this morning. I went to Dr. Coldsnow's office to let him know, and to discuss what further he can do of assistance to me, and I saw Carl there. I asked him for a ride."

"Why not take the car you went there with?"

"I have my reasons." She smiled. Echoes of the night before played center stage as they walked over the spot Mr. Templeton had expired. "Now, there is Carl, ask him."

Carl stood center in the front room. He bowed his head. "Good to see you, Brent, Mrs. Smith."

Brent offered, "Odd seeing you here, Carl. I would think you'd want to spend time with your family." Brent came farther into the room. "Who'd you give a ride to today?"

Carl shrugged. "Ms. Ping. That's all."

"Did you drive past the Pig's Blanket café?"

"Yes."

"Twenty minutes ago?"

"Actually about ten minutes ago."

Becky cut in, "And you had Ms. Ping in the passenger seat?"

"Did you see us?"

"We saw you, but Ms. Ping wasn't sitting next to you. You aren't the reason why Mr. Templeton's body is missing are you?"

Carl soured his face. "No! That's silly."

Brent differed. "Everything about this month is weird. Not silly, but outright weird."

Carl agreed.

Becky continued, "Did you know Mr. Templeton's body disappeared last night from the coroner's office?"

Carl offered, "They must still have the murder weapon."

Ms. Ping echoed from the kitchen, "No, that disappeared from the evidence room."

Brent shouted back. "The police told you that?"

She came around the corner and shrugged. "Call and ask."

Brent studied her. "I suspect you know more about all of this than you let on."

Ms. Ping approached and stood before Brent. "I know lots of things, Mr. Smith. However, many of them would defy your logic, so I feel discussing it with you would be futile."

Brent nodded. "You aren't as polite as Mr. Templeton."

Ms. Ping studied Brent, her eyes in narration. "You think so?"

"I do."

She smiled. "That is perception on what biases you have shown when you make that observation."

"And why is that?"

She continued on to Carl "Because we are the same."

Brent stayed with it, "You two aren't the same. He was jovial."

She turned and proposed, "Often how you act in public is different than how you act in private. Certainly there are times when being friendly isn't possible."

"I suppose that's true, but when are you in a friendly mood?"

"If I told you, you'd never understand."

"Try me."

"Not today, Mr. Smith."

"When?"

"When the day comes that you might be the Guest of Honor."

Brent smiled. "I see. One day I will get this grand welcome like Carl?"

"You never know."

"Well, I can't guess when that might be."

"I will make you a wager, Mr. Smith."

"Yeah, and what would that be?"

"I will bet you one English Pound that you will know exactly when you will be the Guest of Honor."

Brent winked. "Well, since that could be anything I ever come to you with that you declare is my moment, I'll pass on the bet. If I ever feel compelled to find out something, it'll be with more questions."

"That is a lovely quality about you, Mr. Smith; you will be nobody's fool."

Becky cut in, "You know my husband believes last night was a ruse?"

Ms. Ping corrected her. "Your husband doesn't believe it's a ruse, he just can't explain it." She turned to Brent, "By your own logic, I assume all paths that can be explained in the physical world are acceptable."

"Correct."

She returned to Brent's wife. "A ruse is his way of saying your belief that you wish him to explore isn't one of those logical paths. I'm sure he would agree with that."

His wife stayed in the conversation. "What if we have triplets?"

"I don't know; what would you like to have happen?" She took them in. "I hope they display hope, faith, and charity."

Brent hesitated. The mystery that couldn't be explored. "Becky, don't go there. You can't accept what we don't know yet. We'll cross that bridge when the doctor says there's just one child."

Becky held Brent's attention. "And if they don't?" Becky shook her head. "Everything we've experienced and you think this is the thing that won't happen. Don't say I didn't tell you so."

"Even if we do, I'll find out how he knew, and it will be explainable."

Ms. Ping bowed. "Of course it is."

Carl stood, unaware of their conversation. "I'm not sure what you think you saw, Brent, but Ms. Ping was my passenger." He nodded to Ms. Ping. "I need to get back to my family, but I want to thank you for your advice. I didn't plan on going back to the company, so I will be looking for work, and it sounds like the position allows me to feed my family."

Ms. Ping smiled. "Oh, it does so much more than that."

Brent interrupted, "What position?"

"Ms. Ping offered me HR for Templeton Enterprises."

"If Mr. Templeton was tied to Templeton Enterprises, of which I assume makes money if it needs an HR, why was he working as an attorney for Losan and Gellis ?"

"Mr. Smith, who said I was working for you?"

"I?"

"See, logic isn't always what you think it is."

Brent considered her involvement.

His wife came to his side and whispered. "I see what you're thinking, Honey," She rubbed his arm. "It doesn't matter, and you don't have to figure it out. Let's just live our lives. According to her, everyone is accounted for."

Brent turned to his wife. "Accounted for? You mean like they have it all under control?"

His wife shrugged. "I guess."

"I'm not good with that."

Ms. Ping offered, "Reverend Coldsnow felt the same way. Careful getting too involved proving things, Mr. Smith. Sometimes bliss is better."

Becky suggested, "Let's go home."

Brent kept his conversation between them. "Let's go see the doctor."

Chapter 51

Carl made his way across town, not headed home, but to see Mindy. Outside their home, Mindy and Ron held a tense huddle.

Carl stepped out of his car and broke their conversation. "Mindy, Ron, you guys okay?"

Mindy turned. "Glad to see you aren't stuttering after that old man died, but I wasn't that lucky. His mumbo jumbo on me hasn't gone away."

"I know."

Ron turned and took interest, "How do you know?"

"I had heard that you went to see Dr. Coldsnow."

"Who told you?"

"Ms. Ping."

Mindy stepped closer. "How did she know?"

Carl shrugged. "I just came by to see how you are doing?"

She pointed a finger. "My underwear bands are cutting into my hips!"

"Can I offer you something?"

"You have an antidote?"

"If you wish to look at it that way."

"Has that Asian woman rubbed off on you, Carl? Are you about to quote some Chinese?"

"No. Just how I feel."

"Are you going to tell me what to do, where the best place to go is?"

"I'll tell you what to look for, but what decisions you make, they are your own."

"Why do I think listening to a man who has been treated like a dog for a month is a bad idea?"

"If you don't like the advice, you are free to not take it."

"Thank you for mansplaining that, Carl."

Ron tamped down his wife. "Stop it; let him speak." He nodded to Carl.

"Your condition clearly lives on after the death of Mr. Templeton, so I have no idea who there is to help you, but it could come in the strangest of ways."

"And what would those be, lit paths?"

Carl bowed his head. "I'm merely suggesting that if the impossible seems to happen, let it happen."

Mindy put her arms akimbo. "They fucked you up, didn't they?"

"Think what you want. I was just trying to help."

"So does that woman know a way to stop my weight?"

Carl shrugged. "I don't know, why don't you ask her?"

Mindy exhaled. "I'm done asking for things. I'm getting help, but thank you."

"Good, just remember, help is all around you."

"Yeah?" Mindy twirled. "You think anyone can help me with this? You were just stuttering because he hypnotized you. This—" she patted her stomach, "Is not hypnosis."

"Whatever you have, the answer is inside you."

She waved him off. "Carl, go home. I don't need your pep talk. I'm going on a retreat."

Carl tried to say something but Mindy cut him off.

"Buh bye." She waved her fingers "Go away."

Carl nodded. "Good luck, Mindy."

Carl walked back to his car, unsure of what his culpability was for Mindy. Before he reached the door he turned. "Mindy, I lied to Mr. Templeton. I have had to accept firings from departments, even when I didn't agree. However, your department seemed to run like that every firing."

"Boo hoo, Carl. My department runs like a well-oiled machine."

"Someone jumped off a building from your department."

Mindy stiffened. "Are you accusing me of something? Because that's uncalled for and I can have you fired for accusing me of that?"

"You can't fire someone who tendered his resignation, and I'm not accusing you of anything. I'm pointing out the facts. We are here because of your firing Mr. Templeton. I read your report, I spoke to him. The worst feeling overcame me that morning because he asked me upfront why I was there, and I lied."

"Then you admit you are the reason we are here."

"Yeah, I guess we are. I'm here because you affected my life, and I did something I shouldn't have. You are an influence of malcontent."

Mindy's husband stepped in. "Carl, that's uncalled for."

"Is it, Ron? You mean to tell me that how your wife behaves in social settings is kind and sweet?"

"I have no issues with my wife."

Carl shook his head and opened his car door. "Careful about your veracity, Ron. Look where it got me." He motioned to Mindy, "And look what happens to the straw that stirs the drink." He could see her world unraveling.

"Good that you quit, I would have written you up to be fired."

Carl nodded. "I hope you find your path." He stepped in his car, closed the door, and nodded. What more could he do?

Chapter 52

Mindy packed the car.

"Honey, you can't take all that stuff. I suspect you aren't going to be as free to do your own thing as you think."

"Dr. Coldsnow said to bring anything I will no longer be able to wear if I gain more weight."

"Why?"

"He said it will be necessary to study emotions."

"So studying your anxiety about your favorite clothes not fitting is important to study?"

"Perhaps to overcome Mr. Templeton's curse."

"So you've settled on curse?"

"Why not? If it is hypnosis, and no one can figure it out, then isn't that a curse?"

"I guess, but isn't a curse supposed to have a charm that can overcome it?"

"I think my charm might have died with that gunshot." She sighed. "Let's get going."

Her husband pulled the rest of the baggage into the back and joined her in the front. When they made it to the Manor, Mindy checked in and they took her luggage to a guest room.

"Mr. and Mrs. Docket, I'll see you for dinner at the dining hall."

Mindy noticed the time. "That's like four hours."

"You are welcome to order food now, and by all means have lunch. I just won't be able to join you."

Ron nodded. "Thank you."

The doctor left them on their own and they checked into their room, the accommodations surprised Mindy. "This is like a four star hotel."

"Far cry from what Carl said his room looked like."

Mindy plopped onto the bed. "You think the doctor can cure me?"

Her husband pulled her up. "Let's go see this place."

They toured the grounds, inside and out. They didn't go down to the basement. When they hit the dining hall, Mindy pulled her husband's arm. "Look at this."

"Looks pretty swanky, Mindy."

Mindy caught the attention of a busboy. "Where is the maître D?"

He shrugged. "I think you can seat yourself. The maître D is only here for functions."

Mindy questioned, "You mean that this beautiful place is seat yourself?"

"It is at lunch."

He continued on and Mindy found a seat hidden from the few who were there. Behind them a tall young man came by with a wine bottle. "You are here as a guest?"

"Yes."

"Well, in your honor, please enjoy." He twisted a corkscrew into a bottle's cork and popped the wine open. He nodded, bowed, and poured a blood red Cabernet.

Mindy asked, "What's that say?" motioning to the bottle's label.

"Le chemin éclairé."

Her husband took a sip. "It's good."

Their sommelier straightened, as tall as any man Mindy knew. "I hope you find understanding in everything you see." He nodded and turned toward the kitchen.

Ron whispered. "Dude's tall. I wonder if he moonlights as an orderly."

Mindy held the bottle. "Le chemin éclairé,"

Ron leaned in. "Don't ask me, I don't understand French."

Mindy stopped. "What'd you say?"

"I said I don't know French."

"No, you said you don't understand French."

"Same thing."

"Except that Lurch that gave us this wine said 'understand' also, but he said to find understanding in everything I see."

"He works at a mental hospital restaurant. He probably has to calm crazies."

327

"I doubt many crazies eat here. I would guess family and donors eat here."

"So, what's your point then?"

"Nothing. Maybe I'm so skittish that I don't trust anyone."

Dr. Coldsnow rounded the corner and caught Mindy's attention.

"Mrs. Docket. I see you found the dining area. I hope it meets your approval."

"My husband wonders if your patients eat up here?"

"Not often. Sometimes, those who recover have a meal up here, but for the most part, many patients are restricted to confinement, and wouldn't be social if here on their own."

Mindy took a sip of wine.

"Where did you get wine?"

"Your sommelier brought it by."

"My sommelier?" Dr. Coldsnow smiled. "What did he look like?"

Ron interjected. "Tall."

Dr. Coldsnow shook his head. "Sometimes his lack of creativity amazes me."

"The Sommelier?"

"No. His boss."

Mindy asked, "About?"

"He offered the same thing every time, and apparently even after he's gone."

"This wine?" Mindy took another sip. "It's really good."

Dr. Coldsnow tapped the table. "So it begins. Enjoy, we will get back together for dinner. If the sommelier comes back around, tell him good luck." Dr. Coldsnow continued on, his assistant trailing behind him.

Mindy and Ron had a nice lunch. The curing of Carl left Mindy with hope. She didn't feel preoccupied. "Ron?"

"Yes." He reached across and took her hand.

She rolled her thumb over his palm. "I feel like this might be the right place." She eyed him. "I know it could be scary, but I feel better about this than I do about the alternatives."

"I know. I will keep tabs. I really don't like the whole week alone."

"I'm sure Dr. Coldsnow has his methods."

"Just be careful, and keep that phone in a place they can't find it."

Mindy caught something out the window. "Look at that." Walking to a car was Ms. Ping.

Ron craned his neck and cursed. "Damn, why would she be here?" He snapped his finger. "You remember what Dr. Coldsnow did when he saw her? He knew her and was shocked she lived at that house."

"Let's find out why she's here." Mindy stood and pulled Ron up. "Let's go."

Out the doors, and down the steps, Mindy shouted. "Excuse me."

Ms. Ping turned. "Yes."

Mindy and Ron slowed to a walk. When they reached her, Mindy motioned. "Why are you here?"

"I had business this morning with Dr. Coldsnow and had left my car so I could talk with Carl."

"What business would you have with Dr. Coldsnow?"

"Why Ms. Docket, that's personal."

"Dr. Coldsnow seemed to know you."

"He thought he knew me, still thinks he does, but he would be surprised." She grinned. "He had his wish right there in front of him, and he didn't take advantage of it."

"No, I guess Hunter robbed him of that."

"You think?"

"Well, he was hunting for the old man for years, and well, I guess a hunter is what he used to find him, but he never got the answers he needed."

She leaned in. "He's the best thespian out there. He plays his role well. Careful with his treatments. When all feels lost, someone will help."

"If you are responsible for getting Carl out, I would remind you that I am here of my own accord, and I am seeking treatment for what your asshole boss did to me. I don't see you or any of your tall lackies doing me any favors, so back off, Bitch."

Ms. Ping opened her door, put one foot in, and shook her head. "Tough resolve, I like that, but I can't believe I agreed to this for one pound."

She closed her door and pulled away before Mindy could give her a piece of her mind. "Stop!" The taillights getting smaller as she left. "Did you hear that? What the hell did that mean? Is she taunting me?" Mindy felt flush. "Ron, what does she know?"

Chapter 53

Brent took Becky to lunch. They enjoyed the spring morning, weekend foot traffic along the Farmers Market. Under the shade of tent set-ups, they perused the fruit and vegetables, chimes, artwork, and myriad other wares. At the last stall, a man sat alone with several books on having babies.

Becky took Brent's hand. "Let's see what he has."

As they approached, the gentleman stood and stood and stood. Brent whistled. "Damn, you are tall."

His thin stature gave him even more daunting height. "Yeah, a lot of people say that."

A wandering photographer snapped their picture. "Ten dollars for a pic of you two."

"Brent shook his head. "No thanks, we'll take a selfie if we need one."

"Suit yourself." He moved on.

Becky turned and perused the books. She asked about two books on a poster. "Which one would you recommend?"

"I wish I could tell you either one, but the truth is, those sold out." He shuffled through a couple of books. "I do recommend this one though." He pushed a table-book in front of them.

It's title, "Three's a charm–having triplet girls."

Becky pulled the book closer. "Why would you recommend this book?"

He came out from under the tenting, his height stretched to its peak. He shaded them from the sun, a corona around his body. "I don't know, but you look like you could use it."

Brent smiled. "What's your name?"

He held his hand out. "I am Verlicht Pad."

"Where are you from, Verlicht?"

"Netherlands."

Brent greeted him, "Pleased to meet you." He took note if anyone watched. "Maybe I'll see you here again."

Becky nodded. "What do I owe you?"

Verlicht motioned to the book. "That one?" He shook his head. "A gift for you."

Becky eyed Brent.

Brent sighed. "Whatever." He turned to Verlicht. "Thank you. How convenient of us to run across you."

The gentleman leaned down, creating a parasol of shade over both Brent and Becky. He winked. "Not convenient, but fate." He straightened and laughed. "Have a great day, you two." He laid an arm over the top of his tenting. "Hope you find what you are looking for."

Becky eyed Brent again.

Brent pushed Becky to leave. "I'm done, and I'm done walking. Let's go home."

His wife clutched the book and walked along like a school girl. "I had a nice time today."

"Oh yeah, you think you'll be saying 'I told you so,' to me?"

"Nope, I agree with Mr. Templeton. I like that you are smart."

"Oh yeah? You liked that I didn't accuse that guy of setting us up?"

His wife sighed. "You need to accept that there are too many unexplainable things happening to think you can solve them all."

Brent continued walking. He put his arm around his wife. "All the more reason to believe that people are colluding."

"Really, after the death of Mr. Templeton? You don't think that the game would be over and someone would be jumping out of the bushes yelling, 'Surprise, you're on Candid Camera.'?"

Brent smiled. "You aren't old enough to remember that show."

"Neither are you, but you seem to know what I'm talking about."

Peafowl squawked, their shrieks piercing the silence. "That's what I think of all of this."

"Like screaming?"

"They aren't screaming. They are warning that something dangerous has entered their territory."

"But we aren't dangerous." Becky joined Brent in letting a peacock strut in front of them.

"And we know that, but they don't. Sort of like our last month. Those not in the know, don't know."

"Does that mean we are the peacocks in this story?"

"One of us is; you would be a peahen."

"And that means what?"

"The peahen part?"

"No, how is not knowing what's going on a bad thing? If we aren't being hurt, shouldn't we be overjoyed to be having a child."

"The two aren't connected, Becky. Just a coincidence that we get pregnant and Mr. Templeton plays a game with us."

"And you think this book," she held it up, "is part of the game."

"Yep." Brent turned back toward the Farmers Market, "Let's go talk to Mr. Pad." He guided her back to the slope they'd just come down from.

Over the rise, they entered back to the market. Around a corner, Becky huffed. "He's gone."

"He couldn't have taken that down that fast. Where the hell did he go?"

They stopped at the tent next to his. "Do you know where the man who had this slot is?"

A woman nodded. "Don didn't come this week."

"No, there was a tall gentleman, named Verlicht, who was sitting here ten minutes ago who gave my wife this book."

She looked at the book. "Don sells cucumbers." She took out a pen. "What did you say his name was?"

"Verlicht Pad."

She chuckled. "He must be a guide."

Becky joined the conversation. "What's that mean?"

"His name; it's Dutch and means 'illuminated path'."

Becky eyed Brent. "I'm getting to the 'I told you so,' point really fast, Brent."

"I anticipated this."

"Why?"

"Too easy." Brent checked the sod at the event site. As though nothing had been upon that spot, Brent chuckled. "Damn good job."

Becky joined in. She peered at the grass with him. "What?"

"They must have only been here a minute or two. I don't see any evidence a tent was here."

The woman in the booth next to them agreed. "Yeah, since no one was here, that might be why there isn't any evidence."

Brent shot back. "There was someone here fifteen minutes ago. We spoke to him. He was extremely tall."

The woman smiled. "You sure you didn't come in from the other side?"

Brent went blunt. "Ma'am, don't tell me what I saw."

She nodded. "I'm not; I'm telling you what you didn't see."

In the distance, the photographer made his rounds. Brent whistled. "Hey, picture man!"

He hollered back, "You want a pic now?"

"We want the old pic; you still have it in your scroll?"

"I do!" He hurried over, sent a code from his phone to a small printer strapped to his hip. Tics, rolls, and whirls, and out came a pic of Brent and Becky. "Here you go. Ten dollars."

Becky beat Brent to the punch and paid the man. She tendered the picture and stared at it.

"Show the woman, Becky."

She shook her head. "No, you better." She handed a pic that had no stall behind them, no tall man, nothing but an empty slot.

Brent's grin grew. He turned to the photographer. "You are in on this too?"

"In on what?"

Brent dropped the pic and walked away.

His wife followed him. "Honey!"

He was annoyed. "What?"

"Stop it." She had retrieved the photo. If you are going to poo-poo this, don't be a poor sport if you can't figure it out." She stopped him. "If you really believe someone is pulling a big prank on you, I'm in your corner, but don't act like this."

"Let's go home."

Chapter 54

Carl found himself in the Lake District. His path had taken him away from his job and he sensed his destination sat inside the house Mr. Templeton had died in.

As he exited his car, a local detective met him. "Mr. Wickmire, do you have business here?"

"I need to see Ms. Ping."

"Is she expecting you?"

Over his shoulder a shrill voice caught his attention. "Detective! He is requested to be here."

He craned his neck, shook it, and returned to Carl. "Well, there you go. However, we need to speak with you and your other co-workers. We have a missing body and no weapon. So we have someone brandishing a weapon, it discharging and killing someone, and we have to let him go. No one wants to cop to anything, except the perp. Now I have testimonies from all of you from last night, so we know the old man was shot to death. However, we certainly can't take that to court with zero evidence."

Carl tilted his head. "Don't you have bloody rags with his DNA on it?"

The detective eyed Carl. "Funny thing about that, it developed legs along with every piece of evidence."

"How?"

"Walked right out of the evidence room."

"Shouldn't you be investigating your department rather than Ms. Ping?"

"Who says I'm investigating her? She has no reason to not see her partner's death avenged."

"Avenged. Interesting word choice. I agree with you if you are referring to someone who wanted to see a death avenged."

"There is no insurance, Mr. Wickmire." He shook his head. "I'm investigating you and your co-workers. I already know about all the weird things that have happened over the last month. You can't work in a department and not know that whacked out boss of your marketing department."

"She was the intended victim. If you want who pulled that trigger, perhaps Dr. Coldsnow is the person you should be investigating."

"Funny, Ms. Ping said the same thing."

"If you've kept your ear to the wind then you know he has an ax to grind as well."

"Odd that you'd give so many reasons why others might have done this."

"I'm not giving you so many reasons; I'm giving you the reasons as they have been laid out before me."

Another car came up behind Carl's. The detective and Carl turned as a gentleman stepped out his car, and he kept stepping out, until the man who served Carl his wine on his first day at Coldsnow Manor stood before them.

The detective blurted, "Jesus Christ, you're tall."

He leaned in, his presence felt like the Tower of Pisa. "Not my mythology, but thank you."

Carl nodded. "You!"

He smiled. "Yes, I'm hard to forget." He held his hand out. "Name is Verlicht Pad."

The detective asked, "Do you have business here? We've had," he hesitated, "an incident that we haven't resolved."

He folded his arms and extended to his full height. "I live here."

Carl twisted. "What?"

"You think those notes you got were from people who weren't in your corner?"

"I've never heard of you."

"I know, but who talks of themselves anyway?"

The detective cut in. "Excuse me," He turned, but Ms. Ping had departed, "I need to go verify that. Don't move from this spot."

Carl's newest curiosity shrugged. "I'll catch up with Carl."

They stood there while the Detective verified Verlicht's claim.

"Can you believe that? I'm just trying to go home."

Carl shook his head. "Since no one volunteered your information, it might be harder than you think. You better hope Ms. Ping vouches for you."

Verlicht took a deep breath. "Carl I need to concentrate." He closed his eyes and said, "Yes, he lives here. Sorry I didn't tell you, but he has been out of town and I just didn't think to bring him up. Please do me a favor and tell him that Carl is going to be working with me on the next project, and he will be handsomely rewarded."

Carl remained fixed.

"Good luck with the investigation, Detective."

Carl remained fixed.

Verlicht shook his head, inhaled and smiled. "Thank you, Carl."

"What just happened?"

"Nothing, just my silly thoughts running wild."

The Detective made his way back out to the group and waved Verlicht through.

"Thank you, Detective." He took long strides, a handful to make it all the way across the street and a handful more to make it to the door.

The Detective joined Carl in his amazement. "Damn, he's got to be seven and half feet tall."

"Ms. Ping said he lived there?"

"Yep. Shit. I was supposed to tell him that you will be working for—"

"Working for her. I know."

"She already told you?"

"No."

"How did you know?"

"Verlicht told me."

"It didn't sound like he knew."

"Detective, I think he might have been the one who told her." Carl bowed. "If you are through with me, may I go see what I'm going to be doing for them?"

The detective ordered, "Just remember, if I call, I expect you to answer."

"Why wouldn't I?"

He shook his head, pulled out his keys. "Just make sure."

Carl tipped his forehead and took his leave. When he reached the steps, Ms. Ping's voice shrilled, "Door is open, Carl."

Carl came through the foyer, and Ms. Ping sat in her reading chair. "Good afternoon, Ms. Ping."

"I'm glad you came by, I have a proposition for you."

"So Verlicht told me." Carl leaned around a corner. "Where is he?"

"Around. He might have gone up to nap."

"Kind of early."

He had a busy day."

"What does he do?"

"Fixes things."

"And how can I help you?"

I have a job for you, and as soon as my other piece gets here, I'll share it with you."

"Isn't Verlicht a piece too?"

Ms. Ping laughed out loud. "No, Verlicht is not."

They sat without words, Carl catching Ms. Ping with her head buried in her book, the pages never turning.

The doorbell chimed and Ms. Ping lifted her gaze. "Aw, the other piece."

She lifted up and hurried to the door. When she returned, she had Mr. Pearl in tow.

Carl stood. "Him?"

Ms. Ping put her arm around Mr. Pearl's waist. "What's wrong with him?"

"He didn't stop Dr. Coldsnow when he tried to shock me."

Ms. Ping shrugged. "He wasn't supposed to. He was just supposed to stall him long enough for me to shut down the power."

"What if he hadn't stalled him long enough?"

Ms. Ping pointed at Carl. "Then you wouldn't have gone through what you went through, and we might still be there."

"So I was never in danger?"

"Of course you were. Your wellbeing as a good citizen was failing."

"So why didn't Dr. Coldsnow know that you lived here, and won't he definitely wonder why Mr. Pearl is here? Or does he live here too?"

Ms. Ping smiled. "No, he doesn't live here, and Dr. Coldsnow is bound by an agreement."

"The bet?"

"Yes, the bet."

What in the bet would keep him from knowing Mr. Pearl is here?"

"For one thing, Mr. Pearl has had to take over for me as the assistant, and part of that is to swing by here every once in a while to visit me."

"Why doesn't he do that himself?"

She sat Carl, along with Mr. Pearl, and they shared the room. "Welcome to the world, Carl." She began with a clarification. "This doesn't apply to you, but Dr. Coldsnow can only leave sanitarium when he is summoned. If he should leave without a summoning, he would only stutter, and believe me, Carl, that man has not taken the affliction well."

"He wasn't stuttering when he came here last night."

"He was summoned. We were showing our hands."

"So I was part of your hand?"

"You were one third of the hand."

"Mindy and Brent were the other two?"

She shook her head. "Mindy and the Doctor."

"The Doctor?"

"He is always one of the three. To date, he has never won a pound; however, he would have had he not lost himself. Ms. Docket is his first victory."

"And you want me to join Mr. Pearl as your assistant?"

"Yes."

"And why me?"

"Because you won't freak out over what you might see, or think you see, or wonder what that was kind of seeing."

Carl nodded. "Yeah, I sort of got used to it while I was locked up."

She smiled.

"So are we going to have Brent on our team?"

Ms. Ping shook her head. "He was used reluctantly, and it was his family why he was used at all. Brent had mentioned they were trying for a family, and his glow carried citizenship with it, and his services by degrees meant he could fit with ease." She lowered her gaze at Carl, "Pregnancy is off limits in the bet. Mrs. Smith was never in danger."

"But the rest of us were?"

"One of you still is."

"Mindy?"

"Only the second loss; and it happened after we tamed Dr. Coldsnow."

"How was he tamed?"

"He was willing to do anything to find out how far the bet would go, but killing Mindy, someone he sees in himself, caused him to show empathy and fear, what he has never done before."

"And our job is to make Mindy show fear and empathy?"

"Mindy shows fear often. Empathy is in short supply with her."

"Who is the other?"

"Just her. Once Mindy is squared, a new bet will be placed with a new gambler."

"How will you find a gambler?"

"We already have one."

"You do?"

"You see, intelligence is the best gambler, and in eight more months, we will have our next bet."

"Brent isn't a bad guy like Dr. Coldsnow."

"It has nothing to do with good vs. bad; it has to do with someone being wrong."

"What would Brent bet you on that he would be wrong? He's sort of a show-me kind of guy."

"Exactly, and when the lit path is for him, will he take it?" She wiped it off. "Doesn't matter about the future. We have a task, and Mr. Pearl will resume as the doctor's assistant," she motioned to Mr. Pearl, "tell him we are planning our best and that Carl is somehow involved. He will be on Carl like glue when he comes to check on Mindy."

"Why would I do that? He might decide to lock me up again."

"No, he will not. Too much trouble. He already lost you."

"You already lost Mindy, and you are trying again."

"So."

"So, why can't he do that?"

"Because he doesn't make the rules. He's just a gambler."

"So I'll be safe?"

"Yes, but you could be barred from going back, so do play your part."

Carl motioned to Mr. Pearl. "What do I say to him when I'm there?"

Ms. Ping stared at him. "Do you ignore someone in a room if they walk in and say 'hello'?"

"No."

"Then say 'hello' back."

"Will I know what to do?"

"Probably not, but you'll be put in the right places at the right times."

"Is that what you did for him?" Carl referred to Mr. Pearl.

"No, Dr. Coldsnow told him what to do. He hired him."

"What are we supposed to do for Mindy? I mean fear was supposed to get me to stop stuttering. What are we going to do? Starve her to lose the weight?"

Ms. Ping hesitated. "It wouldn't work. Thus, who we are setting up a lit path for."

"She's not too into that."

"Makes the bet all the more valuable."

The three stood and Carl asked, "Why are you still doing this? Seems pointless without Mr. Templeton."

"You are so right." She reached out and fixed his collar. "We'll cross that path when we walk it."

Chapter 55

A day passed and Mindy found herself awakened by a knocking on her door. "Mrs. Docket?" The raps pounded louder.

"Hold your fucking horses, I'm coming." She turned the clock her direction. "Four-thirty, are you kidding me?"

The muffle returned, "Time to get up."

She answered the door, and Mr. Coldsnow and two orderlies blocked her vision. "What do you and the goons want at this time of the day? I only agreed to this as long as you didn't do to me what you did to Carl."

"Read the paperwork, Ms. Docket. I have complete control of you, thanks to you."

"My husband will hear of this."

"Not for a week."

Mindy chuckled. "I will fuck you up, Docter. You better think twice about this."

"God damn; that is what I admired about you from day one. You are a tough human being."

"I have decided that this is probably not for me. I'll be packing up and leaving."

Dr. Coldsnow shook his head. "No, no you won't. You are either going to stop gaining weight, or you are going to explode like baking soda in Pepsi."

"Fine. May I at least shower before I go on this little hike, or whatever you are taking me on?"

Dr. Coldsnow bowed. "Absolutely."

She closed the door and ran to her purse, unsnapped a hidden pocket and reached for her phone. Nothing. She plugged her face down in and searched again. Nothing.

"Fuck."

A muffled voice called out. "You missing something in there, Mrs. Docket?"

Mindy ran to the door and swung it back open. "Where the fuck is my phone?"

"You weren't allowed any electronic devices."

"You entered my room while I slept and went through my personal things?"

Dr. Coldsnow nodded. "And?"

"And that is a violation of the law."

"Read your papers."

"I don't care; I can't give away my rights."

Dr. Coldsnow nodded to his two orderlies. "I think we can."

They nodded along.

"Don't worry about the shower; you won't be needing it where you are going."

"Where am I going?"

"I'm going to take you to a few places you haven't seen yet."

Mindy felt flush. "No, you promised I would stay upstairs."

"I know, but I have a job to do, and it won't happen if you stay up here."

"My husband will be here in six days."

"I'll need more time than that to win this bet, and if you think your husband is getting you out in a week, then I will assume he's just a piece in this hand, and pieces aren't any safer than Guests of Honor."

Mindy backed up and the orderlies forced their way past Mindy's grip on the door. "I don't understand. Please, Dr. Coldsnow, don't do this to me. I'm already afraid."

"Yes, fear isn't a remedy for you, but what it is, is anyone's guess. Hope I can figure it out before you are too big to get in and out of a cell."

"No!" Mindy fell to her knees and the orderlies locked into her arms and carried her out.

From behind her escorts, Dr. Coldsnow offered, "I am going to take great care in getting to know you, Mrs. Docket. You are one for the books."

Mindy cycled back through her thoughts. "You do realize that whether you cure me or not, you lock me up down there and I will get my revenge on you."

"I'm hoping you do seek revenge, but at the end of the day, it won't be me you seek it from. You and I both know who is doing this to you."

"He's dead."

"Is that what you think? His body is gone, and the gun is gone, and the blood is gone. He's no more dead than you and I are. He got past me because I thought he was dead. If anyone thinks Ms. Ping was pulling the strings, they are wrong. She was just one of his lackies." Dr. Coldsnow moved around his orderlies and opened his office door. "Let's show you your room." The orderlies followed the doctor to the elevator in his office. When the door opened, Mr. Pearl came out.

"Is her room ready?"

Mr. Pearl nodded. "Yes."

"Let's get her down there and see if we can flush out that old man."

Mindy fought against being restrained. "He was shot dead. We all saw that."

"Did we, Mindy? Did we?" The doctor had lost patience. "I'm starting to agree with Mr. Smith, there are a lot of people working to make things seem what they aren't. Did anyone check the young man's gun?"

"The police did."

"And what did they decide?" He came around and faced Mindy. "They decided to make the gun disappear. That old man paid the cops off."

Mindy felt ill. "Oh God. I'm bait, like Carl was, for a man you might not know is even alive."

"He's alive."

"And you are fucking crazy."

He entered the elevator, along with his assistant, Mindy, and the two orderlies. As the door closed he offered, "And you are officially crazy. Enjoy your stay."

Chapter 56

Brent couldn't sleep. "Becky."

Becky rolled in and toward his chest. She reached over his shoulder and whispered, "Let's sleep in a little longer."

"I can't."

"Are you still obsessing about the Farmers Market?"

"I'm obsessing about everything. I need to go to the source. I'm going to hound that woman to find out how they're doing this, and why."

"Can't we just leave it alone? We are going to have a child. The last month has been good to us. Can't we just be happy with that?"

Brent shook more life into her. "I need to know what he did."

"And if you find out how he did it are you going to then become a magician too?"

"Prestidigitation not magic."

"Honey, stop, please. Didn't you say you couldn't do anything about what happened to others, and that you wouldn't care until you found out if we are having one child or three?"

"One last time, I promise. I want to ask Ms. Ping to just leave us alone. If I want to know anything, I'll go to her. I don't want her and her people following us anymore."

"Fine, I agree. Now can we nap some more?"

"I can't." Brent pulled the covers away. "You shower first; we're headed over to the Lake District."

"Mr. Smith you are intolerable sometimes, but since I'm off limits, according to Mr. Templeton, I'm accepting your offer to save your life on a trip to Mr. Templeton's house." She grinned and kissed his nose.

They went their separate ways; Brent to the kitchen, Becky to the shower.

After breakfast, Brent gathered up his research; how to hypnotize, exotic drugs, suggestive reasoning, and a host of material on new technology.

"You find in there where the hucksters scammed ya'?"

"Think what you want, but when they slip up, you'll be thankful you're married to me."

She hugged him. "I'm already thankful I married you, but I wish you'd enjoy the ride and stop trying to figure out how it runs."

"I have to know. Everything that has happened seems fantastical, and the root there is fantasy. How did they do it?"

"I don't know, and only one of us cares."

"You should too."

"No I shouldn't too. I have you, and you do enough caring for way too many people. Busybody is going to become your middle name if you don't let it go."

"Let's go." He put his research in his backpack and followed Becky out the door.

They drove to Mr. Templeton's house and as they parked, the tall gentleman, Verlicht, pulled into the driveway.

Becky nudged Brent.

"I see him. I told you he was part of this."

"Wow! You might be right."

"Might?"

"What are you going to do?"

"I am going to let her know when I have questions I expect answers. That's all. You want to come with me?"

She nodded. "Wouldn't miss this."

They hurried across the street and rang the doorbell. A pause before he rang it again.

Footfalls on the other side echoed in thuds against the wooden door. When it opened, Ms. Ping smiled. "Mr. and Mrs. Smith. You two are looking great." She reached out to Brent's wife and placed a hand on her stomach. "Everything looks wonderful."

Brent shook his head. "Ms. Ping, I would like a truce with you for at least until we have an ultrasound for my wife's pregnancy."

"That will be a good news day for sure. I hope I can celebrate that with you."

"I'm not giving you that satisfaction. I'm here because I'm trying to figure this out, and until that fateful day comes, I would like you to stop playing games with me, completely, no electronic devices, no spies, and stop the parlor tricks with trying to hide. Earlier today, we met the tall man who walked in this house a few minutes ago, so I know what happened to us today came directly from you, Ms. Ping."

"Correct."

Brent stiffened. "You're admitting you sent Verlicht to meet us?"

"I am admitting that it came directly from me; that's all."

"Isn't that the same thing?"

Ms. Ping stared. "Is it?"

"Ms. Ping, of all the people who speaks in riddles, isn't that the same thing?"

Ms. Ping stared. "Is it?"

Brent shook his head. "Just leave us alone until I come to you, and that may never happen." He took his wife's hand. "Let's go. I have more things to file away."

His wife added, "This is his thing, Ms. Ping."

Ms. Ping grinned. "He's fine. His intelligence is his charm."

Brent repeated, "Remember what I said, I'll come to you when I want contact."

"I welcome the opportunity to see you walk up that path as a Guest of Honor."

"I won't be walking up a lit path; I'll be coming with questions I want answers to. So I might ask some personal ones."

"I can't wait."

Brent tipped his head and stepped back toward the walkway.

Ms. Ping closed the door, and Brent held his wife's hand with force.

She slapped his hand. "Hey, hey, you are squeezing hard."

"Sorry, I am just heavy in thought."

"Remember your words. Not until we have more questions."

"Fair enough." He helped his wife into the car. "I hope this is the end of it."

Becky winked. "We'll see."

Chapter 57

Mr. Templeton's chapter.

Verlicht entered the house. In the front room, Ms. Ping sat in her reading chair, and Mr. Templeton sat in his lounge chair.

Mr. Templeton nodded. "He is a doubting Thomas, isn't he?"

Verlicht agreed. "He sure is."

Ms. Ping concurred. "He suspects everything as being a personal attack against him."

Verlicht adjusted the view, "Not a personal attack as much as a self-centered view that he is the target."

Mr. Templeton reminded himself, "He actually is the target in some ways. He is going to replace Dr. Coldsnow as my opponent."

Ms. Ping worried, "I just hope making an opponent out of someone who is just trying to figure things out in the understanding he has afforded himself is not deceiving."

Mr. Templeton sighed. "Guess I'll find out."

Verlicht sat on the couch, his knees rising to his face. He stretched, his legs spidered-out in ease of comfort. "Guess I'll find out."

Ms. Ping put her face into her book. "Guess I'll find out."

The doorbell rang.

Mr. Templeton stood from his chair. "I wonder what Mr. Smith and that lovely wife of his are up to today? I hope she liked the book I gave her." A second ring and he took the path to the door.

On the other side, Mr. Smith bowed.

Mr. Templeton greeted them. "Mr. and Mrs. Smith, you two are looking great." He reached out to Brent's wife and placed a hand on her stomach. "Everything looks wonderful."

Mr. Smith shook his head. "Ms. Ping, I would like a truce with you for at least until we have an ultrasound for my wife's pregnancy."

"That will be a good news day for sure. I hope I can celebrate that with you."

"I'm not giving you that satisfaction. I'm here because I'm trying to figure this out, and until that fateful day comes, I would like you to stop playing games with me, completely, no electronic devices, no spies, and stop the parlor tricks with trying to hide. Earlier today, we met the tall man who walked in this house a few minutes ago, so I know what happened to us today came directly from you, Ms. Ping."

Mr. Templeton considered his accusation. "Correct."

Brent stiffened. "You're admitting you sent Verlicht to meet us?"

"I am admitting that it came directly from me, that's all."

"Ms. Ping, of all the people who speaks in riddles, isn't that the same thing?"

Mr. Templeton stared. "Is it?"

Brent shook his head. "Just leave us alone until I come to you, and that may never happen." He took his wife's hand. "Good day, Ms. Ping." He turned. "Let's go. I have more things to file away."

His wife apologized, "This is his thing, Ms. Ping."

Mr. Templeton grinned. "He's fine. His intelligence is his charm."

Brent repeated, "Remember what I said, Ms. Ping; I'll come to you when I want contact."

"I welcome the opportunity to see you walk up that path as a Guest of Honor."

"I won't be walking up a lit path; I'll be coming with questions I want answers to. So I might ask some personal ones."

Mr. Templeton held his hand up. "I can't wait."

Brent tipped his head and stepped back toward the walkway.

Mr. Templeton closed the door and retreated to his spot. Ms. Ping stayed curled in her reading chair. "He'd want to be the Guest of Honor if he saw that," Ms. Ping pointed at Mr. Templeton, "instead of this," she circled her face.

Verlicht chuckled. "True."

Mr. Templeton comforted himself. "Too easy. He needs to learn. Let's see if the triplets change his mind."

Verlicht sighed. "Maybe I shouldn't do that. He would be the kind of person who would try to make a religion out of it."

Ms. Ping shrugged. "Guess we'll see."

Verlicht shrugged. "Guess we'll see."

Mr. Templeton shrugged. He walked past the living room, a bachelor's reward, and went to the kitchen to see if there was anything to prepare, anything to satiate himself with, anything at all. He wondered about Brent's determination and what it might do to him.

He spoke to an empty house, "Guess I'll see."

The End.

www.ingramcontent.com/pod-product-compliance
Lightning Source LLC
Chambersburg PA
CBHW061512020726
47502CB00006B/2044